Best Wishes

Carl A. Kremer

THE PROFESSOR
AND THE SPIES

A NOVEL

O.T. HARRIS
WITH CARL KREMER

PITTSBURGH, PENNSYLVANIA 15238

RoseDog Books
585 Alpha Drive, Suite 103
Pittsburgh, PA 15238
Visit our website at *www.rosedogbookstore.com*

ISBN: 978-1-63661-577-6
eISBN: 978-1-63764-978-7

A CAUTION! THIS IS A WORK OF FICTION: If you happened to attend "the event" or anything surrounding it, you may find parts in the story and think "That is not the way it was or happened," and you may be right. This work is not a history, though real people are depicted as characters. In other words. DO NOT BE FOOLED BY THE TRUTH.

Passages in italics indicate the character's introspection and is intended to convey that he or she is thinking, speculating, planning the next move, analyzing what he just learned or expressing his feelings or ideas to him(her)self.

CAST OF CHARACTERS IN ORDER OF APPEARANCE

SARA O'MALLY : *Receptionist, US Department of Justice (DOJ)*
HAMPTON WEATHERLY : *Retired history professor researching a historical event*
SAM BIDDLELCOMB : *Assistant Deputy Secretary for Security, DOJ*
GRIMSLEY THOROWOOD : *Deputy Secretary for Security, DOJ*
CLIVE ST. JOHN : *2d Officer for Security MI5. British Embassy. Washington DC*
EMILY BUXTON : *Assistant to Secretary of State, Washington DC*
WARREN CHRISTOPHER : *US Secretary of State*
TOM VAN FLEET : *Prominent Fulton Citizen*
"BULLET" MCCLURE : *President of Westminster College*
KATHERINE VAN FLEET : *Wife of Tom Van Fleet*
TRUMAN INGLE : *Superintendent of School For The Deaf in Fulton*
MARY HUGHES INGLE : *Wife of Truman Ingle*
HENRY : *Staff employee at the British Embassy*
FRANK J. WILSON : *Chief of the Secret Service*
CHARLOTTE GREENWAY : *Secret Service agent*
TOM HARRIS : *Secret Service agent*
WARREN HARRIMAN : *Secret Service Agent*
MARY BETH RIDLEY : *Special Secret Service agent*
CLARK BARNES : *FBI agent*
OSCAR TRAUTMAN : *Doorman, MI5 residence (Washington DC)*
IAN MCTAVISH : *Provost of Strathclyde University*
JOHN STONE : *Editor of The Fulton Sun*
ROBERT H.C. SLOCUM : *British MI5 agent*
HUGH WAGGONER : *Missouri Highway Patrol Superintendent*
DUKE RICHARDS : *CIA agent*
TOM BLEDSOE : *Fulton Chief of Police*

ERNIE WOOLERY : *Owner of Woolery Cafe in Fulton*
ERNESTINE AND HELEN WOOLERY : *Daughters and employees at Woolery Cafe*
J. FRANK HENSLEY : *Mayor of Fulton*
KRIS LARSEN : *Special agent, MI5*
MRS. MARKLEY : *Executive Secretary, MI5*
SHARON BINGHAM : *Secretary for Frank Wilson*
WILLY WESTBROOK : *MI5 agent*
MRS. EDWARDS : *Secretary for Ian McTavish*
ALBERT : *Factotum in Administration building, Strathclyde University*
MR. BOYLE : *Maître 'd, hotel in Glasgow, Scotland*
DANIEL : *Dining Room Waiter, hotel in Glasgow*
BEN : *Innkeeper in Quoyloo, Orkney Islands (Scotland)*
KIRIL METREVICH : *Russian Naval Security Officer*

TABLE OF CONTENTS

PROLOGUE

SARA O'MALLEY, RECEPTIONIST at the U.S. Department of Justice, looked up when a trim, neatly dressed man approached her desk. His appearance and confident manner suggested that he expected to get what he wanted. He sported a well-trimmed white beard and introduced himself with a business card reading "Hampton Weatherly, BA, MA, PhD, Litd, OBE, Professor Emeritus of British History, Westminster College." He also showed a new Department of Justice Research License, which explained in general terms what information he could access. A more detailed request was explained in the Freedom of Information Act request form he also presented. When Miss O'Malley punched in the file number, she looked up and said, "Professor Weatherly, this is a restricted file under the fifty-year clause of The Act."

"Yes, I am aware of that," he replied, "and today is January 30, 1996, fifty years to the day after it was classified under the restrictive clause."

Miss O'Malley responded, "Due to the sensitive nature of this file, I would like you to speak with my supervisor."

Very professional, he mused, *cool, direct, modestly dressed and confident. She could be a valuable ally in my research.* The professor nodded agreement, and after leading him to a nearby vacant office, she called her supervisor. Ten minutes later, a balding, middle-aged man appeared carrying Weatherly's documents; he introduced himself as Sam Biddlecomb, assistant deputy secretary for security.

Weatherly noticed that *this first-level supervisor wore a somewhat worn, blue, three-piece suit. Presuming that junior officials, even with years of service, could probably not afford* to *update a wardrobe frequently,* Weatherly rose and shook his hand.

"Professor Weatherly, I am sure you realize that this is a file linked with MI5 in London and that they cross-file with Scotland Yard. British security allows no release date on this type of file. If we release it to you, the linked file at MI5 will be released as well."

"That is correct."

"And if we release it, the authorities at Whitehall may object."

"Quite possibly, yes."

Biddlecomb looked at the professor for a moment, then picked up a phone and dialed a number. "Mr. Secretary, there is a gentleman here asking for a double-linked security file, and he would like to speak with you." He listened for a moment, then nodded and hung up the phone. He turned to the professor, folded his hands, and spoke without meeting Weatherly's bland gaze. "The deputy secretary will be down shortly." He turned and walked briskly away carrying the documents, his back straight.

A few moments later, a tall, slender man of middle years, with a full head of silvery, wavy hair appeared, documents in hand, and in a soft British accent introduced himself as Grimsley Thorowood, Deputy Secretary for Security. He took the chair across the plain metal desk from Weatherly, gesturing to the professor to the other seat. "I understand, Professor, that you have asked for access to file 1612WSC1945. I assume you are aware that this file is a double-linked document that may have implications for Anglo-US relations if we release it."

Awed by neither Thorowood nor his title, Weatherly suspected a run-around. "I do understand that," he replied, looking the Deputy Secretary in the eye, "but the file I requested is no longer restricted as of this date. Would it be possible for me to speak to your superior about it?"

"Unfortunately, the Secretary is out of the city this week. However, you are correct as to the particulars." He smiled broadly, revealing small, but otherwise perfect teeth. "You've obviously done your homework, Professor, and may I ask why you want this particular file?"

Carefully containing his elation, Weatherly nodded briefly. "You may. I am preparing a book on Winston Churchill's visit to my college fifty years ago. I was a student there. Some of the security measures were evident— the FBI agents' dark suits, fedoras, and bulges in their jackets, but I am sure that there were also agents from MI5, and possibly from Scotland Yard or other agencies who were not so obvious. I intend to explore all the security measures involved in the event."

"Well," Thorogood replied, "I haven't the authority to release the documents, but I have forwarded copies of your request to those who will make the decision, stamped 'Reply Immediately,' but that still might mean a few days. Agencies of both governments are involved, and some may be contacting you. He gave Weatherly a conspiratorial smile. "You should also know that under Department Policy, a copy of your request will go to Attorney General Reno. Any FOI requests involving international relations is reported to the appropriate cabinet level." He handed over his business card and Weatherly's documents and offered his hand, which Weatherly shook, thanking him. He nodded politely at Sara O'Malley on his way out. It would not have surprised him that messages were already flying between Washington and London.

CHAPTER 1

MEETING CLIVE ST. JOHN (1996)

PROF. WEATHERLY WAS sipping a cup of tea while updating his notes the following morning in his apartment when his phone rang.

"Hampton Weatherly here."

"Professor Weatherly," the distinctly cultured female voice responded, "Second Officer for Security St. John at the British Embassy would like you to call him back concerning your request from the Justice Department for a certain linked file. The number is 202-435-9000, and the switchboard is expecting your call."

"Thank you very much; I'll call back directly."

Professor Weatherly smiled to himself at the bureaucratic handling of telephone security as he dialed. "Her Majesty's Embassy," a voice answered. "How may we assist you?" The switchboard operator had been alerted, and St. John was on the line.

"Professor Weatherly, thank you for taking my call. I know of your book plans and something of your reputation as a scholar, and I would like a chance to discuss this project with you."

Always alert to new contacts, particularly those with access to information not otherwise available, Weatherly quickly agreed and invited St. John to his apartment that same evening, giving St. John his Macomb Street address.

Macomb is a short, quiet, residential street in northwest Washington where there was little traffic and residents parked in the street without worry. Stately sycamores line each block. Though he had retired four years before undertaking this new book, he had been invited occasionally to lecture at American University and at other schools in the District. He had leased this small apartment, convenient to Wisconsin Avenue, where there were several bookstores that Weatherly frequented, often with colleagues.

When St. John arrived, Weatherly invited him in and offered a drink, surprised to discover that St. John's favorite, like his own, was bourbon and ginger. *Over six feet,* he mused. *Prominent features, especially large nose, ruddy complexion. Quiet-spoken, with a Scottish accent. A hint of after-shave... No bath since Wednesday?*

As Weatherly was preparing the drinks, St. John took in the small, tidy living room, stuffed with more books on nearly every level site than he expected in the temporary quarters of a retired college professor. Weatherly delivered the drinks and seated himself in what was obviously "his" chair, a once-handsome, over-stuffed leather recliner, aged but of excellent quality. It fit the professor like a favorite garment.

Motioning toward the tobacco canister on his chair-side table, Weatherly said, "I hope you don't mind. I enjoy my pipe with a drink."

St. John waved it aside and, smiling, pulled a box of Players from his pocket, saying. "Professor, when you have access to the 1612 file, tell me how you will approach those fifty-year-old security measures. I suspect that they are not so different from what would be employed today—though we're somewhat more sophisticated now."

"I expect that will be the case. I think I will find many similarities, but I hate to guess before I have really even begun my research. I intend for the book to detail the security measures taken to protect Mr. Churchill, President Truman, and their guests primarily, but it will of necessity deal with the college and its surroundings to establish the scene. If I can so presume, I would like to prepare a series of questions for you to consider—and perhaps answer—about how security was designed and executed on the British side on March fifth, 1946. Of course, if any of my questions exceed protocols or if the answers to which might raise concerns about classified data, I would not expect you to answer. And I will bear any expenses attendant to this research. I realize that I am imposing on you, but I would be very grateful for whatever assistance and guidance you can give me."

St. John responded with a small smile, raising his glass in a light-hearted salute. "I am pleased to be of service, and interested to see how far the Service has come in dealing with such situations." He lowered his glass, leaned back, and crossed his ankles, looking directly at his host. "In fact, I took it upon myself to access some of our files through March sixth, 1946, including 1612, and would be interested in what you already know about that event. Since you were there, you must have some memories of it. Have you contacted the principal participants, other students, teachers, and townspeople still living who might have been involved?

"I have indeed," Weatherly replied. "I was in my first year there, but I had a small role in the proceedings—I could even claim to have been part of the security measures that day: I handed out press passes to the several journalists who were there to cover it." He paused and shook his head in a self-deprecating gesture and went on.

"In the past year, I have read all the news accounts I can find, even consulted my college yearbook's handling of it. And I have tried first to determine who of that considerable number are still living, and then to interview them. Some I simply could not find, and some, for whom I had only an address, did not respond. A few agreed to answer specific questions in writing, but some of them never responded to my queries. I contacted the local law enforcement entities and picked up some interesting tidbits, but some have either lost any records they might have made or declined to cooperate with me in getting access to them. Despite my disappointment, I respect their concerns about opening them to the public, as it were."

St John nodded. "From what I gleaned in skimming over our files, I think your government's agencies at the federal level have considerably more detail about the security measures of that operation than ours, but, based on my dealings with them, I think it unlikely they will make them all public."

"'They're called the Secret Service for many reasons," the professor said wryly, "but now I must ask you, with some understanding of your position, is there any chance that I could examine a copy of what you have in your files? I know it is forward of me to ask on such short acquaintance, but frankly, I may be stymied—stonewalled, as we call it—for months or years getting access to it through available channels."

St. John's expression altered slightly; still smiling, his gaze locked on the professor's. "I will need to clear it through our ambassador, Sir John Kerr, and I can promise you nothing about his response. Having examined the file, I can assure the ambassador that I did not find much in it I would deem particularly sensitive. He could read it himself before deciding, and he might want some confirmation from London before allowing it. My superior, First Officer McPhail, is reviewing it, and he will probably accept my recommendation at our weekly briefing with Sir John in two days."

Weatherly's eyes widened, and he leaned back in surprise. "You're telling me there's a chance I could see that file in a matter of days?"

St. John chuckled at his eagerness. "Don't get your hopes up. We're dealing with bureaus here—as in 'Bureaucracies,' with a capital B. As an amateur student of history, I am intrigued by your interest in this topic—which occurred when I was just a boy—13, to be exact. I had forgotten Mr. Churchill invented the term 'Iron Curtain' in Fulton, Missouri, though I knew it happened in The United States."

St. John smiled, then stood, and unwilling to set his empty glass on a book, he handed it to his host. "I won't impose on any more of your time, and I look forward to having a small part in your research. I know you will do what you Yanks call your 'homework,' and I would love to find out what you learn, in so far as you want to share it. I will do my best to answer what I can." Weatherly thanked him profusely and promised that he would work on the questions over the weekend and that they would meet for lunch on the following Monday at a local restaurant called The Lame Duck.

Over the weekend, Weatherly reviewed his notes and then listed questions he felt St. John might answer as a full-time administrative security officer of long experience. Weatherly determined to limit his first draft of questions to no more than a dozen, not all of which would require written answers, but serve as discussion points when they talked. He made two copies and folded one into a manila envelope with St. John's name on it.

#1. Was security for Churchill's speech, from England's position, strictly a function of MI5? Or were Scotland Yard and other agencies involved as well? And what were the functions of each?

#2. I have tried to read everything printed about the event and have found no reference to British security agents. How was their identity concealed? We know that there were about twenty agents from the Secret Service and the FBI (and some from OSS). Their protection was due almost entirely to President Truman's presence. The FBI agents were easily identified because they wore "uniforms:" black or dark blue suits, neckties, brown fedora hats, their suit pockets bulging with their side-arms and ammunition.

Here Weatherly chuckled to himself: They looked like baseball umpires with side pockets full of baseballs.

#3. How many agents from each of those agencies were assigned to this duty?

#4. Of those so assigned, how many were to be admitted to the gymnasium and how many had "outside" duty? What were those duties? Did they file reports with their headquarters? Are those reports extant? And, if so, where?

#5. I assume that those assigned to duty inside the gymnasium carried some sort of identification to get past the "gate keepers." What was it? Are any of those available? I will need some illustrations.

#6. Did any British agents arrive early to learn the lay of the land? If so, how did they avoid being spotted by the press?

#7. Did any of those agents (#6) accompany the presidential party on the train? Both ways? Were they made aware of any fallback plan?

#8. Who could issue the order to activate that plan?

#9. Were President Truman and Mr. Churchill aware of a possible change in plans? If so, when? What about President McCluer?

#10. Where in England are these planning and execution files located? How can I gain access? And with what results?

#11. Final acceptance of President McCluer's invitation was not sent to McCluer until Truman's letter on December 19, leaving only a little over two months for security planning. Did this not put MI5 and the Yard under a lot of pressure to get plans in place?

I am working on some further questions, but these will get you started. Do not jeopardize your position by answering any that make you uncomfortable. DO NOT ANSWER IF NOT COMFORTABLE FOR YOU."

CHAPTER 2

AT THE LAME DUCK (1996)

WEATHERLY'S FIRST IMPRESSIONS of St. John proved quite accurate: *Rather more casual than one might expect of a mid-staffer at the British embassy; (short-term?) veteran of Washington protocols; probably willing to protest establishment standards but in a reserved, respectful way; knowledgeable; probably knows his way around Washington; likely has contacts who know how to get things done by ignoring or bypassing higher level appointees. Probably of a very old and respected family, he is bound to protect his reputation and to stay out of trouble, though not out of timidity.*

Early Monday afternoon was usually a time for quiet conversation at The Lame Duck, but today there was one table of about ten chatting women. The men were seated as far as possible away from the ladies' group. The waitress poured water for the two men, saying, "I'll be right back to take your order."

The ten ladies paid their tabs and left, talking as they went. As a hush descended on The Lame Duck, the waitress disappeared through the kitchen door.

St. John looked at his watch and then toward the kitchen door. Weatherly said he had a couple of general questions and pulled a small, lined notebook from one pocket and stuffed envelope from another, which he handed over to his guest. "These are the questions I mentioned the other night, and I'd like you to take the time to study them and determine your answers."

Clive slipped the envelope into an inside pocket of his jacket.

Weatherly opened his notebook and quickly scanned the first page, looked up at St. John, and asked, "Even though this event took place in the United States, I assume that your security people were involved because Mr. Churchill was such a prominent figure." St. John nodded, and Weatherly continued, "Now, this planning involved MI5 and perhaps Scotland Yard?"

"Very likely the Yard as well. I can tell you that most of the security measures designed for 1946 are no longer appropriate today. I have had access to file 1612 and can say that most of the measures mentioned in 1946 are no big secrets now. Some others are likely still in effect which might be of interest to you in your research.

"I noticed that you are a prodigious reader, and I understand that you have published several books as well. Mostly English history, I believe."

"All history, but hardly several. And your off-duty interests, Clive?"

A brief smile crossed St. John's face as he nodded. "Certainly. History as well, but only a few modest publications. And, by the way, I must request that when this present work is finished and the book published, there be no mention of my name anywhere. I would prefer it not appear in your notes as well. I'm sure you understand some of the delicacies of my position."

"Of course. And I give you my word as a gentleman and a professional," Weatherly replied, somewhat stiffly. "But I do want you as a resource—respectful of your professional duties and expectations. With the commonality of our interests, I trust we shall get along easily. I will try not to probe deeply enough to compromise your position."

"Thank you, Professor. That does clear the air. And I wonder how the ginger is holding out?" Professor Weatherly took both glasses and went through the kitchen door, returning with the waitress following, carrying the two drinks. She apologized for the delay and recommended the quiche, "Which you can't rush." Both men smiled and ordered the quiche, thanked her, and returned to their conversation.

"Now, how do you plan to proceed with this research?"

Weatherly folded his arms and studied St. John before responding. *Not what I expected in a top British security officer.* When he met St. John's steady glance, he realized the man was studying him as intently as he was studying the British officer. St. John's smile widened briefly. *Competent, but without the self-conscious firmness, the studied pleasantness of most security personnel. Interesting, likeable. Seems almost eager to cooperate. A very smooth operator.*

"As to background, you already probably know a bit about me, and I'll answer any relevant questions about my background, qualifications, and character you might ask. And, as I would like you to be a principal source of information, would you mind telling me a little about you and your family; how old are you, by the way?"

The waitress arrived with an apology for the delay. "You can't rush a quiche, you know."

Clive folded his arms and answered, "I am sixty-three—nearing retirement, and a bachelor, never married,"

"Thank you. Now, go ahead with your story, Clive."

St. John sipped his drink, then clasped his hands on the table, took a deep breath, and spoke in a steady professional tone. "Well, we're blood 'n bone Scottish with roots in twelfth century, and, I might add, while we are generally well-regarded, we are not wealthy. Quite the contrary. My father, Sir Hugh St. John, was born in 1910, and my parents married in 1930, my mother at eighteen. Of course, finding a job in the early '30s was bloody tough everywhere. My father joined the Royal Navy in 1930. The military was one of the few options available, and I suspect that the family name helped him enlist as a junior officer. Father had many postings, from Ireland to South Africa, India. I do not recall them all. He was not on leave so frequently that we had a close relationship. He never talked about his experiences or his work. Maybe he was protecting me, or maybe it had to do with the type of work he was in. I know he had a top-level security clearance, and he was often out of touch, especially during the war."

Wow, Weatherly thought, *this chap's very talkative for a high-level security official, but he's pleasant enough, and though he sounds a bit like he is delivering a prepared report. Maybe I can steer him back to the particulars of the document I need.* "Please go on," he said, nodding.

"Well, during the war years, I had little understanding of what was occurring in London. All the major cities were severely bombed, especially our manufacturing centers and major ports. They were trying to starve us out. The situation was untenable, so in order to protect them, many thousands of youngsters were sent to rural areas to live and go to school. I went to live with a family near Cardiff, in Wales, but my mother stayed in London because she had a good job there, some kind of office work. We were told little about the war and what it meant, again, to protect us, but lads are inquisitive and some war reports got through. Early on it was spot-on exciting for an eleven-year-old. Reality came along, though. Older boys went into service; some didn't come back—food rationing, patriotism. All part of the war-time scene." He paused, looking down.

"And how did you wind up in Her Majesty's Security Service?" Weatherly asked.

"I did well in school, particularly in mathematics and the sciences, so in 1943 I was admitted to Neath College, at that time a technical school not all that far from Cardiff. They had a 'Cadet Corps,' a quasi-military prep school for youngsters with particular interests. I was especially interested in radio-telegraphy, various signals disciplines and the entire and rather new electronics studies.

"At age sixteen, having taken a Certificate, I was almost automatically in the navy through the Cadet Corps. I say 'almost' because had I not enlisted, I would have owed many thousands of pounds to pay for my schooling. I was sent to signals school through advanced training and into cryptography, code-breaking, and the like. And that's what got me into security during the Cold War and ultimately to my present posting here in Washington. A right plum job, I might add, for a crusty old bachelor, nae? I have no formal graduate work, but I have picked up a few hours here and there, some at American University, just up the road here."

Weatherly nodded, and both men concentrated for a time on the quiche.

"And your parents? He asked at length, "Both gone now, I gather?"

St. John glanced down briefly, then raised his eyes to look directly at his companion. "My mother is still with us. She is presently in a retirement home at Taunton in Somerset, up near Liverpool. Her body is 84 years old but, God bless her, her mind has been gone for ten years and more. And it's a blessing too. She often thinks Hugh will be back from Kabul today and he will walk into her room any minute now." Now, Hamp, what is your program?"

He has the highest possible security clearance and has achieved a high level posting to the one of the largest and most important embassies in the world. He has spent several years on the Washington scene and knows his way around town. I must become better acquainted with St. John.

He noticed the waitress leaning languidly against the kitchen doorframe, and he glanced at his watch. "I will, of course, spend a lot of time working through DOJ file 1612, if I ever get it, but I will begin with the newspaper files and available books at the Library of Congress for any data from the mid-forties that might be helpful. And I hope that I may be in contact with you for guidance and clarification. The Washington bureaucracy has refined the art of the run-around; the paperwork is extensive and the process of getting information often very slow. So getting file 1612, even the British file, would be a coup for me because the British perspective is an important aspect of the operation. You now have the list of questions I prepared over the weekend. But there will be more. Of course, you should decline to answer any that might be uncomfortable for you—"

"I appreciate that, Hamp," St. John interrupted.

"But I may argue on some points," Weatherly added, smiling.

"That's all right," Clive responded. "I appreciate a good argument."

CHAPTER 3

THE STATE INTERVENES (1996)

WHEN HAMP WEATHERLY rolled out of bed the next morning, his thoughts focused on new questions he would propose to Clive St. John. After a second cup of tea, he spent a few minutes trimming his beard. Precisely at 8:00 a.m. his phone rang, and a pleasant female voice said, "Good morning. Is this Professor Weatherly?"

"Yes."

"Sir, this is Emily Buxton, executive assistant to Secretary of State, Warren Christopher. Would you have a few minutes to speak with the Secretary?"

"Certainly, I would be pleased to speak with Secretary Christopher.

"Very good, Sir. Please call back at this number, and I will alert the switchboard to put you through."

While waiting a minute to call back, Weatherly recalled that Christopher was from a western state, possibly one of the Dakotas. Weatherly himself being from South Dakota, there was a possible future contact that might prove useful. Pretty top-drawer stuff.

He dialed the number and was immediately put through to Ms. Buxton, who thanked him by name and said, "I will put you through to the Secretary."

After a single ring he heard, "Professor Weatherly, Warren Christopher here. Let me state my business, and then I will be glad to answer any questions you have. This concerns your request under the Freedom of Information Act for a certain file that has been held under the restrictive clause of that act. Releasing the file to you would mean the British file would also be released, since they were linked. We have received a cable from John Major asking for everything we know or can find out about you, your background, integrity, your honesty, etc. You get the picture. They are more concerned about that fifty-year-old file than I would have thought. There must be something in it that makes them nervous."

"Yes, Mr. Secretary. I understand all of that, and I am sorry that the powers that be have blown this out of proportion."

"They may have," the Secretary said, "but I will have to respond promptly. We have a pretty complete dossier on you already. My point in contacting you is to ask if there is anything at all in your background that we should not forward to them or anything we may not have and that they might dig up."

Now let's play the Dakota card. "I know of nothing, Mr. Secretary, except that a few times back in South Dakota, a friend and I smoked corn-silk cigarettes out behind the barn."

"Ha!" exclaimed Secretary Christopher. "A kindred spirit! Except I am from North Dakota. MI5 would probably discover that on their own. Now, Professor, is there anything you want to ask me or anything we might assist you with?"

"Only one thing, Mr. Secretary. Would it be appropriate for me to ask for a copy of Mr. Major's cable?"

"I do not have the original, Professor, but I will have Miss Buxton get a copy to you. I think she has your address, and we will send it by department courier." *Prime Minister! The Secretary of State! Official courier! His self-confidence was boundless, and he was honored that his efforts had received attention in such high offices.* "I can't think of anything else, Mr. Secretary, but I may call if I need help later. And thank you."

"Please call Miss Buxton for anything that might be helpful. Good day, Professor."

The courier arrived in less than two hours.

Prime Minister to Secretary of State, Washington. London, Feb. 1, 1996: HMG most earnestly requests that doc. 1612WSC1945 not be released. It is requested that all measures be taken to prevent this action. Further, HMG requests that your government supply HMG with all information detailing the loyalty and reliability of Prof. Weatherly, including dossiers at the FBI, CIA, NSA, and any others that may exist. We request also that you inquire of Prof. Weatherly if he would receive a representative of HMG to discuss his intentions. A security officer at our Embassy would be appointed soonest. We await your reply.
John Major

That Secretary Christopher was working on a Saturday made Weatherly smile; he thought to himself, *Wow! To have aroused the interest of Whitehall and of Foggy Bottom in the same week! An accomplishment indeed for a small-time college professor.*

His self-confidence was boundless, but had Prof. Weatherly bitten off more than he could chew? *I'm a one-man team, and I must get to work on the questions for St. John. I know I was treading on thin ice in asking St. John for information that was still in a restricted file in England. If I push St. John, a security officer after all, to answer questions about classified information, I might endanger his job and thus lose a valuable high-level asset and possible friend. Their correspondence might better be conducted outside embassy channels, perhaps bypassing documents by hand. These points had not been covered. Why had they not settled this over lunch? Damn!*

Weatherly picked up the phone and called the Embassy. "My name is Hampton Weatherly, and I need rather urgently to contact Second Officer St. John. Could you possibly give me his home telephone number if he's not in the office?"

"Yes, Professor. Officer St. John has spoken of you." She gave him the number, but he refrained from calling before noon, since St. John might be sleeping in.

Following a light lunch, Weatherly called St. John's home number. "Clive here."

"Clive, this is Hamp. One matter we did not touch upon yesterday is how we can communicate with each other without jeopardizing your job."

"Yes, Hamp, I have thought about that as well. My calling you from my home to your apartment should not be a problem. However, if you called frequently at the embassy, you would likely trigger something in our security system. All perfectly innocent, of course, but it could cause some temporary problems."

"Exactly. I see from your telephone number that you live out in Maryland."

"Yes. Just over the District line, actually, so not a bad commute at all."

"Then how about lunch one day to discuss this issue?

"The Lame Duck, as I recall, is not open on weekends. So how about one o'clock Monday?"

At The Lame Duck, the waitress again recommended the quiche. After ordering, Hamp said, "It seems they always recommend the quiche. It is pretty good."

Clive said, "You know, Hamp, this is all perfectly innocent and maybe we are trying to make it look like some sort of plot."

"It could appear that way. Could you not explain to your ambassador what we are doing?"

"I think not beyond what I have already, Hamp. Sir John Kerr can be a bit difficult at times, and he has a lot on his plate right now."

"We can always use the mail. Slow, but it would avoid the embassy altogether. I will need your address."

"I think we can make that work. My address is 1528 Crescent St., Bethesda 20816. I do want to help you but there is some risk—for me."

Weatherly jotted the number on a notepad at his desk. "I understand perfectly, and I don't want to jeopardize your situation in any way. And you already have my address. Now here are a few more questions that I came up with on Friday." He handed an envelope to Clive who put it in his jacket pocket without opening it.

"I do intend over the next few days to spend a lot of time working on the newspaper files at the Library of Congress. I will concentrate on *The Times* and *The Guardian* for any contemporary articles about the upcoming speech. Any others where I should pay attention?"

"Well, Hamp, you might try a Glasgow or Edinburgh paper. I don't have a name, but those northern sheets are usually critical of anything the conservatives propose, and they very likely opposed Winston's proposed speech even without the slightest idea what it might be about."

Service was fashionably slow for the early afternoon crowd, and the conversation lagged. Their waitress brought more water and said, "Your orders will be out shortly. You can't rush a quiche."

"But might you rush a couple of bourbons with ginger?" Hamp asked.

She gave him a puzzled glance and disappeared through the kitchen doors.

"You know, Hamp," Clive said, "I can't help wondering how in the world Westminster College pulled this off. While we have a minute or two, could you fill me in?"

"Well, I do have some background that may be of interest to you. I am not at all sure that it belongs in my book, but it explains how Churchill's visit came about."

"I have plenty of time and, all together now: 'You can't rush a quiche!'" Both men laughed. "I would like to hear that story."

"It's going to take more than a couple of minutes, but we can start.

"Back up to 1946, Clive. Franc McCluer, the President of Westminster College, was looking for a speaker for the Leadership Foundation Lecture the following spring. He called on his friend, Tom VanFleet, for suggestions..."

CHAPTER 4

IT'S A GO (1946)

TOM VAN FLEET, a tall, angular fellow, set his lightly watered bourbon on the small table between him and "Bullet" McCluer (so called because he was short, rotund, and bald, and he tended to speak rapidly) and leaned forward in his chair on McClure's patio, almost in Bullet's face. He started counting off points. "Churchill has been thrown out of office and is now a private citizen. No political responsibilities at all. Therefore, he can speak his mind freely. Further, he is a marvelous orator, and it would be a great PR event for our town. Dammit, Bullet, you've got to do this. You will never have a better chance for the college. Also, Churchill is continually broke, and he just might listen to the possibility of a small honorarium."

"It would sure as hell be small, Tom." They laughed, but both were serious; the college was always searching for funds.

Tom went on, "If you issue the invitation and he accepts, it's a boon to Westminster. If he declines, you are out not even the price of a postage stamp."

"Let me think about it."

"Don't think about it too long, Bullet. As soon as it's announced, the big dogs will be foaming at the mouth to invite him."

"Okay, Tom. Ida Belle will not be that happy, but I'll do it."

"She'll get over it, Bullet, and she will be the perfect hostess."

"What should we do to get started?"

"I think that you should write a letter of invitation to Mr. Churchill and let me forward it to General Harry Vaughan to deliver to the president."

"You're sure you are serious about this, Tom?"

"Dead serious. We're pretty damn lucky to have Harry Vaughan as an alum to cut through the red tape to get to the president. I think you should call on Percy Green. Since he's on your Board, he should be willing to

handle some bottom-line costs to the college. Churchill's presence alone—
and President Truman—would make rather than lose money for the
College."

"You're real sure?"

"Bullet, it's a win/win situation."

Katherine Van Fleet appeared at the kitchen door. "Bullet, Ida Belle
says 'time's up'"

Katherine was a handsome woman—tall, stately, full-bodied but firm,
her carriage erect, a full head of carefully styled snow-white hair, and
perfect, well-bred manners.

McCluer got the message and parted with, "Tom, we've got work to do."

Within a few days, Bullet and Ida Belle called on Truman and Mary
Hughes Ingle. Truman was the person of choice when a community project needed leadership. He was the "go to" guy. In his middle years and
slightly balding, paunchy, Truman was the Superintendent of the State
School for the Deaf in Fulton. It was a comfortable late fall evening when
the four of them were seated on the Ingles's screen porch. Truman knew
what the problem was. The word had already made the local gossip circuit
even though the official announcement had not been published.

"I had a conversation with Tom Van Fleet, and he…"

"Never mind the sales pitch, Bullet. What do you want me to do?"

"Let's not dance around this, Truman. I want you to take charge of all
of the local arrangements for…this is the first time I've said this…Winston
Churchill's visit to Fulton. He has accepted my invitation to speak on
March fifth, and here's the icing on the cake: President Truman is coming
along and will introduce Churchill…and your job would be to see to the
organization and oversee the operation of everything local. And this will
be a huge crowd, larger than the annual Santa Claus parade." All four
laughed.

"Okay, said Ingle, picking up an approving glance from Ida Belle.
"You've got your man for this job. What's next?"

"Not sure," McCluer replied. "Let's get together and see what jobs are
needed. How's your calendar tomorrow?"

"It's okay. Come to my office about ten, if that suits. We won't be disturbed there."

CHAPTER 5

A BREAKTHROUGH (1996)

"AND THAT, CLIVE, is how it came about. You know the rest. I don't know if it belongs in my book, but it's a pretty good story."

"I'd include it for sure," Clive said. "It's history, and it should be recorded somewhere—and where better? I will start to work after hours tonight. Have you heard anything of your request to the Justice Department yet?"

Weatherly shook his head. "No, nor do I expect to any time soon. It's on its way up the chain of command, and I am low priority at every level."

"Well," St. John said, standing, "I haven't given up hope that our embassy will release file 1612, in what we hope will be a timely decision. If it does, I will see that you are the first to get access to it." They shook hands and parted.

Two days later, Weatherly's phone rang before he had even dressed for the day. It was St. John, who first apologized for calling so early. "I wanted to catch you before you went out to ask if you might be at home this evening with time for a short chat. Something has come up I need to clear with you, and I will be in the city after five."

"Yes, I can be back here by then—"

He was interrupted by St. John, "I'm sorry, I have another call coming in I must take. I will see you by five-thirty." The hum of the dial tone from his phone prompted Hamp to hang up.

Though not given to fretting over things outside his control, Weatherly found himself wondering what had prompted St. John's cryptic request. Was he bringing good news? Bad news? Advice? Warning? Questions of his own for the professor? He shook them off, turning his considerable powers of concentration on to the material he was retrieving in the Library of Congress.

St. John arrived at his apartment just before eight the next night. Weatherly invited him in. "I hope you have at least time enough for a bourbon and ginger."

His briefcase still open, St. John reached in, unzipped a small compartment inside, and produced a pint of top-shelf bourbon. "I don't think I could match your ginger syrup," he said, handing the liquor to Weatherly, "but I wanted to make a contribution to our labors together, and also propose a toast to some of the good folks in the British Embassy."

"Well, they do seem to have excellent taste in American whiskeys," Weatherly responded.

St. John moved a step closer to Weatherly. "Upon the recommendation of an American acquaintance in the Secret Service, with whom I had a brief meeting this afternoon, I was delegated to inform your Department of Justice that on the advice of MI5, the British Foreign Office has authorized the release of file 1612WSC1945, and I took the liberty of having a copy made for you, which you can pick up at our embassy at your convenience. I passed this file to my superior, who, along with other specialists, redacted significant portions as a condition of releasing it under special permission, with the understanding that no further inquiries into its contents will be considered." Obviously enjoying Weatherly's growing curiosity, he paused. "I think you will find reading it both fascinating and frustrating, and while I objected to much of the redaction, I was denied, and urged to limit its circulation to you, with your word that you will not reveal to anyone that you have it, and will make every effort to prevent the agency's connection to it. They can deny its official authenticity, but I can personally affirm it is what it purports to be: Frank Wilson's official report of the Churchill-Truman Team with a number of supporting documents."

So shocked was Weatherly that his eyes widened, and he wanted to jump into the air and click his heels, but instead he grabbed St. John's hand and pumped it vigorously. "Oh, thank you, Clive, thank you so very much. I can't think of any more welcome news you could have brought—and with a fine bourbon to boot! Uncork that lovely elixir while I find a couple of glasses, some ice, and ginger." He released Clive's hand and hurried into the kitchen, muttering "Oh wow! Oh wow!" and shaking his head.

After a second bourbon and ginger, Hamp said, "There is probably a lot more information in that file that can be useful to me. I confess, though, that I was reluctantly considering asking if in your position at the embassy you could obtain a copy for me—even possibly the entire file. So I am very grateful I don't have to do that. I am greatly in your debt for the great service you have done me."

"Think nothing of it, Hamp; the staff knows of my interest in history, and particularly in Churchill's prime ministry, and I merely got the ball rolling. And I must confess, I got a small measure of satisfaction from informing one of your biggest bureaucracies, the Department of Justice, that we'd made their fuss over the release moot."

Weatherly courteously refrained from reminding St. John that the British bureaucracy was the first to raise objections—at the very highest levels. *I wonder what changed John Major's mind—a conversation with Secretary Christopher, perhaps?*

St. John rose, stepped to the door, and paused, smiling. "I dare say you will find some surprises in the record of the events of that day, and I'm looking forward to our next conversation." He nodded briefly and stepped out, closing the door softly behind him.

The next morning, Weatherly was at the British Embassy when it opened. The armed and uniformed guards stationed inside and out never met his gaze, but he felt he was being watched. The tall, slender receptionist had a pleasant face and carefully coiffed gray hair. Her makeup was perfect, her smile lovely, and her blue-eyed glance at him cool, firm, and professional. "How may we help you?" her voice was controlled, low, and precise.

"I am Professor Hampton Weatherly," he said with a slight nod. "This a happy day for me. I am here to pick up something left here by Second Security Officer Clive St. John. What must I do to get it?"

"The file is in the first room down that hallway." She nodded to the left. "There is a release form you must sign and leave with me, but you should know this is quite a large file. I could have someone bring it down, or even have it delivered to your address."

"I don't think that will be necessary, but I appreciate your offer. You have been very kind." He nodded to her and hurried off to retrieve his prize. It consisted of a cardboard carton about eighteen inches by three feet square, and four inches deep, tightly sealed with plastic tape. The release form lay beside it, with a ballpoint pen neatly aligned beside the box. He scanned the form and signed it, then returned it and the pen to Ms. O'Malley. "As you warned me, there is rather more to the file than I anticipated. I must impose on your indulgence again."

"Despite our legalistic reputation, Professor, we are pleased to be of service. What can we do for you?"

"My car is in the public garage nine blocks away. I wonder if I could temporarily park my vehicle in the drive in front of the office—just long enough to load the carton in the trunk."

"Of course, and I will have someone carry it out. Henry will be waiting for you in the drive with the file when you return."

Henry turned out to be a husky young black man wearing an identification card on his dark blue shirt with matching trousers. By the time the professor opened the trunk, he was there with the box on his shoulder, moving it smoothly into the open trunk. When he had finished, he stepped back while Weatherly closed the trunk and stepped up on the curb to shake the man's hand.

"Thank you, Henry; I wish you could accompany me back to my apartment for the unloading."

"Glad I could help, Professor." He lifted his arm in an informal salute as he turned back into the building.

Since he was less than two miles from the Department of Justice, Weatherly called at the Library of Congress to look for anything in *The Times of London* or *The Manchester Guardian* about Sir Hugh. He had used the resources of the LOC extensively in gathering information about Churchill's visit, including British newspaper coverage of the event. Not too deep into a 1947 issue of *The Guardian*, a small headline jumped out at him like the first shot of a fireworks show: "Naval Officer Charged With Espionage"! It was dated January 1945. The brief announcement stated that one Sir Hugh St. John of London had been charged with espionage and colluding with the enemy, both capital offenses. His rank and age and other specific details were omitted in the short announcement.

This could not be Clive's father, but there must be a connection. Perhaps the appellation "Sir Hugh" was carried by a more distant relative, some second or third cousin even. Surely if it were Clive's father, Clive himself would not now be the embassy executive security officer. Still, a nagging thought.

CHAPTER 6

INVITATION ACCEPTED (1946)

MCCLUER RECEIVED CHURCHILL'S acceptance on December 19, and March 5, 1946 was confirmed as the speech date so security plans had to be made in a narrow window—no time could be wasted. The job fell into the lap of the Chief of the Secret Service, Frank J. Wilson. A better qualified person for the job could not have been found. Wilson had been director of the Service since 1937. He had played a major role in the case against Al Capone and was one of the lead agents in solving the Lindbergh kidnapping case. He was meticulous and unrelenting in his duties, and highly sensitive to and adept at handling the political aspects of his job. These competencies would be tested and serve him well in the operation he was assigned.

A twenty-five-year veteran of the Secret Service, one of Wilson's principal duties was safeguarding the President, his family, and important guests from all over the world. That duty was clearly stated in the agency's charter, but even Wilson did not know why the Service was an arm of the Treasury Department.

Wilson's professional qualifications and his complete dedication to the mission of the service were never questioned. If the President was in Jakarta while the First Lady was sponsoring a bridge party at the White House and their children were in two different schools, his resources might have been stretched thin, but there was never a question that the job would be done.

In such cases, a provision in the law permitted officers of the Service to be posted temporarily with the Federal Bureau of Investigation, and vice-versa. FBI agents were as well trained as Wilson's officers. There was rivalry between the two bodies, but when assignments called for it, rivalry was set aside—mostly.

Wilson's style, however, was vastly different from that of FBI director J. Edgar Hoover. Hoover had been the Bureau's director since its inception, and he was fiercely protective of its turf. His style was dictatorial while Wilson approached problems quietly and analytically. Wilson would frequently visit the sites of his assignments. One story told that the daughter of the President returning from school one afternoon spotted Wilson standing at the front door of the White House and said "Hello, Mr. Wilson" and addressing her by name, he said "Good afternoon, and how was your day in Miss Singleton's fifth grade today?" Despite those basic differences, the two men got along well enough to cooperate when necessary. The occasion of Churchill and President Truman traveling together required such cooperation.

Wilson ordered that a task force be formed immediately, composed of high-level representatives of not only the Secret Service but also of the FBI and CIA, the British MI5, and Scotland Yard. He himself would head the task force, but the individual chairmen might be from other agencies, and he was determined to convene their first session before the end of 1945. Surprisingly, given the sluggish movement of some government agencies, this happened. With the aid of top Secret Service agents and experts from other national law enforcement, he broke the task down into five areas of responsibility:

#1 Security screening of Jefferson City and Fulton communities and the campus and coordination with local authorities.

#2 Security screening of the speech venue both inside and the immediate environment and development of security plans for the site.

#3 All rail travel.

#4 Auto service between Jefferson City and Fulton.

#5 Development of alternative plans to meet emergencies.

Since the Secret Service had the primary responsibility for the security of the President and therefore of his guests, a representative of the Service, when possible, was in charge of each task force, and Wilson himself took on the duties of coordinating the work.

Chairman Wilson recruited all the task force leaders, who met on December 23 along with a few select representatives from the other agencies. He had developed the task force job descriptions and made it clear that holiday season or not, their schedule was significantly accelerated.

Assigning the British personnel to task forces was not difficult since the personnel of all five services available to him were highly trained and competent. While some adjustments were made later, the early task force assignments were in place by the deadline. Wilson assigned #1 and #2 to the Secret Service and the British National services, #3 and #4 to MI5 and CIA; the FBI and Scotland Yard were charged with Task #5.

Each task force was led by an agent of the Secret Service appointed by Chief Wilson. He assigned a bright young agent, Charlotte Greenway, to head Task Force #1. Chairmanship of Task Force #2 went to Tom Harris, a Missouri native whose reputation in the ranks was that of an up-and-coming leader. Clark Barnes headed Task Force #3. Agent Warren Harriman would Chair Task Force #4. Special Agent Mary Beth Ridley assumed the chair of Task Force #5. Mary Beth was an expert organizer. Wilson asked for ten or twelve agents from the British agencies. The Task Force chairs immediately began combing through top-secret personnel files to recruit the best qualified teams they could on such short notice.

Wilson called the first meeting of the chairs at a secure conference room in the Treasury building. "Ladies and Gentlemen, we have a formidable job before us, protecting both Mr. Churchill and President Truman. The travels alone are complicated, and plans for their safety and convenience must be executed with very tight timing and each agent's job must be handled 100% as assigned, with no excuses. Our duty to protect President Truman and the former Prime Minister of the British Empire is as difficult an assignment as I could imagine. I am confident that everything down to the last detail will be handled flawlessly and with the least notice by the public that we are there. Now it is up to you to find the most skilled agents in all these services to serve with you as the plan is prepared and executed. Each one must hold or be qualified to hold the highest security clearance. Do not accept any with the slightest question in his or her record. You have authority to co-opt whomever you need from the US agencies. Let me know what who you need from the British agencies, and I will see to it that such persons are assigned to you. This is probably the most important assignment you will receive during your career. Are there any questions?"

Clark Barnes of the FBI, as expected, said, "Frank, in case anything were to happen to you, will you appoint a vice chief?"

"Yes, Clark. Since this is a joint operation, I intend to appoint a representative of either MI5 or Scotland Yard. I anticipate that the appointment will be made within the next day or so. Thank you, I intended to mention that."

Barnes was not finished. "Since this entire operation is on U.S. turf, do you consider it appropriate, should problems arise, to have a Brit in charge?"

"Yes."

This abrupt response by Wilson was not lost on veteran members of the assembled audience. Over years of association between Wilson and Barnes, there had been little love lost. Both men were highly capable and smart, but Wilson, with the Secret Service, had a contemplative nature while Barnes, who was with the FBI and had his training under Director Hoover, wanted to jump onto any problem, wasting no time. There was between them a large portion of respect, each for the other's talent. Even with personalities that were poles apart, as professionals they worked well together.

"If there are no further questions then, my friends and associates in this undertaking, I wish you God speed."

CHAPTER 7

FULL SPEED AHEAD (1946)

THE CHAIRMEN ANSWERED to Chief Wilson in Washington until their assignments were complete and approved by Wilson, who met at least weekly with all five task force leaders.

The work of the task forces was intense and exhausting because of the critical importance of the assignment, and also because of the tight schedule. The task forces usually met in conference facilities in their home offices or at the British embassy, and their work together developed into some very close friendships. These occasions became social events in neighborhood bars and restaurants. None of this, however, stood in the way of their jobs.

These little affairs concerned Wilson from a security perspective. He spoke with the Task Force chairmen about it and received little more than shrugs in response. In fact, one of them, a close associate, said, "Let it go, Frank. It's natural." Frank did.

Members often paired off. A dinner party or other social affair might be in progress when couples would quietly disappear, to show up the next morning ready for work. Two of the women on Task Force #1, Sharon Billingsley and Betty Hall, said they were willing to testify that a couple of the British agents, whom they declined to name, were indeed professional. Frank Wilson was not particularly pleased with these activities, fearing it could compromise the work at hand on a very tight schedule. He mentioned his concerns to the Task Force Chairs and got little more than shrugs in response. One of his own agents suggested that since they were all intelligent, professional adults, he should ignore their off-duty activities. He vowed to do so as best he could.

Careful notes were taken of all official interaction between and among the task forces. These records, however, were given the highest level of classification and were available only to Wilson's "executive" group.

Task force members, security conscious in their regular jobs, of course, were trained to look at even the most minor details of the responsibilities before them.

Task Force #3 addressed the President's rail car. For some years, it had carried the name "Ferdinand Magellan" on its sides. It was well known as President Roosevelt's favored mode of travel, and whenever the Ferdinand Magellan passed through a station, people would gather to watch it, waving and cheering as it passed. If the general population knew that this was the President's car, then certainly anyone who intended to harm the President, his family, guests, or other important persons would also know about it. This detail was handled by removing "Ferdinand Magellan" and substituting simply "Pullman."

Task Force #5 raised an interesting question: Rather than routing the presidential train through the huge and quite busy Union Station near downtown St. Louis, might it be better to use the less-used Wabash station on the northwest side of town? Some considered that the more remote location would make for better security, but it was a divided opinion. The decision was finally made to stay with Union Station, principally because this would avoid re-routing in St. Louis to the Wabash tracks which would place the train north of the Missouri River as it traveled westward and bring it into Mexico, Missouri. There would thus be no visit to Jefferson City, upsetting Governor Donnelly's plans as well as those of the Highway Patrol.

However, when this was considered, the Task Force was made aware that the Wabash tracks for most of their way were on higher and therefore dryer ground and could possibly serve as alternate routing in case of early spring rains. A subcommittee was charged with assembling data necessary to determine the alternate routing.

Several merchants inquired about developing souvenirs. The Service's Legal Department advised that they could not be prohibited unless they proved a safety hazard. They were encouraged to use good taste. Most cooperated and set up their souvenir stands some distance from the sites of major activities.

The great rivers of mid-America created routing problems for the planners. It would have been possible to send the presidential train over several tracks. The rivers involved, depending on the route selected, might have been the Allegheny and the Monongahela, which join to form the Ohio at Pittsburgh, and the Wabash, Mississippi, and Missouri Rivers. These were headaches for planners. They had to consider which route might be the most convenient, but, as mentioned earlier, possible flooding or accidents might cause changes to be made, perhaps on short notice. As these rivers were crossed in daylight, Churchill would look out of the windows and proclaim them "magnificent!"

While Mrs. Truman had an intense dislike for flying, plans had to be made concerning the proximity of a major airport able to handle the new Constellation. The B & O route took the party close to Pittsburgh, Cincinnati, Columbus, Louisville, and St. Louis—all with airline service. But would they handle the President's plane? All had to be investigated should an emergency arise, and it became necessary to use the Connie.

In their early years of increasing commercial air traffic, airports in major cities were located near downtown for convenience. Thus, the airports of all of the cities under consideration, except for St. Louis, were considered too small to handle the presidential plane, though they might be used in an emergency. St. Louis's Lambert Field was far enough from the city center that it could be used safely. Scores of such details were handled by the task forces.

On February 6, all of the members of the task forces were back in Washington where Wilson addressed them: "... due to the cooperative spirit that you have demonstrated over the past few weeks, you have brought to the table the talents and the assets peculiar to your agencies. By so doing, we have cooperatively built the best security system ever. But now, my friends, a word of caution: I sincerely compliment you for your work, but as you know from your regular jobs, no system is perfect. While I will demand perfection in the application of the security system we have developed for this event, I know that unforeseen situations can arise. Therefore, continued review of your assigned areas is necessary until all of the principals are safely delivered. I truly believe that for the next few weeks you will have the second most important job in the world: protecting those who have the most important job. There are some out there who would do harm to those we are directed to protect. They are smart! So are we. Thank you and good luck."

On February 9, Wilson sent the following letter to President Truman:

Mr. President:
Pursuant to your request, this letter confirms that in connection with the visit of Mr. Churchill next month, every plausible security matter has been addressed and appropriate responses are in place. I have

every confidence that the safety of all participants in the event is as close to 100% as humanly possible. My personnel will, of course, be immediately available to assist you and your guests at all times. Respectfully, Frank Wilson

CHAPTER 8

ST. JOHN'S REQUEST (1996)

FILE 1612 CONTAINED CONSIDERABLE detail on the organization of various agencies, both in the US and in Britain. The task of gleaning the information he needed was somewhat tedious, and Weatherly's small apartment was soon crowded with stacks of material, each carefully labeled. He arranged and re-arranged his notes as new facts and insights revealed themselves, but most surprising was how little information there was about the events of March 5—the date of Churchill's speech—and no indication of reviews or follow-up in the days afterward. Obviously, parts of the file were incomplete, or had been removed. Perhaps the American file, if he ever got it, would have more detail. The nature of the bureaucracies involved made it unlikely it would be available to him for some time. He determined to speak to St. John about that and about the St. John who was charged with espionage about a year later.

Professor Weatherly had a long-standing commitment to deliver a series of lectures on sixteenth century British Naval history at Glasgow University over three days, and he had to put aside the file to prepare and to make arrangements for his travel.

The St. John question still nagged at him. *When I am in Glasgow, perhaps I can find time to look into this. But for now, screening of file 1612 must continue.*

Now that the file was in Weatherly's hands, he began to feel pushed for time to practice his delivery and make needed adjustments in the texts of the lectures only two weeks away. He decided to call Clive St. John before he left; time permitting, he might be able to do some research of his own on the matter of Sir Hugh's arrest and what his case had to do with Clive's family.

He reached St. John that evening at his apartment. After exchanging pleasantries, St. John asked, "Tell me, Professor, how you are coming in your researches—was file 1612 as useful as you had hoped?"

"Actually, Clive, I'm finding it a bit overwhelming." That brought a chuckle from St. John. "However, I have discovered that there is almost nothing there about the actual event, and nothing at all in the way of reviews or follow-up, and, of course, the redacted portions are intriguing. I plan now to resume my discussions with the Justice Department to see if the American version differs from yours, if I can pry it out of them."

"I would be interested in knowing that myself," St. John responded.

"However, it will be a few weeks before I can get back to my research, as I am off to Glasgow shortly to deliver a series of lectures at the university there."

"Glasgow!" St. John interjected. "That's where my family roots are. I still have cousins there, though we haven't been in touch for years."

"Well, that brings me to a rather delicate question I want to ask you, possibly concerning your family, if you don't mind."

"Well, I suppose that depends on the nature of the question, but go ahead."

Weatherly paused, noting that St. John might have some reservations, but he plunged ahead. "While I was perusing *The Guardian* from the midforties for information on Churchill's visit, I came across a brief announcement that a certain Sir Hugh St. John had been charged with espionage and collusion with the enemy, but that was all I learned. You understand that it piqued my interest, as I understood your father was a naval officer." He paused, gauging St. John's response.

It was a soft, bemused chuckle. "Intentionally or not, you've encountered a topic I am very much looking forward to discussing with you, but in person. Have you a free hour any time tomorrow when we could meet?"

"I'd invite you over for what we call 'brunch' here tomorrow," Weatherly answered, "but every free level space here is occupied by file 1216. You understand."

"Most assuredly, Hamp. Could you come here for brunch tomorrow morning? Any time that is convenient for you."

"Thank you; that's kind of you, and if I may, I'll bring a beverage. Say around nine o'clock?"

St. John gave him clear, precise driving directions to his flat.

Clive's apartment, located not far from his embassy, featured a doorman in a rather plain uniform with a plastic badge identifying him simply as Oscar Trautman, who bowed slightly as he opened the door for the professor and followed him inside the lobby, asking, "And what is your name, sir?"

"I am Hampton Weatherly, here to see Clive St. John, at his invitation."

"Very good, Professor Weatherly," Trautman answered, turning to lead him through a set of double doors to a bank of four elevators. Oscar walked to the farthest door and typed a code into the small keypad under the call button. The elevator doors opened, and the doorman ushered Weatherly in, saying, "When you exit the lift, turn right. Mr. St. John's flat is the second on your right down the short hall." He stepped back, gave a little nod; the doors closed, and the car rose with a quiet hum. Weatherly estimated the speed and duration of the ride and concluded he got out on about the fourth or fifth level—the top floor or the one immediately below. He stepped out onto a dark gray carpet, looked to his left and then turned right, passing a door and stopping at the next. He knocked, and St. John's voice through a hidden speaker asked, "Professor Weatherly?" When he responded, the door opened, and St. John reached out to shake his hand and draw him inside. Weatherly was shocked to see his host in faded blue jeans, white socks, sneakers, and a sweatshirt advertising Montana State University. Hampton Weatherly owned neither blue jeans nor sweatshirts, so he felt slightly stuffy in his button-down dress shirt and creased khakis. St. John grinned at Weatherly's look and waited for his guest to remove his jacket and hat, which he took to hang in a small closet near the door. "Have a look around," he said. "I have omelets to attend to. And do you prefer coffee or tea?"

"Strong black tea, if you please, with honey and cream, if available."

"Coming right up. We'll eat in the 'dining nook' as I believe it is called here. Make yourself at home."

The living room, not large, was simply furnished with a comfortable looking couch flanked by small end tables, two easy chairs, a small television, and an elaborate looking sound system. A large, healthy looking succulent plant rested in one corner. Two medium-sized paintings, both rather abstract landscapes, hung on one wall. Weatherly's closer examination revealed them to be original oils, but he did not recognize the painter's signature. A short hallway led to a closed door at the end, but on the left side was a compact bathroom, and across from it what was obviously St. John's study. Weatherly glanced inside, but did not enter. Two large south-facing windows admitted light enough to reveal a long wooden table, a three-screen computer in the center, with rows of what seemed manuals, perhaps of a technical nature, on each side against the wall. In front of them were stacks of papers and files and the usual desk array of pencil and penholders, notepads, a small clock radio, and a large ashtray, clean. Beneath the table was a large empty waste basket and a double tier of books, both hardcover and paperbacks. Some could have been reference materials, others texts or novels. He was pleased to see three of his own history texts, but he could not be sure of the rest without entering the room. He did not open the door at the end of the hall, assuming it was St. John's bedroom. He returned to the breakfast nook, a small alcove off the kitchen, where St. John turned and poured a good-sized mug of tea from a large ceramic pot clad in a heavy knit cozy. He set it on the counter and carried the mug to the nook, which held a small, round table covered by a tan tablecloth and two silver settings with tan napkins in plain wooden rings. "Please sit down, Hamp." He gestured to a chair. "The toast is coming, and I just have to finish the omelets." He turned back to the stove, and flipped the two pans simultaneously, and turned off the burners beneath them. He poured another mug of tea and asked, "Would you like some fruit juice? I have some fresh cantaloupe and strawberries as well."

"Just the fruit sounds good to me," Weatherly replied, sitting down and pulling his chair to the table.

St. John stepped to the refrigerator and pulled out a platter of fruit, neatly arranged, with small serving forks, which he placed in the middle of the table. He turned back to the stove and opened the omelet pans to dump the steaming omelets on two plates close by on the counter. Four pieces of perfectly browned toast popped up from the toaster on the counter near the stove as he served the omelet. He placed the toast in a small basket containing another napkin, which he folded over the warm toast and placed on the table, and seated himself across from Weatherly. Each slipped his napkin out of its ring and arranged it on his lap. Weatherly, smiling at his host, said, "That was impressively done, Clive. A hot, fresh breakfast on the table in less than ten minutes of my arrival."

Clive grinned back at him. "Well, I was sure you would be punctual, my friend, and omelets are not quite so complicated as a quiche."

Hamp noted that the small glass pitcher of milk was heated, the sugar near it in a matching covered bowl. Steam hovered over their mugs as he prepared his tea. Clive offered the toast and cut into the delectably fragrant omelet, releasing the melted cheese with diced ham, and a fresh whiff of steam. Hamp buttered his slice of warm toast and complimented Clive on his culinary artistry. "I get the sense that you quite enjoy cooking, and I envy you. I consider myself competent, but it's a bit of a bother at times, and I admit to resorting to dishes already prepared and frozen."

"I do rather enjoy it and often spend most of a Saturday putting together entrees for the week, things I can freeze and thaw out when I get home in the evening. I have friends in for meals as often as I can, but not all that frequently. I often eat out, of course. There are lot of parties hosted by the huge international populace in Washington, D.C., and I am obliged by my position to appear at more of them than I genuinely enjoy."

"I think I understand, Clive. It sounds glamorous but wearisome to attend often."

"It's not my favorite part of the job, but I do pick up useful intelligence data occasionally, sometimes just by eavesdropping. And I often meet interesting and attractive women."

St. John was both a courteous and pleasant host. He guided their conversation subtly, encouraging Weatherly to talk of his career, his tastes, his acquaintances and interests, offering just enough of his own contributions to keep his guest entertained. They lingered over their tea when they had finished the omelets, and St. John made quick work of clearing the table and loading the dishwasher while Hamp went to his coat and returned with a silver flask and a small bottle of ginger mix, as well as his pipe and a leather tobacco pouch. "This being a weekend, and a social call, I thought you might agree to a wee dram of a fine bourbon, eh?"

"Such thinking is one of the things I like most about you, Professor," Clive responded, heading into the small kitchen for two sizable glasses and ice. He moved one of the small tables in the living room next to Hamp's chair and the other next to his, setting ash trays on each and producing a cigarette from a wooden box he left on the table between them.

Hamp stirred the ginger syrup into a generous shot of the bourbon, gently swirling the mix. "Now then," he began, "may we bring Sir Hugh into this very pleasant conversation?"

St. John's smile and slight nod suggested he was genuinely pleased. "This is a bit of a tale, Hamp. You see, I knew a bit about you before you made your audacious request, and I was elated when I heard your name. You may have noticed that I have what I believe is every book you've written, and many of your articles and presentations, several of which I acquired after I learned you had requested the release of file 1612."

"I suppose I should be flattered by your investigation," the professor said, folding his arms. "It seems I was a person of interest to your agency—the British government."

St. John laughed, then reached toward him, his palm outward in a reassuring, placating gesture. "Not so much, actually. My genealogical research piqued my interest in British history, and when I was posted to the United States, I came across your book *King James and the American Colonies*. I thought an American perspective on the king should be interesting, as I was aware of his support for the venture. I was impressed by the depth of your scholarship, and I acquired your other books on British history. When I arrived here, I made it a point to find out more about your work, but I never expected to meet you."

St. John's regard discomfited Weatherly momentarily; as was his habit, he removed his glasses, closed his eyes, and rubbed the bridge of his nose to gather his thoughts. "I hardly know how to respond," he admitted, replacing his spectacles and looking at his host. "Now I wish I had taken the time to look up your publications. I am curious about them, but I've been so involved in my research that I postponed that endeavor."

St. John shook his head. "I must say that I am relieved that you have not," he said. "I make no pretension of academic scholarship. I'm just a history buff and a member of a couple of organizations of like-minded amateurs, and I write for them occasionally. I would rather talk about your work, but in answer to your question, the Sir Hugh who was charged with espionage and collusion is my father." He paused and lit a second cigarette, awaiting Weatherly's reaction.

The professor peered intently at St. John, noting the trace of a smile on his lips, though his gaze was leveled on his guest. *Wow!* was his first thought, and then perplexity. *How could this guy be deputy head of security in the most important embassy in the world with that in his personal history? Actually, I've never questioned his validity, but I have never asked for his credentials or anything.* Neither man's gaze at the other wavered as Weatherly asked, "Did not that detail snag your career in MI5?"

St. John leaned forward, his hands on his knees. "Not so much as you might think. The charges, brought by the admiralty, were dropped before he was ever actually tried, and he remained an officer in the navy until his death." He leaned back, and his smile widened, knowing Weatherly was again stunned.

Weatherly smiled back and shook his head. "Well, you promised me a tale, and now you have me hooked, so please go on."

"Well, first of all, ours is a very minor name in the ranks of the nobility. By the time my father inherited the title, it was little more than an honorific, and I was never much interested in keeping it up, once the adolescent romantic appeal of it wore off.

"At thirteen I remember being disappointed that my father wasn't coming home immediately after the war. His job in the navy, I was told, was something very important, very secret, and that I could never talk about it, except with my mother. She missed no chance to remind me in the severest tones never to answer any questions should I be asked about it, never so much as mention it to anyone, not friends, acquaintances, or relatives. Occasionally a man, a naval captain, would come to our home in London, and he would converse with her, then talk to me briefly before he left. He assured me my father was in good health, that he missed me and Mother, and was hoping to see us before long, when he had finished his affairs with the admiralty. Father and I exchanged occasional letters, which I foolishly discarded or lost." St. John paused for a moment, and he glanced away from the professor; his look for a moment was serious, but when he spoke, his voice and gaze were level, and the Scottish burr in his voice was modulated.

"He returned when I was 14 and home on holiday. For the first time I was aware that he was aging. He looked older than I remembered him, his hair thinner and turning gray, his face worn, though not yet wrinkled. Then he was called away again, I think to India, and I saw him only sporadically. He occasionally mentioned that he had been to two or three countries for varying periods of time, though usually less than a year. So you see, we were never very close, and I knew his picture better than his face. There were a number of them in our flat, and in a scrapbook my mother kept and shared only with me—it was another of our very important secrets. To this day she keeps it locked away in a wooden box, and if she ever looks at it or thinks about it, I don't know. She became very emotional the last time I asked to see it some years back, and I haven't asked about it since."

"What do you know about the charges?" Weatherly asked.

"Frankly, very little. When I applied for the necessary clearances for my work in the navy, I was grilled about my relationship with my father, but I was in no position to ask them about him. The nature of their inquiries seemed to suggest that there was something highly confidential about him, but they didn't discuss it with me. By the time I learned of the charges, years later from my mother, he was dead."

"When did that happen?" Hamp interjected.

"In 1970. He was sixty years old, and returning, sick, from Afghanistan aboard a navy vessel when he died. At his request, we were told he was buried at sea. I was in London at the time and got the news of his death just minutes after the commodore personally delivered it to my mother, also by phone. I left almost immediately on a bereavement pass and went to her flat, to be there when the commodore came the next morning with Father's personal effects. There weren't many." St. John paused, opened the box to retrieve another cigarette, and lit it while Weatherly pondered the details he'd just absorbed.

"If you don't mind, could you tell me what rank he held at the time of his death?"

"He was a commodore, second class. Fortunately, his monetary benefits, which went of course to my mother, were sufficient for her comfort and well-being for the rest of her life."

Weatherly hesitated a moment before he asked, "With your connections you must have access to files, even secret or secured files that cover his career, right?"

St. John's manner changed, Weatherly noted. *He's making a report, and probably half his time in MI5 he's making reports, written and oral. He looks alert, confident, attentive.*

"Aye, 'there's the rub,' as Hamlet put it. My father was in Naval Intelligence, under the direct command of the admiralty. For a time, we were both in the Royal Navy, and he advised me not to pursue that kind of duty, but I rather backed into it, you might say, by my interests in the electronics, coding, etc. I don't remember my father actually encouraging them, but maybe there's something genetic in our aptitude for that sort of thing. When my enlistment was up, I resigned my commission, having already applied for a position in MI5. I had the feeling that someone or some agency influenced my acceptance into the Service. My father never spoke of it, beyond congratulating me on my career choice. And I soon learned how tightly controlled data and information is disseminated in these circles, and a proven 'Need to Know' precludes personal fishing expeditions."

"If I may ask," Weatherly interrupted, "what were among his personal effects? Anything to give you a clue as to his duties in the Service?"

"There was a sidearm, with holster and gear, but no ammunition, his full dress uniform with all its service ribbons, and a packet of official papers, mostly dealing with survivor benefits, and several letters of commendation, official notices of his promotions, but almost nothing about his actual career or the nature of his relationship with the admiralty.

"He had earned medals we never knew of, and a couple were not represented in the ribbons on his dress uniform, though he had earned them years before his death. Some of the papers bore the signatures of admirals and rear admirals, but I have always wanted to know more. I was and am constrained by duty to the Service and the Crown." He paused and gave Weatherly a long, speculative look before going on. "Professor Weatherly—Hamp—I'm asking a personal favor of you, but please understand that I am placing you under no obligation." He paused again and raised his hand to stop Weatherly's response. "I want to engage you to do some research for me, and I am prepared to compensate you for your time and efforts."

Weatherly shook his head and raised his palm toward St. John, who stopped him by interrupting, "I know a lot about you, Hamp, and find you in person to be both highly respectable and highly respected. I know that you are fully trustworthy and skilled in your profession."

Weatherly was again about to respond, but something in St. John's face, his strong, steady stare, gave the professor pause. *That's the look of a professional interrogator; brooks no disseminating. Yet, there is something else behind the gaze: a look of hope, a hint of warmth, even sincerity. He's almost smiling.*

St. John's manner relaxed as he leaned forward in his chair and snubbed out his cigarette in the heavy ashtray. "You are not entirely comfortable with my compliments, Professor Weatherly," he went on, "but I intended no flattery. Our research, though we had only days to investigate you, was hardly exhaustive, but enough to prompt me to volunteer to interview you as part of the investigation."

"You are quite right, Clive. I am flattered and somewhat abashed by it, but please tell me what I can do for you; I am in your debt for securing file 1612 for me, and for looking into your agency's role in the event, so ask anything of me."

St. John studied Weatherly for a moment, considering his words. "Well, you've already begun to, quite inadvertently I am sure. I wasn't aware of *The Guardian*'s announcement of the charges against my father, though I have combed through many newspapers and other publications and documents to learn all I could about it, which wasn't much. The charges were filed, and then they were dropped. When I inquired of the Admiralty about Father's service with them, I was firmly told those records were not available to me upon my personal request; if it was part of an investigation by MI5, I must provide proper authorization." He smiled, seeming for the moment to drop his smooth professional manner. "All I am asking of you, Hamp, is that in the course of your research, if you should turn up any reference to my father, Sir Hugh, please let me know—discretely, of course."

"I will do all I can, Clive, as discretely as possible, but would it be too much to ask what you already know, so I won't be duplicating data you already have? It would help sharpen the focus of my research."

St. John rose, excused himself, and walked into his study. Weatherly heard a drawer open, the rustle of papers, and the closing of the drawer. St. John reappeared, holding a large manila envelope, about three inches thick. "Over the years," he said, handing it to his guest, "I have made many notes, many copies of the data I gathered, including from history books dealing with the Admiralty, and especially its intelligence agencies. He paused and shook his head. "As it happens, my grandfather St. John was commended for his service to king and country during the First World War in the War Department's coding and encryption unit, so I come from a long line of government spies." Both men smiled, and St. John went on. "I've tried to summarize here what I have uncovered and added some of my speculations and questions I'd like answered. I have no other family to speak of—Father was also an only child, preceded in death by two stillborn sisters—and with little contact with his two uncles, both of whom emigrated—one to Canada and the other to South Africa—and a few cousins. So, I really haven't anyone to ask or even discuss our family history with, and I want to know more about my father's life." He paused and leaned slightly forward. "You understand very well the obligations of an only son, with whom this part of the family tree finally ends." St. John's stare for a moment compelled Weatherly's full attention, then both men looked away.

Either Clive is sincerely opening himself to me, or he is so good at opening people up that he has me wanting to believe the former. He is compelling, but not overtly manipulative—and identifies himself as a spy. As a joke maybe, but revealing.

"You know, Professor, I never really knew my father, no real contact with Mother, and being an only bairn, I have always felt rather orphaned. As a lad, I always looked forward to getting to know Father, have a game of bowls with him, drink a few beers together, and now...well. And to add salt to the wound, the military transport carrying him home for burial was lost on its way home in the Adriatic. All of his papers gone. I suppose that his military career was no more interesting than many others..."

Hampton waited a few moments, then asked, "Did your father talk to you or to her about his service?"

"He did—very circumspectly answering my questions up to a point, but always careful, I understand now, not to divulge anything specific about what he did. At some point, I learned, either from him or from her that he was in Naval Intelligence, had very high security clearances, and was subject to sudden assignments anywhere in the world. Even after I was in the navy and had high-level clearances myself, we never spoke of his duties. As an only child, I am left to carry this burden and, if possible, to resolve it. I am not looking for sympathy. It's a challenge, but if there is any way to do it, I want to learn the truth of the matter and, if possible, to remove this blot on our family name. My research thus far into my father's service career has been limited. There's a gap—the war years—in my knowledge and in family papers as well. Of course, he was in Naval Intelligence service and remained in the navy after the war ended, but I do not know what his duties were beyond what I have told you. I think that when you have reviewed this material, you will understand there is much I do not know, and may never know, but I want to fill in the blanks, so even what may seem trivial details you might uncover could be useful. But don't waste any of your valuable research time on it."

He sat back in his chair and smiled at Weatherly. "I can't tell you what a pleasure it is to talk about this with you. It brings up memories I had forgotten, and I am eager for your return from Scotland when we can discuss what you find there."

St. John rose and walked to the closet and retrieved the professor's jacket and hat and handed them over. Weatherly extended his hand. "Thank you very much for a most interesting conversation. I am looking forward to being in touch. And the brunch was outstanding."

"The pleasure was mine, Hamp. I hope we can talk a bit before you fly off to the place of my family's indigenous roots, if not quite my present home. I will make some inquiries and would like to discuss my connections there with you. And a reminder, do not let this digression at all influence or take time away from your research and professional endeavors." St. John's handshake was firm and warm as they nodded briefly at one another without smiling.

CHAPTER 9

OFF TO GLASGOW (2006)

WEATHERLY SPENT MUCH OF the following week brushing up his lectures and practicing his delivery. Evenings he spent going through St. John's paperwork. He was not surprised that nearly all the materials corroborated what Clive had told him during and following their brunch. He learned that Sir Hugh had graduated from the University of Strathclyde there in Glasgow, and St. John had some of his father's student records. And, assuming that Clive had given him all the pertinent information he had gathered over the years, there was a significant lack of any records of Sir Hugh's life and service in the navy. Parts of some letters of commendation and other official correspondence had been redacted—names and signatures, descriptions of his actions and achievements, even parts of the Admiralty letterhead were blacked out. *The work of a zealous guardian of naval intelligence, or of Clive St. John?* Another topic to be discussed when next they met. He spent much of the flight reviewing his lecture notes.

The overnight train delivered him to Glasgow early in the morning. He located the rooms he had taken at the university for the days of his lecture and left his suitcase. His first lecture was scheduled for that evening, leaving him almost an entire day. Clive had suggested that some old files from the offices of MI5 were archived in the library of the University of Strathclyde in Richmond St., only a twenty-minute walk from his rooms at Cowcaddens Rd. on the Glasgow University campus. He visited the library and established his credentials there, giving him free access to the data in the library's stacks and document files. He located the MI5 archives and would be able to visit them without losing time.

His first lecture went well. He was introduced by the university Provost, Sanford McTavish, who said he was pleased with the attendance. The students and dons in in the audience were attentive and curious. He was able to handle most of their questions without trouble. A few loaded inquiries were posed by mischievous students anxious to display their knowledge of the subject most likely gained just that afternoon. One student asked, "Why is it, Professor Weatherly, that you, a recognized scholar in English history, chose to teach at an obscure college in the middle-west?"

"It is my *alma mater*," he responded, smiling, "and when I finished my doctorate at American University and a two-year fellowship at Oxford, there were few positions available for professors of English history. I was flattered by the offer, and having considered others over the years, I concluded that I enjoyed teaching and learning English history among colleagues I respected and liked with the support of an institution I am proud to represent." A light smattering of applause followed his answer. Weatherly came to realize he was addressing an audience whose members had not been born when Churchill was Prime Minister, or even an elder statesman, and that he was therefore including in his lectures assumptions many in his audience could not share. Consequently, and chastising himself for not recognizing it, he worked until the small hours revising his notes for the other two lectures.

He was introduced by McTavish, and later the two men retired to a nearby pub for a pint to get better acquainted and to polish off the evening. Weatherly found McTavish a most agreeable companion. He was tall and lean with an unruly shock of white hair, bushy white eyebrows, and piercing blue eyes, and a bluff, direct manner. He had lived in Glasgow all his life, had achieved a prestigious position there, and took serious interest in local area history.

I may never have a better opportunity than right now, presumptuous though it may be, to get some insight into Sir Hugh's early life—if McTavish can spare me some time on Tuesday...

"Dr. McTavish's office" was the pleasant response to his call.

"Hampton Weatherly here. Is Dr. McTavish available?"

"Certainly, Professor Weatherly. I attended your first lecture and found it quite interesting. Please hold."

"Good morning, Hamp. Sandy here."

"Thank you and good morning, er, Sandy, if I may?"

"Certainly. How can I help you?"

"I have a rather interesting question about some family history here in the Glasgow area. The family is St. John, and I hope you might be able to provide some insight for me. Are you free for lunch tomorrow…or even today if your schedule permits?"

"Oh, yes, Hamp. I do have some information on the St. John family in the Glasgow area. Quite well regarded, although we have lost touch over the past few years. My schedule is open today. Suppose we meet at The Andrew. It's on Richmond Street…"

"Yes, I recall the location," he answered, preferring not to discuss their having consumed several pints there the previous night. "Will noon be suitable?"

"Certainly. I will see you then."

CHAPTER 10

MCTAVISH OPENS UP

PROFESSOR WEATHERLY WAS ten minutes late for the appointment and apologized to McTavish as he entered the pub. The barman asked their preference, and McTavish called for two pints of the local stout and ordered lunch as well.

"Aye" the barman replied, "and a fair brew it is, you would agree, Professor?" Weatherly nodded but preferred not to recognize this obvious breach of the international barkeepers' code of ethics. Pressing a bit, the barman said, "A true Scot's beer, you might know. From Aberdeen."

"The beer please, Curly," McTavish interrupted, his Scots accent more evident than it had been on the phone. A glance upward by Weatherly revealed two thin strands combed over the barman's shiny pink pate. The three men laughed.

"So, my new friend, Hamp. What might be all of this St. John business?" McTavish asked when they were seated.

"Well, Sandy, this is a rather winding tale, but please indulge me. I am preparing a book on the security measures in place during Mr. Churchill's visit to my college in 1946. It seems that some of the U.S. State Department's records of those plans are still classified. One of the British files very important to me was obtained for me by Clive St. John, Deputy Chief of Security at the British Embassy. Those files are linked, but I got only the British records. An interesting factor is that these fifty-year-old files hold little of current interest—unless one is writing a book."

McTavish laughed and said, "Okay. I begin to see the connection."

"And more. Our State Department (roughly equivalent to your Foreign Office) received a cable from John Major objecting to the release of the file and asking that a security officer at your embassy in Washington be permitted to contact me. Of course, I agreed. I need all the connections I can get. And that's how I met Clive St. John, the security officer. It turns out we have some common interests, and I decided to pursue this a bit. I am not sure I have ever met a titled gentleman before, and his story was intriguing."

"All right. I think I see where you're going with this. I know you are pressed for time and need to get back home, but there may be information here in the Glasgow area that you need for your book. Let's finish lunch and go back to my office..."

"Oh, no, Sandy," Weatherly interrupted. "I would not impose on your time..."

"My schedule is free. Let's do it."

Back in his office, McTavish relaxed behind his desk and pulled out his pipe. "The trustees officially forbid our smoking on the premises. They know I smoke in my office, but they haven't sacked me yet. Now, about this St. John business. I am not surprised that Clive St. John is sticking to you. You see him as a source for your book. He sees you as his source with access to some of his family history that he can't get without compromising his status and career in MI5. The St. Johns are very sensitive folks. Good people, for the most part, but very protective of their heritage. They all seem to feel that any blemish on the family name is their personal responsibility to erase. It's an obsession with them. Sometimes they are almost reclusive. I have known a very few of them personally. The one I knew best was one Sir Hugh St. John."

Bingo! A connection, Weatherly thought.

"He was a few years older than me, in the Naval Service. A very private, quiet, unassuming man. We had some pleasant visits during the times he appeared here in the north. He and the Lady St. John had one child, a son, who would be your friend, Clive. Their flat was next door to our house."

"So you knew him when he was a boy?"

"Nae, not so much. While I know he spent some time in Scotland during the war, he was seldom here, and as I say, rather reclusive by nature, like the rest of the clan. I may have met the lad Clive occasionally, and even less often as an adult. He's done well in his career, I assume."

"Indeed. He is second officer for security at the British Embassy in Washington, a few years away from retirement, and a very impressive agent. As we discussed the file, I asked how he got into MI5, and he told me his father's career had been in Naval Intelligence and his grandfather with the Admiralty's Coding and Encryption services in the first war."

"Perhaps here's an angle worth considering," McTavish said. He leaned forward, jabbing the air with his pipe. "I mentioned that Sir Hugh was a very private person. He never made much of a splash in the social world, as one might expect of nobility; he married a commoner. And yes, it is a noble family but at the same time rather impecunious. They simply could not compete financially in the expected circles, so you might say they sort of withdrew. Another factor could well be that when Hugh and—I can't recall her name—were wed, the depression of the thirties was upon us; jobs were few. Military service was honorable, but good postings were scarce. To support his family, and no doubt leaning on the family title, Sir Hugh entered the naval service. You know the British naval history better than I. The war came along, and it is likely that Clive was evacuated to a rural area during the worst of it. They did this to protect the children and to ease the strain on essential services in the metropolitan areas, particularly London, Manchester, the major ports. Where the Lady St. John was, I do not know."

"Well," Weatherly said, "what you have told me confirms what Clive talked about. I am almost of a conviction that he feels himself something of an orphan—an absent father in the Service, a mother quite alone in London and perhaps evacuated. Clive during this period of his life lived in Wales with a family not his own."

McTavish leaned across his desk, his eyes bright behind the smoke curling up before his face, smiling at his guest's fascination. "There's more to this winding tale of yours, Professor. Intrigue and treason!"

"Involving Sir Hugh, you mean?" Weatherly asked.

"Yes!" McTavish responded, almost exultantly. "Sir Hugh St. John, noble neighbor and family acquaintance, was charged by the Admiralty Court of Treason—collusion with the enemy!" He sat back, gauging the effect of his shocking announcement.

Weatherly nodded, his look bland, and he asked, "Do you happen to know what was his sentence?"

"The sentence for treason is death, of course, but the sentence was shortly repealed, and Hugh St. John was banished to the Orkneys pending the outcome."

"I am shocked," Weatherly said evenly. "That information was not carried in *The Guardian* or *The Times,* nor has it come up in any of our conversations. But why was he sent to such a remote, inaccessible place as Orkney and why in such a small town?"

McTavish leaned back in his chair. "There may have been several reasons. First, he could have been quite an embarrassment to the Admiralty Court and, from their point of view, the less attention he got, the better for them. Some think he was essentially a double-agent—a mole—sending misleading information to the Germans and maybe the Russians, messages that they may have felt had some value. Not only was there quality transmission from that far northern location, but he also was of more value for his reports of convoys headed for Murmansk around the North Cape of Norway. He may have worked to confuse the German submarine command and steer them into interception by Allied forces. A lot of shipping to Murmansk was lost, but what did get through was valuable. Also, the North Cape area was well within range of any air cover that might be available in Murmansk or naval units hiding in the Novaya Zemlya fjords."

"Am I to understand that Sir Hugh was a double-agent? A spy for Britain and a mole, trading secrets with Germany?"

"I believe he might well have been, and with the Russians as well." McTavish sat back, pleased at Weatherly's surprise at these revelations.

"Why did the Russians care much about what was going on in the North Sea? Their naval presence there was very small, so why were they there in the first place?"

"The obvious tactical reason," McTavish responded, "would be to keep them informed what kind of junk we were feeding the Germans. They were our allies, after all. There could be many reasons. Another, as I mentioned earlier, could be to provide some cover for incoming convoys. I doubt that carried much weight with them, but maybe a small factor. Actually, I place more weight in what I would consider a 'pride' factor. For many generations, the Russians have felt locked out from the oceans of the world. Think about it. Ports in Siberia, Vladivostok, and other smaller places and these ports are too remote to be of much value. Their outlet to the Atlantic through Leningrad—soon to be St. Petersburg again—is closely restricted. They formerly owned Finland and what are now the Baltic States, but not in 1944. So, look for a warm-water port. Sevastopol is one, but it is only an outlet through the Black Sea and Turkey controlled the Bosporus.

"You know all of this—it's your field. What needs to be added is the Russian mind-set, almost paranoia on this very subject. Just look at us! A world power, from the Pacific to the Black Sea! Six thousand miles! And we have to ask some nabob in Turkey for permission. A ridiculous situation. Some might say 'Who can blame them?' but thrashing about with little peanut things like this make no sense...except to them. Sorry, Hamp, I've made a speech. But it is a fascinating little piece of Scots history."

Weatherly removed his glasses and massaged the bridge of his nose. "Yes, that all speaks to the Russian mind-set, but you are suggesting that Moscow would look for such a small niche to gain what? What are they going to do with the data gained through the interception of radio transmissions and reports by St. John they could observe for themselves by similar means? They value recognition or an enhanced reputation or regard in the eyes of the rest of the world that much?" Weatherly was openly skeptical.

McTavish replied, "Yes."

"And so," Weatherly continued, thinking aloud, "they found a man of the nobility who may have been shunned by his peers, and by his sensitive nature he was susceptible to Russia's overtures... He may have even read a little of Marx or Engels." He paused and smiled. "Might have read it while a student here."

"Hardly likely," McTavish responded, looking away, "but I suppose possible. But I'd be interested to know what Sir Hugh might have shared of these experiences with his son."

Weatherly shook his head. "He claims his father advised against his getting into Naval Intelligence, but he did mention that he suspected strings were pulled to get him into MI5 after his term of enlistment in the navy was up."

McTavish rocked back in his chair and drew on his pipe. "What I can tell you is that Sir Hugh St. John, as a junior officer in the navy, was posted in civilian clothes to the Orkney Islands in the last year of the war, sent to a small town to host his radio-telegraph operation. His job was ostensibly to report on ship and air traffic around this far-northern route and make it possible to intercept German submarine and even commercial traffic."

"Do you know how long he was up there? When he was court-martialed, the war was over."

"Aye, and the Cold War was opening," McTavish reminded him. "Except," he continued, pointing at the professor with the stem of his pipe, "though he was court-martialed for it, his real job up there probably was to feed false information to the Germans, using known reports, representing perhaps 80% accurate data, news and the other 20% or so designed to mislead them into making a major mistake. These broadcasts were in the current German code as soon as possible after it had been broken by experts at Bletchley Park, and they were shared with the Russians."

Weatherly, suspicious, retreated for a moment. *Why is McTavish, whom I met only yesterday, spending so much time with me on a subject that is not my reason for being here in Glasgow? The subject is fascinating, but...I like Sandy. If I had not called him this morning, would he have called me? And how does he know all this?* "Why with the Russians?" he asked.

"They were our allies, remember, though hardly trusted by the English or most others. I don't have a full and convincing explanation for that. One theory that fits what we know of the St. John mentality could reveal the best and the worst of motives. The worst would be for money, but I think the risk was too great for any amount the Russians would offer. He may have been paid by the KGB, but the Admiralty would probably have been aware of that, though he could have hidden this source of income from his superiors."

Is something going on here? Weatherly thought. *Sandy undoubtedly knows a lot more than he's telling me. I need to think more about this.* "This is hardly a pattern for the St. Johns, is it?

"No, Sir Hugh was the very embodiment of personal honor and the service of God, Crown, and Country, but he would do the best he could for his little family too."

"So, those intelligence reports were of sufficient value that the Russians were willing to pay for them?"

"Exactly, and Sir Hugh might have been vulnerable. This would have put the Admiralty Court in a difficult position, but even more it put the St. John name in a possibly compromising situation, something that the proud St. John family could not abide. Your friend Clive I'm sure is fully aware of all of these circumstances."

"He knows that his father was charged and on appeal cleared of all charges and returned to duty in Naval Intelligence, but aware that his father took bribes from the Russians while spying on the Germans for the Admiralty? Where is the proof?"

"Here's the next chapter," McTavish replied, refilling his pipe as he considered his words. "Whitehall and MI5 were aware of his obsession with keeping the family name pure, which must have weighed very heavily on his conscience, along with the very real danger he was in while collaborating with the enemy, Germany and Russia, whom few trusted. And how do I know these things? Because I know more about the secretive St. John family than anyone else in the UK."

Weatherly, though intrigued by this boast, responded by asking, "Where would you suggest I go to research data on Sir Hugh's history, especially any records of his naval service? Since he was in Naval Intelligence, I expect that few records of specific assignments are open."

McTavish leaned back in his chair and studied the professor for a moment, squinting through the smoke of his pipe. "I think," he said after a moment, "that I can say without boasting that our university probably has more records and files of British military history, especially any involving Scottish soldier and sailors, than most. There is more in London, of course, but access is very limited." He paused again, looking upward as though gathering his thoughts. "Clive St. John is undoubtedly aware that the Strytheclyde Library has more data on MI5, and undoubtedly he would like you to see how much of what he wants to know you can dig up for him. I will arrange for you to have full access to all our library resources, as allowed by law and our chief librarian, Mr. Ballard. He will handle your requests for specific files. And, of course you can call on me at any time if you think I can be of help."

Weatherly stood and thanked the provost for his time and advice. When McTavish rose, they shook hands; the Scotsman was smiling as Weatherly left.

The next afternoon, Weatherly prevailed upon McTavish to arrange for him to make a private call to Warren Christopher in Washington, DC. McTavish declined all the professor's efforts to reimburse the university for the long-distance international charges. He led Weatherly to a private office, briefed him on the procedures for making the call, and closed the door softly when he left.

This is really pushing my luck, he thought. *Will Christopher be in? Will he take my call?* Miss Buxton greeted him with cool professionalism. "How may I help you, Professor?"

"I need to speak with Mr. Christopher briefly on a matter we discussed in an earlier conversation. It is not urgent, but I am in Glasgow, Scotland, and need to verify the qualifications of a source here. It should take only a few minutes of his time."

"Please hold while I check with the Secretary." There was a click, and shortly Warren Christopher was on the line.

"Good afternoon, Dr. Weatherly—though it's still morning here. Is Scotland proving a good ground for your researches?"

"More than I would have expected. My question is can I trust Sandy McTavish without question or qualification, and can I take as accurate any information he gives me? He indicated in a recent conversation that you were acquainted."

"The answer," Christopher said, "is a qualified yes, based on my few brief conversations with the man. You are lucky to have run into him. If he can help you, I think you can trust what he says. And, Hamp, we Dakota boys have got to hang together, so if any further questions arise, call Mrs. Buxton and me. Between us we can handle most things. Now, if you can help me on this Irish problem...."

Both men laughed and hung up.

This is becoming hard to understand, thought Weatherly. *I can't keep track of who is using whom. I am using Clive; MI5 is using Clive and me; Clive is using me. What else is out there? I hope all are as honest as they seem.*

Weatherly still spent most of his daylight hours searching the MI5 archives, both for his book and for anything relative to the St. John case. Eventually he found copies of the court records of Sir Hugh's case. A surprising entry, dated August 1946, reported that Sir Hugh would likely be charged with espionage because of the following report received from the Royal Audit Office:

"...We find, however, that the re-transmission to German naval authorities was sent using a code that had been compromised on June 25 resulting in damaging information being sent to German naval authorities. Sir Hugh was in control of re-transmissions to German naval headquarters who viewed him as an 'unauthorized source.' Our inspector viewed this finding as 'inadvertent' and so classified it. However, further research reveals a pattern of similar transmissions, and this pattern can only be viewed as probably intentional and, if so, subject to possible criminal action."
(signed) Reginald Billings,
Chief, Admiralty Division of Audits

CHAPTER 11

THE DIARY (1996)

THE RESEARCH OF HIS WORK on security surrounding Churchill's appearance at Westminster was soon exhausted. He would never have all the facts he wanted, but the broad outlines of MI5's involvement were clear, and he had examined everything he could in the university's holdings. But he had only scratched the surface of the Sir Hugh story.

His last two lectures went well and were applauded in the campus newspapers as being a significant contribution to sixteenth century British naval history. This recognition gave a boost to his self-confidence that he lacked going into the St. John obligation. *Could I extend my stay here in Glasgow for further investigations? It makes sense since I am already here. And nothing is pushing at home. My publisher has a queue of books ahead of mine; I shall indulge myself and do my new friend what favors I can. A lot of naval history is right here in Glasgow, and should I find it necessary to visit the Orkneys, they are only a day away.*

Weatherly's search began in the library of Strathclyde University, where getting access to all but the most highly classified data in the MI5 files was fairly simple. He presented his credentials from the Department of Justice and The Library of Congress as well as his special pass from Glasgow University to the head librarian, who disappeared with them into a private office. He emerged in five minutes and smiled at Weatherly as he explained that he had been in contact with the Vice President for Campus Security, who had promised that, if approved, the professor could pick up his pass at the front desk after no more than twenty-four hours. In the meantime, the staff of the library had been alerted to aid him any way they could in his research. After a brief tour of the facility, he was shown to a spacious cubicle just outside the MI5 archives. The valuable and classified documents were behind a windowless wall with a single door accessible with a swipe card, which he would get if his application was approved. After thanking the young lady who had been guiding him, he picked up the lined tablet from the desk and headed to the row of computers that functioned as the library's card catalog. Avoiding all the files marked 'Secret' or 'Top Secret,' and some identified only as 'Enter MI5 AS ID Code,' Weatherly nonetheless found something that so elated him he felt like dancing. Not secreted or hidden in any way, he found reference to a small volume, hand-written, in something like the style of a diary. The reproductions on his screen were almost unreadable, but the next day, with help from one of the librarians, he ordered the original file. It was delivered to his cubicle in about twenty minutes. The title page read "My Experiences in the Orkneys by Hugh St. John." It was mid-morning when he found this treasure. The entries in this volume were written in the first person. *"Upon the advice of my father, I enrolled at the university as a Scottish History major. One afternoon, my adviser, Professor Ian McDowel, asked me to remain for a brief conference after his lecture. I had never received such a request before, but I was more intrigued than alarmed by it. He invited me to sit, then leaned back. The squeal of the mechanism in the old chair startled me, and he smiled, crossing his legs and putting his fingertips together. He said, "Mr. St. John, you are a better writer than most at this level of your progress. You might do well to attend Mr. Nichols's series of lectures on 'Writing Creatively' in the next term. I have spoken with him about your talents, and I think it would be a good learning experience."*

With McDowel's endorsement, I was accepted, and I enjoyed the class immensely. I learned that creative writing did not mean poetry and fiction, but thinking about one's subject in creative ways, telling a story in ways that engage one's reader. This journal is intended as such an exercise. The next thing Weatherly knew, the librarian was saying "Closing time, please, Professor Weatherly."

Weatherly called Clive. It was near lunchtime in Washington, and the embassy operator located Clive in the dining room. "Clive, Hamp here. I find that I must delay my departure from Glasgow for perhaps several days. There is so much naval history here, much more than I had thought, that since I am here and nothing is pressing at home, I must visit some museums and libraries devoted to my field. I will call when I know more."

"Certainly, Hamp. I will meet your schedule."

The next morning, Weatherly asked the librarian if he might have the entire file copied at his expense to save a lot of time. She said that policy prohibited copying classified documents. The professor, recognizing he could not win this little skirmish, spent the rest of the afternoon in tight latex gloves copying from the diary.

CHAPTER 12

ESPIONAGE (1996)

SOME OF THESE OBSCURE FILES, many of which verified Sir Hugh's account of his wartime service, while not the actual records of the Admiralty Court, contained data sufficient to demonstrate what happened after Sir Hugh's arrest in 1946. In his initial interrogation, Sir Hugh, citing the top secrecy of the allegations against him, refused to confirm or deny them. Several further interrogations brought the same results. These refusals to cooperate with the court resulted in his conviction, which was immediately appealed. There, at the option of either party, proceedings could be closed to the public. Despite many misgivings, Sir Hugh eventually opened up in closed sessions, detailing his wartime experience as a special agent for the Admiralty. Some of his testimony inexplicitly reached the Glasgow press. Since the payments he received from both Germany (the enemy) and Russia (an ally) were documented as valid, defense stipulated that Sir Hugh had been in the pay of Russia for some fourteen months, feeding them military information from the Admiralty. Information was also fed for eleven months to the German government, each in their own codes. It was thus necessary that each new code had to be broken before traffic could be sent. Sir Hugh kept careful records of all messages sent to both governments and details of his payments from them; these were admitted into evidence at the closed hearing where they established that the information to the Germans and to the Russians was 80% accurate, necessary to validate his transmissions. Much of it was either outdated or already leaked, however, and so of little or no value. The remaining 20% of the messages were false or misleading.

His personal log of these transactions, verified by the Admiralty, was sufficient proof that Sir Hugh's activities were not only sanctioned but explicitly ordered by the Admiralty over the signature of the First Sea Lord,

A.V. Anderson. The prosecution, aware that the war was winding down, had no desire to see Sir Hugh convicted under the wartime clause, which required the death penalty. Therefore, delay after delay was entered in the court docket and automatically agreed to. The case was finally called up in November of 1945.

Thus, the prosecution had the problem of protecting the clandestine activities of the Admiralty while prosecuting the already public case against Sir Hugh, while recognizing that the false information fed to the Germans had, very likely, caused considerable damage to the enemy's navy, which was the operation's intent. He was following Admiralty orders while recognizing his responsibility for English deaths in which he might have been complicit, which was at the base of the charges brought against him.

The prosecution moved, and the judges agreed that Sir Hugh should be sentenced to house arrest in or near the village of Quoyloo in the Orkney Islands while an appeal was being prepared and filed. Thus, he was sent back to Quoyloo, which he had frequented during the last year of the war. Very shortly the appeal was heard and the charges dropped; he retained his rank and security clearances in the Admiralty.

The Strathclyde library on Richmond Street also held a Decree of Clemency, confirmed by Elizabeth II in August of 1975. The Decree absolved Sir Hugh of all charges against him and recognized his considerable contribution to the war effort and post-war international operations. When he had read and re-read the decree, Weatherly laid aside his pencil, removed his glasses, and massaged the bridge of his nose. Sir Hugh knew that he had been absolved of the espionage charges by the Decree of Clemency. Still, he apparently felt some lingering guilt, for clandestine actions which probably caused damage and injuries to British military personnel. And, while his actions were justified because he was following orders from the highest echelons of the Admiralty, these actions were regarded as a form of treason in some circles. His family's reputation for adhering to a rather rigid moral code, protecting the family honor, plus his dedication to the Naval code all must have weighed heavily upon him.

Although Hamp's luncheon conversation with Provost McTavish gave him a disturbing picture of both Sir Hugh and Clive, still on his mind was the nagging question of whether this amateur analysis was what St. John was looking for when he asked Weatherly to help him research his family history. *I hate not to trust Clive; he's such an agreeable fellow. But his interest is unusual. Surely if anyone should have credentials granting access to this material it would be a security officer at the most important embassy on earth. I want to trust him, but I am not sure what he really wants of me nor what all his motives are.*

In the end, Weatherly decided to face Clive with his uncertainty, realizing that his distrust of St. John, once revealed, could very well mean the end not only of their relationship but also of any further assistance for his book. The issue had to be confronted and resolved.

He called Clive's home number late the next afternoon. "Clive? Hamp here. Glad to have reached you at home. Is everything going well?"

"Oh yes, Hamp. The usual exchange of insults on Capitol Hill but nothing major. I am surprised by your call. How are your researches going?"

"Quite well, thank you. With full access to the MI5 archives at the Strytheclyde library, and I have turned up some fascinating documents. But we've got to talk. I was planning to take the overnight on Tuesday, as I told you. Could you possibly..."

"Yes, Hamp, of course I will meet your plane."

CHAPTER 13

CONFRONTATION (1996)

CLIVE PLACED WEATHERLY'S SUITCASE on the floor of the crowded apartment and said, "Now, Hamp, what have you found in Scots country that is so important?"

Weatherly returned St. John's slight smile and answered, "Well, not enough, not yet. I find myself curiously intrigued by what I learned about your father, but it is teatime, and we're in need of refreshment. Have a seat—clear any of the chairs. I do apologize for the disorder, but it is how I work. There's more space in my quarters in Fulton, but my sources are more accessible here. And I have few guests."

St. John waved him off. "Sorry to inconvenience you, Professor, but I've taken some holidays to devote more time to our research. And yes, some tea will make it even nicer."

Weatherly quickly prepared the tea, then made his way to his recliner. St. John perched on one end of the small sofa near the door. "I have brought or sent several copies of the materials I uncovered in Scotland, thanks to the good graces of Dr. McTavish, who knew you as a child." St. John raised his eyebrows and shook his head at the provost's name.

"I do remember him, and I always knew there was something a bit odd between him and my parents. They treated him with reserve, and I knew they were not fond of him, though we never discussed it."

"Well," Weatherly responded, "he went out of his way to accommodate my research, introducing me to the head librarian and requesting his support in finding what I was looking for. I even asked him if he would consider talking with you about his knowledge of your family, and he responded with more than polite assent. 'Speaking with Sir Clive would be interesting for both of us,' I think were his words. I also sensed he wanted me to pursue this. Just a feeling I had, perhaps, as he didn't ask me about it when I called to thank him for his help just before I left, but he again offered his help 'at any time.'" St. John's brow wrinkled slightly, and his face tightened in intense thought. Weatherly, waiting St. John's response, rose and made his way to the kitchen for the tea things.

When he returned, St. John's smile was relaxed. "You have done me a great favor, Dr. Weatherly," he said. The professor's eyebrows rose slightly. "I have had no personal contact with Dr. McTavish other than a sympathy card at my father's death, in which he wrote above his signature, 'I am truly sorry for your loss; your father and I go back a long way.' Now, please go on with your findings. I shan't interrupt again, except for clarifications."

Weatherly nodded. "Well, as to Sir Hugh's exile in Quoyloo, it put him in familiar territory. He probably renewed some old acquaintances, and no one would likely have asked him his business any more than they had while he was assigned there. I know by reference there were letters exchanged with the Admiralty and other naval authorities, but no copies were in the files I accessed, and no records of his responsibilities and limitations under exile were available. Following his exoneration, he was given several short-term postings in and out of the country, none for more than a year, and all evidently completed successfully. He was offered early retirement but turned it down. But that's not the main thing that I learned. In Glasgow, most of my days were spent in the library at Glasgow University, and some at The University of Strathclyde, and in that research I again ran across the 1944 case in which Sir Hugh St. John was charged with espionage."

Clive started to speak, but Weatherly cut him off by raising his arm, palm out. He had organized and planned the report he had prepared for St. John, though he wanted St. John's responses—in the appropriate order.

"Please wait just a minute, Clive. Let me finish. This is, of course, what brought me into this intriguing saga."

"Let's refocus a bit here, Hamp," St. John insisted. "My father passed on during his return from his last posting at Kabul years ago. I have known of this case since I was old enough to understand it. I hope that you can give me some factual details and suggest sources where I might learn more."

"I would advise you to cultivate McTavish," Weatherly said over his shoulder as he rose to pour the tea. "He claims to know more about the St. John family than anyone else in Glasgow. If you'd like, I can send him a letter of introduction. He even invited me to call if he could be of help in my endeavors."

St. John stood to accept the plate which bore a sturdy looking mug of steaming tea and three large oatmeal cookies on two neatly folded paper napkins. "Thank you," he said, sitting down and neatly balancing the plate on his lap. Weatherly returned to the kitchen to refill his own cup while St. John examined one of the weighty-looking cookies before taking a tentative bite.

Weatherly returned with his tea, sat down, and picked up one of the cookies. He dunked it about an inch into his tea and held it there as he resumed his report. "The Strathclyde University had information indicating that most MI5 data was at Glasgow, your father's *alma mater,* quite a large collection, in fact. Some of these may still hold secret information or, more likely, data the powers that be in MI5 would rather not become public. My research pass was not enough to get me access to all of them. I did uncover a kind of journal your father apparently wrote when he returned to the Orkneys while his conviction was under appeal. I have made a copy for you. Here's the gist of what I could extrapolate from it. During the war, your father was employed by the_Admiralty on a secret assignment and stationed in a remote village in the Orkneys. A copy of his 'orders' is in the file, signed by First Sea Lord, A.V. Anderson. His assignment was to track and report German ship and aircraft movements. That type of surveillance was fairly common knowledge. What was not is that his real duty was to encourage the Germans to recruit him as double agent willing to feed Allied military information to the Germans. About 80% of this information was accurate enough to be considered secret, and the other 20% was deceptive, some of it to lure the Germans into traps. An occasional duty was to alert the Russian naval authorities of the approach to the area of Norway's North Cape, of supply convoys headed for Murmansk and requesting as much naval and air protection as possible.

"And Clive," Weatherly continued, "I must tell you that in the Strathclyde University library are copies of some letters he wrote following his conviction. One was to Sir John Cunningham. Sir John was the new First Sea Lord. Apparently, they were acquainted because your father addresses Cunningham as 'Johnny.' In that letter he implores Cunningham to order his retirement or a transfer to 'anywhere away from here.' He goes on to describe the Quoyloo climate: rain every day, cold all year 'round, wind off the Atlantic all day every day, etc. I have made copies of these letters. I did not find any direct reference to his being paid by the Russians. Perhaps that can only be established through Exchequer, as he surely reported any payments, favors offered, and requests of both the Germans and the Russians, if they ever actually paid him."

Clive, who had nodded at several of Weatherly's revelations, leaned forward, again interrupting. "This is the best example I have of his sense of conscience and his morals. On the few occasions when he had leave and came home, he wore a naval uniform. I recall only one conversation my father and I had about his top-secret duty in and after the war—ordered by the Admiralty. It was during the time we were both officers in the Royal Navy. He told me a bit about his espionage duty and was shaken in the telling, though steady and clear. He never mentioned the constant fear and the danger he was in. What troubled him most was the extreme guilt about sending false information because some of it may have caused several deaths, some of them Scots, Irish, English. We had this conversation only a few years before his death while he was on a short assignment near Cambridge. I suspect that he felt a certain relief in unburdening himself to me, his son, the last of our line. It was one of the few and maybe the last time he clearly spoke to me as a father, overriding for the moment his loyalty to the country and the Navy. Perhaps no one else ever saw that side of him—uncomfortable, even pained at sharing details that violated his official word not to reveal. He owed his life to the Decree of Clemency, but that did not clear his conscience."

Weatherly, taken back a bit by these personal details, ventured, "His exploits both during and after the war were hard for me to reconcile with the man Dr. McTavish described: reserved, cool, sensitive about his station, and private. The Navy describes him as heroic and valorous in some of his commendations. How do you remember him, especially as an adult? I'm not asking you what he did, but your interpretation of him, his picture in your mind."

St. John, now as relaxed as Weatherly had ever seen him, seemed to relish sharing the story of his father. He smiled slightly and paused, preparing his words, and reported, "His sense of duty was perhaps his defining trait, hereditary, if you will. His father was willing to give up the small remaining estate, and did, by giving himself over to his call to duty to King and Country. He possessed a unique talent for code-breaking and was in the employ of His Majesty's Secret Service in World War I. Already struggling to keep a modest country home on a few acres, it was a severe financial drain on his modest resources, so he sold it at auction. With a small pension, he lived modestly on the investments but was eventually obliged to sell them to meet his obligations, including a university education for his son.

"And that son, my father, also answered the call and gave his life over to what he considered a critically important service, requiring his unique intelligence, courage, and skill: spying. He was adept and bold and brave— and directed, handled, in your words, by the highest echelons of Her Majesty's navy." Despite the intensity of his words, St. John's voice and manner were without emotion, his gaze on Weatherly serious, but not noticeably concentrated. It was clearly a personal report well presented, a story he had rehearsed countless times in memory for three decades.

"While quite effective for a time, it seems likely that, like most operations of this sort toward the end of the war, it began to unravel. This put the Russians on the alert that some of their secret operations might be compromised. From my own researches, I learned that the codes used by Germany as well as those of the Soviets had indeed been broken by the experts at Bletchley Park, but the Germans were quite adept at changing their codes immediately at the first sign of a break. To have a British expert code-breaker dumped in their laps was deemed very helpful to their cause. Sir Hugh had to be aware that he was essentially a pawn of both the Admiralty and the Germans; he could be brought to trial at any moment and face execution. Given reason, the Germans or the Russians would dispose of him without hesitation.

"So," (a deep breath here), "the Russians, one of our Allies, may have been paying him for sharing secret German code transmissions and were thus aware that he had information valuable to Germany."

Are we really just playing games with each other? thought Hampton. *He's a highly trained MI5 agent, but he's conversing with me like a trusted friend. He could be manipulating me, but international intrigue might sell better than fifty-year-old security measures. Who knows? I may have material for two books!*

St. John again picked up the cookie, looked at it, and held it as he broke the silence. "Hamp, I can't tell you how much this means to me— verification of what I'd hoped you might find. It's more than I expected. I am looking forward to going through all the data you brought back." He looked doubtfully at the substantial treat in his hand and placed it carefully back on the napkin. He drained his tea and stood. "I am in your debt." He glanced down at his wristwatch and shook his head. "And I am going to be late for another appointment. I will be in touch." He shook Weatherly's hand warmly and left.

CHAPTER 14

HOW TO ASSURE A SAFE TRIP (1946)

PLANNING FOR THE EVENT in Jefferson City and in Fulton was a major concern for Task Forces #3 and #4; local officials had never faced such a formidable assignment—and they had less than three months to prepare.

The Jefferson City portion involved security for only a short parade from the train station through the downtown district and across the Missouri River Bridge. From there the drive to Fulton was twenty-five miles through a rural countryside—not heavily populated.

In the state capital, the task force members had ready access to local police forces, the Highway Patrol and the Capital Police. Those agencies were accustomed to handling local crowds, so plans there were quickly completed, including an escort to Fulton by Highway Patrol vehicles. Those plans were forwarded to the Secret Service office where Frank Wilson's team coordinated them with those of the other planning groups. Security plans for Fulton, however, were another matter. Fulton, a town of fewer than ten thousand population, did not have the resources to manage a crowd some estimated could be twenty-five thousand.

Westminster's President McCluer did not wait for the Washington teams to contact him. Ever since the invitation had been sent to General Vaughan, he had seriously pondered what he would do if it were accepted. One evening in late August he called his friend, Truman Ingle, the Superintendent of the School for the Deaf in Fulton. "Truman, if you're not too busy, I'd like to come over and run an idea by you."

"Sure, Bullet. I'm just listening to a bad football game, so come on over." Truman Ingle's wife, Mary Hughes, overheard the conversation and said, "Truman, tell Bullet to bring Ida Belle along; we can gossip in the kitchen while you two lie to each other outside."

After a few minutes' walk down Fifth Street, the two men, good friends for several years, were comfortably seated in Ingle's backyard with highballs in hand while the ladies worked up a platter of cheese and crackers.

"Well, Truman, I'm in trouble," Bullet said, but with a smile that said "I've got a job for you."

Ingle, a balding man of fifty years, average height and build and well above average in energy, had been Superintendent of the School for the Deaf for twelve years. In a small town where everyone seems to know everyone, Ingle had gained a reputation as the man who could get things done. He knew the right sources; he knew whom to call on for what jobs, and he knew whom he could approach—and he was an organizer. He was the right man for the job; Bullet knew it—and so did Ingle. "What now, Bullet?" Ingle knew not to jump the gun on Bullet. *Let him tell his story in his way.*

"I had a conversation with Tom Van Fleet a while back—"

And Ingle interrupted him, "And he talked you into something, right?"

"Well, yes, Truman. Tom has such a fertile brain, and he's just full of ideas. Ida Belle and I were over at their place. The girls were in the kitchen talking, and Tom and I were sipping a little bourbon in the backyard. He's smart as a whip, and he could propose selling rice to China and make it sound plausible.

"Truman, I have stuck my neck out. Tom suggested that the college should invite Winston Churchill to deliver the Leadership Foundation lecture next spring."

Ingle again interrupted, "And you took the bait?"

"Well, yes, I did. Tom is so convincing. When he mentioned it, I told him that it would never happen. But you know Tom has connections... Harry Vaughan, Clarence Cannon. He knows Champ Clark, and you know that Frank Briggs was raised over in Howard County. Tom also knows Truman. I don't think they are very close, but Tom says that Truman would remember him by his nose."

The men laughed, and McCluer continued, "You know, Tru, chances that Churchill would accept our invitation are slim to none, but here's what we've got so far. Yes, I took the bait. Should he accept, it would be quite a feather in Westminster's cap. But he would be entitled to an honorarium, a lot of plans would have to be made locally, and probably a lot of expense, and who knows where I could find the money. In short, I have a bear by the tail until Churchill says no. Still, there's that chance…and I want you in charge of local planning."

Ingle chuckled. "I knew when you called that it would be a job. Shoot, Bullet, I've got a school to run and prying money from the state is a never-ending job. I don't know if I could find or manufacture the time."

"I know, but there is just nobody else who` can do this job and do it right. I will—"

Ingle held up his hand. "Never mind, Bullet. I'll do it."

They clicked their glasses, and the conversation turned to MU football. "What do you think about Chauncey Simpson as coach?" asked Ingle.

"Well, his record hasn't been too hot, but he's just holding things together until Don Faurot gets back from the Navy."

Ida Belle McCluer opened the kitchen door. "Time, gentlemen! Bullet, you have to be up early tomorrow; we'd best be getting home."

"Thanks, dear," said Bullet. And to Ingle, "That was not a reminder; it was an order. So goodnight, Tru, and many thanks. I'll be in touch."

CHAPTER 15

CURIOUS (1946)

TASK FORCES #1 AND #2 combed the gymnasium and discovered several problem areas. The most glaring was a press box located high above the main floor, perfect for an assassin with a direct line of fire to the platform. The Task Force concluded that if anyone were planning to inflict the most damage it would be to assassinate Churchill and/or Truman for a double victory.

Who would be the likely suspects? It was quickly agreed that because there was no love lost between Churchill and Stalin, Soviet sponsorship of an assassination was the most likely. Another possibility, considered remote, was the fast-moving drive for an independence movement within some of the colonies. This was a plausible threat. The war was over, and many of Britain's colonies, having spent heavily of their lives and treasure, were pushing for independence. Talks between London and several colonies had been under way for many months, but no violence was expected. The Colonial Office was in agreement that none of those ongoing negotiations posed a threat to the event in Fulton, Missouri.

Another possibility, deemed remote, was the long-simmering independence movements in Scotland and Ireland. A long history of violence with the Irish (often described as "the Irish temperament") had had London on the alert in that area for many years, and it was determined that there was no threat outside the talks already in process there. The only remaining possibility, MI5 considered, was the long-standing, sometimes lively, sometimes dormant dispute with Scotland on the question of independence. The Scottish advocates of independence were loud and, on occasion, violent. The movement, of course, also included the Orkneys and the Faroes, but the greatest activity was in mainland areas and mostly centered around Glasgow.

While all of these potential areas of threat were real, Wilson felt, with Sir David's and others' concurrence, that there was no credible danger within the Empire or the Commonwealth, so they might safely concentrate their efforts elsewhere.

In addition to the main entrance to the building, there was a small back door that led to the basement and access to the main floor. This was not considered a serious threat, since anyone bent on mischief who might reach the main floor area would be under the bleachers to be constructed there. It should be sufficient to see that that entrance was locked and to station an agent there.

Every security agent was to be armed, of course. In addition, each would be equipped with a "walkie-talkie," a rather cumbersome radio device that had been developed by Motorola and improved by the US military during the war. This would permit guards to be in touch with each other and with the security headquarters that would be set up in Westminster Hall, a classroom building next to the gym the security personnel would control. They further concluded that no students should be allowed in that building, and the security program for Mr. Churchill's safety while he was on the campus required that no students should be allowed anywhere on the main campus. McCluer objected:

"Special Agent Frank Wilson.

Sirs: I have read your proposed plan and find it well thought through. There is, however, one proposal with which I cannot agree. You intend that students not be allowed anywhere on the main campus during Mr. Churchill's presence. I remind you that our purpose in inviting Mr. Churchill is to provide an educational experience for our students; that is the reason we exist. Therefore, I ask that you remove that requirement. I am sure that Mr. Churchill's safety can be assured without so stringent a measure as you propose. F. McCluer."

McCluer sent copies of his letter to Task Forces #3 and #4. Wilson agreed with McCluer. Both task forces revised their plans to accommodate McCluer's request.

Security for the exterior of the gym presented more of a problem. It was a rather large building, and its rear portion was considered inaccessible. The ground dropped off immediately into a declivity to a creek bed below. On-site surveillance of that area would be sufficient.

The north side of the building and the front (east) end were the most accessible and vulnerable. Churchill would be having lunch at the president's home, Washington West House, immediately north of the gym. Others included President and Mrs. McCluer and the platform party, including President Truman, a total of about sixty guests. North of the President's home was a student dormitory, Reunion Hall. It was agreed that the second floor of that building would be accessed only by security personnel. There they would have a clear field of vision not only to cover the president's home but also of the front sidewalk area where the dignitaries would walk to the gym.

The plan was that following lunch and a short time for Churchill to rest and gain some fortification from a glass of his favorite brandy, the platform party would leave the President's home by its front entrance for the short walk to the gym. A wide stairway gave entrance to the gym, and anyone ascending those stairs would present an easy target for someone who might be concealed in any of a large number of locations, including a small tree located between the auditorium and Swope Chapel, which security agents would occupy.

CHAPTER 16

THE MISSOURI TASK FORCES (1996)

WEATHERLY READ THROUGH the early pages of the file St. John had presented him, as he said later, like a kid on Christmas morning. Each page offered more insight into the planning of security for the two principals and others. Making meticulous notes for his book, Weatherly realized it was dark outside and he had had nothing to eat since a meager breakfast. He put together a few bits of leftovers from the refrigerator and then went back to the notes. *There was mention somewhere about a tree. Where was that? Something about a photographer. That would be that little tree in front of Swope Chapel, in the driveway. It's huge now...*

The tree was, at first, not considered a problem until it was learned that a foreign press photographer had asked permission to station himself in its branches for good pictures of the platform party approaching and leaving the gym. Since pictures of the event would be valuable to the history of Churchill's speech, the photographer's request was granted, pending his passing a background check. Security in that area would be simplified somewhat since in early March the tree would not be leafed out and the photographer would be clearly visible. However, this presented a new concern for local planners. All press representatives would be required to submit requests to the local committee on press relations. Ingle appointed John Stone, editor of the local newspaper, to handle this function, working with Task Force #2 to issue the passes.

When Task Force #4 first met, there was concern that no member of that Force had experience with such a large and complex assignment as this. It would require not only security on site but also close collaboration with the local police and the Highway Patrol. The Task Force required expert personnel for this specific assignment be assigned to them. Wilson complied and responded to their request:

January 12, 1946 to Chairman, Task Force #4. (by secure mail) Pursuant to your request for additional personnel, please be informed that I contacted the British embassy here in Washington with your request. The British are well known for their resourcefulness and expertise in the area of security. The first assistant to Lord Halifax immediately suggested a young but extremely capable young man who has been on his staff for a couple of years and is now deputy security officer. Robert H.C. Slocum is of a distinguished family and presently serving as Assistant Security Officer. I have arranged Mr. Slocum's transfer to your Task Force effective immediately.

Slocum reported promptly to the chairmen of Task Forces #3 and #4, meeting together, and he was cordially introduced as a new member. He responded, "My colleagues, it is indeed a compliment to me to be assigned to work with this distinguished group from the FBI, Secret Service, and even the CIA, all agencies that are considered to be preeminent in their fields of security. I am grateful for this opportunity. Now, what say we have a turn at the wheel."

His expertise in security matters was quickly recognized as he reviewed the campus security plans. He suggested that agents placed in the second-floor classrooms of Westminster Hall be stationed on the roof, thus being less conspicuous and offering a better line of sight.

It was immediately agreed that the press box overlooking the speaking area would be occupied by two agents to deny occupancy by anyone else. There was then the question of agents to be stationed inside the gymnasium, some to simply mingle with the crowd. Since the Secret Service had the primary responsibility for the President's safety, that job was assigned to the Service, and Mr. Slocum was asked to work closely with them. He accepted the assignment readily.

Task Force #3 was in the hands of the Secret Service. Their experience in providing security on railroads was considerable since the Trumans used trains almost exclusively. Because of the shared responsibility for rail and auto security, the Secret Service worked closely (and sometimes reluctantly) with the FBI.

The Task Force estimated that six or eight agents aboard the train would be sufficient. And since the White House travel office was handling routing, scheduling, and equipment procurement, all that was needed was the number of passengers. The Secret Service undertook that assignment with the cooperation of the FBI.

Focus for Task Force #3 was divided between rail and ground travel. They held that the same number of agents aboard the train from Washington to Jefferson City and return would be sufficient and should be the responsibility of the Secret Service. Wilson agreed, and therefore all rail travel would be covered by that agency. Task Force #1 readily accepted their assignment, and their plan outline was approved by Wilson.

With this transfer of duties, only the movements by automobile remained to Task Force #4, and this became an interesting assignment. Meanwhile, President Truman had issued an invitation to Governor Phil M. Donnelly, and the text of his invitation was included in file 1612.

Hon. Phil M. Donnelly
Governor, State of Missouri
Jefferson City, Missouri

Dear Governor Donnelly:

On March 5, Winston Churchill and I will arrive in your capitol city by train on our way to Fulton where Mr. Churchill will deliver a speech that afternoon. I would be pleased if you would join us in welcoming him. If I recall correctly, it is only a short walk from your home down the hill to the station, but I am sure that I can arrange for you to be picked up at your front door. Also, I have requested that Westminster President McCluer arrange for you to have a seat on the platform. He agreed and said that you should also have lunch with him, Mrs. McCluer and the platform party before Mr. Churchill's speech. Details can be worked out by your secretary and Rose Conway at the White House.

With all warm wishes,
Harry.

Several personal letters and memos had become part of the 1612 file, perhaps attached later for lack of some other place to preserve them. The story that they reveal was that Clark Barnes was the FBI agent in charge of Task Force #2, which was to handle security for automobile transportation for Mr. Churchill and the President. He was early on in contact with the State Highway Patrol Superintendent, Hugh Waggoner, a bright and ambitious member of the Patrol. Only 34 when he was appointed to the job by Governor Donnelly, he was determined that any involvement of his office would best be done under his leadership.

When Waggoner met with Barnes, it became apparent to the former that the role planned by Barnes for the patrol was modest. Barnes was about twenty years Waggoner's senior; he had piercing gray eyes as a predominate feature. Waggoner understood from their first handshake that Barnes intended Waggoner to follow his orders. It was felt in the Patrol—and not just in Missouri—that Mr. Hoover did not think highly of local law enforcement agencies. "Mr. Barnes," Waggoner greeted Barnes at the Patrol office. "I am pleased to meet you. Please have a seat. Would you like a cup of coffee?'

Not one for needless formality, Barnes replied, "No, thank you. I won't take up much of your time. I am here to organize security for the visit of President Truman and Winston Churchill to Fulton. Your role in the exercise will be fairly minimal. We need two patrol cars driven by your troopers to escort Mr. Churchill and President Truman from Jefferson City to Fulton. In addition to the limousine, there will be several vehicles transporting staff people and some of the press. There will be a very short parade here in Jefferson City and a larger one with larger crowds in Fulton. Some are estimating up to twenty-five thousand. Your escort needs simply to follow the routes that will be provided to you. Please let me know with whom I should work on your staff."

Sounds like a recitation, Waggoner mused. *Sounds rehearsed, like he's almost tired of saying it. Puts himself right in charge from the first.*

Somewhat taken aback by Barnes issuing orders so abruptly, he responded, crossing his ankle over his knee and examining the spit shine on his boot. He looked up at the agent and responded, "My office will cooperate fully with you and your people. I understand that the matter of a parade in Fulton is not fully settled yet. Some discussion of security: I believe that you will find it helpful to have more troopers working with your security team, particularly should trouble develop. We will also need to coordinate with the local police both here and in Fulton. I will take care of that."

Barnes replied, "Thank you. I will let you know what we need," and he turned to leave.

Waggoner, still seated, stopped him with the commanding tone of his voice. "Mr. Barnes!" The agent stopped and turned abruptly to Waggoner, who remained seated. He placed his foot back on the floor and looked hard into Barnes's eyes, his voice level. "I have an idea for a more appropriate escort. In addition to the two patrol cars you have requested, and which we will be pleased to provide, we will post six more patrol cars to the escort, three leading and three following. This will enhance security with a dozen troopers.

"That's good," said Barnes. "Now thank you for your time—"

Waggoner interrupted, "And that's not all. I will station a motorcycle trooper every mile between here and Fulton. As the caravan approaches, ten of those will take the lead, and the others will fall into line behind as it passes. That will mean about sixty of my troopers will be available for any traffic problems. My office will work with you on details later." He paused for a moment, holding Barnes's gaze. "Good day, Mr. Barnes."

Barnes did not know quite how to respond, so he simply said, "Good day to you too, sir." and left. He was not used to addressing very many people as "sir," but Waggoner's compelling attitude had taken him by surprise. On his way back to Fulton, Barnes considered Waggoner's suggestions and decided they would make quite a splash that would enhance his report to Hoover in Washington. *I'm going to put on one helluva parade,"* he chuckled to himself.

The next morning, Barnes called Waggoner to concur with Waggoner's plan to expand the Patrol's participation in the parade. Waggoner explained that "the only member of the Safety Squadron from Callaway County is Russell (Poodle) Breid; he is a cycle trooper, and Fulton is the seat of Callaway County. I think we should arrange for Poodle to lead the procession into Fulton and back to Jefferson City."

"A nice touch," said Barnes.

But I promised sixty motorcycles! Why in hell did I do that? There aren't sixty cycles in the entire Patrol, and a lot of them are down swamp-east. I wonder if I could get say, twenty, from nearby police departments. Worth a shot or I'll be badly embarrassed. Barnes would have a ball with that.

Waggoner had his receptionist contact police departments in Columbia, Boonville, California, Fayette, and Mexico to explain the problem. He asked for police officers who owned or had access to white Harleys and promised that they would be legally deputized as Highway Patrol troopers. Before the week was out, she had rounded up over thirty, and more if needed. *I didn't realize there were that many Harleys around. That's why it's so noisy at night.*

It occurred to Barnes while driving back to Fulton that as the motorcade left the campus following the speech, the drive down the circular driveway passed the Hall of Science. The dignitaries would make perfect targets from there. Agents would have to be stationed on the second floor. *I wonder if those dolts on my Task Force thought of that? It seems I have to do everything myself.* As he pulled over to the curb to park, he noticed two of his FBI colleagues standing in the doorway. They waved; he waved back and drove on down the hill.

Duke Richards was a twenty-year veteran with the CIA and its predecessor, the OSS. He headed Task Force #1, charged with developing relations with local law enforcement agencies. Clark Barnes had called Richards to report on his visit with Col. Waggoner.

"Duke, Clark Barnes here. I had a visit yesterday with one Hugh Waggoner. He is Superintendent of the Highway Patrol and an arrogant bastard. He tried to tell me how to run my security assignment. He is quite young, I'd guess about 35, but an authoritative s.o.b. Anyway, he is going to take care of relations with the Jeff City police, so you don't need to worry about that."

"Thanks, Clark. That's a big help. I have to deal with Tom Bledsoe."

"Who's that?

"He's the Fulton Chief of Police and tough as nails. I doubt I'll be giving him any orders. He'll soon enough realize how much help he's going to need, so I'll work with him."

"Yeah," Clark replied. "We just have to deal with these yokels. Talk to you later, Duke."

After calling Bledsoe, Barnes met him at the front door of the City Hall, where his department was located, along with the fire department and all city offices.

"Welcome to Fulton, Mr. Richards," said Bledsoe, extending his hand. "Pleased to meet you."

"Likewise, Chief, and thanks for giving me some of your time this afternoon."

"Not a problem. Things are pretty quiet. Probably get a little more active tonight. Friday's payday lots of places, so the local bars will see some activity, and my boys will have to haul in a few customers to sober up. Them that's married will be picked up by their wives. Now, pull up a chair and tell me how we can work together."

After hearing Barnes's assessment of local police personnel, Richards was pleasantly surprised at Bledsoe's hospitality. He pulled up a very hard oak chair, probably war surplus.

"Some folks are predicting crowds of maybe twenty-five thousand. What's your take on that, Chief?"

"Call me Tom. There won't be nowhere near that. The report that there might be twenty-five thousand is a load of crap. People are throwing numbers around, and they haven't the least idea what they're talking about. That is irresponsible. My prediction is that there will be one helluva lot of ham sandwiches left over."

Both men laughed, and Richards said, "Probably right, Tom. It's pretty hard to estimate the size of the crowd, isn't it?"

Bledsoe replied, "I'd guess half of that might be close. Will your people help us with crowd control?"

"Yes, of course. That's why I'm here. We will provide as many licensed and trained law enforcement personnel you feel you need. If you over-estimate and a dozen or so of them sit around your office with nothing to do, that's okay. All of those assigned to your crowd control contingent will be under your command, regardless of where they came from."

"That's what I need, no question. Thanks."

Bledsoe glanced around his small office. "If I overestimate, it could be a little crowded."

Richards grinned. "Tom, just let me know by mid-January what re-inforcements you need and I will see that it's done."

"Thanks, Luke, I'll be in touch before that."

Contrary to the Waggoner/Barnes encounter, Richards was pleased with his meeting with Tom Bledsoe.

Bledsoe filed his estimate of needs with Richards well in advance of his deadline. The only issue remaining for Barnes's assignment was to discuss with Bledsoe whether he might need a temporary lock-up in case some drunks showed up. He asked Tom about this, and the reply was "we can handle that. If we find a few bad boys around the streets, they'll never want to be in jail in Fulton again." That satisfied Richards, and he filed his report.

CHAPTER 17

ROTARY CLUB (1946)

AT NOON ON THURSDAY, as usual, Truman Ingle walked three blocks to Woolery's Café for the Rotary Club meeting. This Thursday he stepped into John Stone's "Press Relations" office and invited Stone to be his guest at the Rotary luncheon meeting.

"Thanks, Truman. There is one matter I need to discuss with you."

Ernie Woolery was a big guy. They said he had a good sense of humor, but he seldom showed it. He always had a cigarette either hanging from his mouth or lying on the counter next to the cash register, but he did know how to run a restaurant. His daughters, Ernestine and Helen, were waitresses at Woolery's Cafe.

Rotary lunch, as usual, was fried chicken, green beans, mashed potatoes, and gravy followed by a large slice of apple pie and a ten-minute report from Mayor Hensley on Tuesday's Council meeting.

Back at Stone's office, Ingle observed with some concern, that the "Press Relations" office was simply another pile of papers on the table behind Stone's desk. Print journalists are not known for their neatness and organizational skills, and Stone's office was no exception.

"I haven't heard much from our PR office lately, John. Are things moving along okay with you?"

"Oh, yes, no problems. But I do have a concern about the estimates of the crowd size. Requests for press passes are running well ahead of what I anticipated. Here are requests from two New York papers and from the *Chicago Tribune* yesterday. Apparently, the press feels that Churchill will make a major speech."

"I share your concern, John," Ingle responded. "The security teams think they have all of the bases covered, and I trust them. They're supposed to be the best."

"I sure hope so," Stone responded. "Thus far almost all requests for passes have been from reputable papers and for well-known names. But I do have one that I don't quite know how to handle. It's for a reporter named Bransky from a newspaper I never heard of in Tiblisi, Georgia."

"Okay. I'll bite. I'm supposed to ask if that is near Atlanta."

"Tiblisi is the capital of Russian Georgia, which happens to be Stalin's birthplace."

"One can easily understand their interest," Ingle said dryly. "What's the problem?"

"What they want," Stone continued, "is a picture of Churchill leaving the gym. Triumphant, smiling, flashing 'V' sign."

"I'm confused," said Ingle. "Why would they want that sort of shot? They're no Winnie lovers."

"Don't know, but we can't write their captions for them. Probably something derogatory. But they are our allies...at the moment. And here's the kicker," Stone continued. "They have obviously surveyed the site. You know that tree in the circle drive, maybe a sycamore, between the gym and Swope Chapel? Since the event is in early March, that tree will not be fully leafed out, and they want to post a photographer there to get what they call 'the shot of the century' as Churchill leaves the gym. My problem is that if I refuse them that pass and later issue it to some more friendly sheet, we would be severely criticized ... and properly so."

"You're thinking we should issue it to them and let the chips fall?" Ingle asked. "I would support that decision. I take it that those arrangements are being made through the British embassy there."

"How comfortable are you with the British handling what is, at bottom, our problem?" Stone asked.

"I am very confident. The Brits and we are in complete agreement about what is important and what is not."

"Okay. Thanks, Truman. I'll take care of it."

"And while we're on the matter of security," Stone continued, "we have set up a security system for the press. You know that all applications for press passes have to be submitted by mail."

"Yes, that was early on."

"Additionally, passes will not be mailed but will have to be picked up in person on the day of the speech and the reporter will have to show his credentials for identification."

"That's pretty severe, isn't it?" said Ingle.

"Maybe so," Stone continued, "but you don't know the press like I do. Reporters will go to any extreme to get a story. They're a sneaky bunch. It would not be unheard of for a reporter to check in, claim his pass, and then leave to sell his pass to someone on the outside and spend his day at Stine's Grill where he can hear the speech on the radio."

"You're betting Bransky won't show up."

"It sounds like you've got it covered if he does," Stone replied.

"Anything else?"

"No, Truman. I think everything is ready and we're ready to go. And thanks for lunch."

When Ingle returned to his office, he found Clark Barnes, the FBI agent who was working with Frank Wilson in Task Force #2, waiting for him. "I just happened to be in town, Mr. Ingle, checking some details with President McCluer, and we have uncovered what may be a security problem. I need to discuss it with you."

"Come in and have a chair." When Ingle was seated, Barnes closed the door and remained standing, making it clear that he was in charge of their meeting.

"A very serious security matter has arisen. We have discovered that a reporter for a Russian newspaper has applied for a press pass. It may be perfectly innocent, and not connected at all, but there are indications that the Russians might attempt some serious mischief against Mr. Churchill and President Truman. And, of course, this occasion provides a perfect opportunity. So, Mr. Ingle..."

Ingle knew instinctively that Barnes's visit with President McCluer had not gone as Barnes had wanted; McCluer, in effect, threw Barnes out of his office.

"Mr. Barnes, I have been informed that the work you and your Task Force have done is top-notch, and I want to thank you for a good job. Now, as to the application for a press pass by what you call 'a Russian newspaper.' I am aware of the application. You did not mention—and perhaps you did not know—that the application is by the leading newspaper in Tiblisi, the capital of the USSR state of Georgia. Tiblisi is an important city in its own right, but Georgia also happens to be Stalin's birthplace. So, it was no real surprise they had applied for a pass. After all, a favorite son made good."

"Yes," Barnes said, "but that does not alter the fact..."

Ingle interrupted again. "Just so, Mr. Barnes, it does not alter the fact that freedom of the press is one thing we would like to encourage in the

USSR. Issuing a press pass to a Russian newspaper is a splendid example of this freedom, I have already given our press relations people clearance to issue the pass."

Obviously miffed that he was no longer in charge, Barnes said, "Mr. Ingle, I understand your position, but we are talking about the possible assassination of two world leaders and—"

Ingle interrupted again, "Proof to the Russians that freedom of the press is real and alive in the west and should be so in the east. I have every confidence that your people will protect Mr. Churchill and Mr. Truman. Now, is there anything else, Mr. Barnes?"

"No, Mr. Ingle, that is all; except if anything happens, you will bear most if not all of the responsibility. And you may be assured that Mr. Hoover will receive a report on our conversation."

Rising to his full five feet, eight-inch height, Ingle said, "Please send a copy of your report to Frank Wilson and give Mr. Hoover my regards. Now, if there's nothing else, I have a school to run."

Frustrated, Barnes said, "Of course, sir." Barnes did not bear very well that twice in a matter of a few days, he had found it necessary to address as "sir" two men he considered his inferiors. As he left, Barnes closed the office door a bit more firmly than necessary.

Ingle called Stone as soon as Barnes had left. "John. Truman here. If you have not already issued the press pass to the reporter for that Tiblisi paper, I suggest that you notify him of his approval immediately. There's a lot of meddling going on in other people's business."

"Right. Truman," Stone replied. "The pass was approved and issued to one Feodor Bransky this afternoon and notification of the approval has been sent to his paper through the British consulate in Tiblisi. It seems that our consulate there is not yet in full operation, so the Brits are helping us."

Ingle asked, "Don't the Brits have a lot of paperwork in their password department?"

"Well, by George, I believe they do, come to think of it."

Ingle chuckled. "Do you think Bransky's newspaper will get that notice?"

"Now, how would I know about that?"

"Highly doubtful," Stone responded.

CHAPTER 18

THE BRITS HAVE A TARGET (1946)

THE INTERCOM SIGNAL in Kris Larsen's MI5 office at Thames House lit up. "Mr. Larsen," his secretary intoned, "Chief wants to see you as soon as possible".

"Thanks, Mrs. Markley. Tell him I am on my way."

Larsen was a specialist, called on occasionally for difficult or complicated assignments. When the Chief called, Larsen knew he had a tough, often delicate assignment, and the Chief knew that if he gave the job to Larsen, he could expect it to be done to perfection. He was aware that certain details of Larsen's work were occasionally omitted in his official reports, but the Chief trusted him in ways he did not other agents, and they had a tacit, unspoken agreement that some details of Larsen's assignments were best left unreported. He was often informed by the head office that Agent Larsen was out on a special assignment and would return to his office at a later date. They never discussed these special assignments.

The Chief's door was open, and Miss Smedley motioned for him to go on in. Sir David Petrie was seated behind a massive carved wooden desk. The décor fit Sir David's large office with heavy drapes, thick dark carpet, and oak furniture—a place that demanded conversation in hushed tones.

"Pull up a chair, Kris. I have a job for you."

"I assumed that to be the case, Chief. It's nasty raw out there. How about a job in the Caribbean or Mediterranean? Majorca would be nice."

"You're used to London in December. You can get the details from Miss Smedley, but Russia in December is not all that different from London." Petrie turned and looked out the huge window behind his desk and drew slowly on his pipe.

"You're kidding me, of course," said Larsen, hopefully. "Or at least the job won't start until early May?"

"No kidding this time, and the job starts tomorrow. But it's not Moscow. Here's the brief. Feodor Bransky again."

"Aw, the filthy Armenian. He's an internationally known assassin, and he has stolen enough secret material from us to start his own country. Bransky is just one of his many aliases. Don't tell me you've found him."

"Not yet, Larsen. That's part of your assignment."

"We've been chasing this guy for years; you want me to find him and that's only a part of my assignment? Okay, Chief. Drop the other shoe."

"Kill him."

"Find him. Kill him. Maybe in his own backyard. Just a nice little thing to knock off before Christmas. I assume you have some instructions that are a bit more helpful."

"Yes. You can pick up the file from Miss Smedley on your way out, but here's the sketch of it, and it's not in Russia or Armenia. Mr. Churchill, as you may know, is wintering in Florida at a beach home belonging to a Colonel Frank Clarke, a Canadian admirer. Keep this under your hat for now. Mr. Churchill has been invited to speak at a small college in the Midwest—I forget the name—and he has accepted. I spoke with Mr. Churchill just yesterday, and he intends it to be a major speech. That means, of course, major security undertakings. The speech is scheduled for March fifth. It also means that we might have an opportunity to locate Bransky in the west and not have to chase him all over Siberia."

"Great snakes, Chief! And you want me to plan the affair including security measures to be taken?"

"You might have had that job had you volunteered yesterday. No. Since it is on US soil their FBI and Secret Service have that responsibility, but we are involved, of course. How Leningrad learned of this speech and its date before we did I'll never know. Frankly, I am getting pretty damned tired of being scooped by those bull-necks in the Kremlin. We are fairly sure that Bransky will be there with instructions to assassinate Mr. Churchill and, if the opportunity arises, Mr. Truman also. We only want one death on that occasion—Bransky's."

"Okay, Chief. I'll give it my best. I assume we have a pretty good make on Bransky. I've never seen a picture of him and so far as I know, never met him in person."

"We have some photos, but they're all a bit fuzzy. They are in the file that Miss Smedley will hand you."

"And that's all we know?"

"All except that he is extremely clever and probably the second-best marksman in the world—after you. You know that you can call on any of our resources that you might need."

He stood. "I do believe the weather is moderating somewhat. I think I'll catch a few minutes' fresh air in the courtyard."

This was a clear signal for Larsen to join him. The air was a bit more fresh than either of the men wanted, but Sir David said, "Every room in Thames House is bugged, even my own office, and what I want to say must go no further than the two of us. I trust you implicitly."

"Thank you, sir."

"You must know that you have every MI5 asset on hand so you and Wilson can protect Churchill and President Truman."

"Should I know who this Wilson is? Or is that a surprise for later?" asked Larsen.

"Frank Wilson is the FBI agent in charge of the US Secret Service part of this occasion. Their principal job is to protect the President. His reputation is very good. Get acquainted with him soonest. And further, perhaps you may find the time to get acquainted with Mr. Bransky."

"I'll do the best I can, Chief."

Larsen stopped at Miss Smedley's desk to pick up the file. "I'm Kris Larsen, Mrs. Smedley, I am supposed—"

"It's *Miss*," she interrupted, "and this is the file that Sir David mentioned." She pointed to a well-stuffed folder on her desk. "Sir David said that I am to supply whatever you might need."

Kris briefly eyed her low-cut blouse. The briefest smile flickered across his face.

"Thank you very much," Larsen replied. "There is something that has occurred to me already." His piercing blue eyes met her soft brown ones for a second or two. "I need to locate someone in the department who is about the same height, build, and complexion as this Feodor Bransky. I understand that we only have some fuzzy photographs that are allegedly of him, but do what you can to find a look-alike in our ranks or among our contacts. Just locate him and that's all for now. I don't want to scare him off. The personnel office should be able to help. And I'll be back in touch with you as soon as I get my feet on the ground." Kris turned on his "charm" smile and thanked Miss Smedley again. Her eyes followed him out the office door and down the hall.

Walking back to his office he mused, *That Smedley is a knockout. And she did say "Miss." And I get Markley. She's efficient and competent, but a Smedley at her desk would make this job more interesting. I suppose there's a reason for it.*

He closed his office door, sat down at his desk, and scratched his head. *This is huge! Where do I start?* He thumbed through the file Miss Smedley had handed him. *I need to talk with this Wilson guy. He's in charge of security and most other plans for this event. If I have to work around security to get to Bransky, no one needs to know about it except Wilson and me.* He reached for the phone. "Connect me with Frank Wilson with the Secret Service in Washington, please. And don't give me that business about 'how will I get the number if it's so secret?' Not likely in the directory. If it's any help, look under the Treasury Department in the Washington directory. And never mind asking why it's under Treasury. They do things strangely over there." *It's eight a.m. there. I wonder if he gets to work before noon.*

"Mr. Wilson's office. Sharon Bingham speaking."

"Miss Bingham—"

"It's Mrs."

"Sorry. Mrs. Bingham, this is Kris Larsen with MI5 in London."

"Yeah, and it's damn cold here at the North Pole in December. Did you want Mr. Wilson?"

"Well, yes."

"Mr. Wilson will be back in about an hour. May I have him call you?"

"For security, ask him to call the switchboard at Thames House. I will alert the operator."

"Will do, Mr. Larsen."

Wilson returned Larsen's call within the hour, and they introduced themselves. Larsen had ordered a photo of Wilson earlier, and it was on his desk as they spoke. Voice and appearance were thus fixed in Larsen's brain.

Without explaining the details of his assignment, he simply told Wilson that they needed to meet within a few days. They agreed that Larsen would fly to Washington the next day to meet with Wilson the following morning.

"Mrs. Markley, would you please make arrangements for me and one other agent to be in Washington by early tomorrow evening. Either the Foreign Office courier or a commercial flight will be okay."

"Yes, sir. Would you like for me to inform Sir David's office?"

"I'll take care of that, thank you. I'm going that way anyway."

Larsen walked briskly out the door and down the hall to greet Miss Smedley. He walked into her office wearing his most charming smile.

"Good afternoon, Miss Smedley. Is the Chief available?" Larsen noticed that she had covered her cleavage with a soft, clinging lavender sweater.

"He's on the phone and may be a few minutes. Please have a seat."

His conversation with Miss Smedley involved mostly nothing. She continued reading from a small stack of papers and taking notes in shorthand. He did notice that she turned to her typewriter perhaps more frequently than necessary, each turn revealing a bit more of her shapely leg. Her phone rang, and, after checking caller I-D, she said, "Oh, I'm sorry, Ginnie, we'll have to arrange one evening next week. Yes, I'll call Brunswick House."

Larsen, while standing by her desk, was able to see that that the telephone code under which the incoming call had registered was not a London number. He was as adept at deciphering telephone codes as she was at receiving fake calls. When she hung up, he ventured, "I couldn't help overhearing that your dinner date for tonight has fallen through. I wonder if I might take the place of your caller."

She looked up sharply into his carefully innocent smile. She demurred and returned to her transcription. After a moment, Kris said, "You're not making a lot of progress on whatever it is you are coding. Sorry if I am distracting you." When he made her laugh twice in less than a minute, they agreed to meet at Brunswick House at seven-thirty.

The hallway door opened, and Sir David came in. "Why, Sir David," said Miss Smedley, "I thought you were in your office."

"I used the private entrance. Sorry I did not tell you I was leaving. I'm going to a late lunch now, and I won't be back this afternoon. If anything important, er ... arises, er... just ... just handle it."

Sir David smiled and went into his office. Susan was visibly flustered, and she blushed as she turned to her work. Kris noticed that the reverse cleavage filled her skirt as nicely as the obverse cleavage he had noticed earlier.

As Kris started to leave, she went to the office bookcase to reach a book from the top shelf.

"May I help you?"

"Yes, please. The one with the green binding, there."

He reached it, and she turned as he handed it to her. Kris caught a very brief whiff of a delicate perfume. Their eyes locked briefly.

Back at his office, Larsen called the Chief's number, and it was answered "Sir David's office, Miss Smedley speaking. How may I help you… " and softly "Kris?" She was pretty good at recognizing numbers as well.

"It occurs to me, Miss Smedley, that I have a dinner date with you tonight, and I don't even know your first name. Miss Smedley certainly won't do."

A laugh on her end of the line and, "It's Susan, and I have work to do. The Chief said I am to provide whatever you need."

They both laughed out loud, and Susan said, "I'll see you at seven-thirty."

Brunswick House was an older, French revival structure that housed not only the restaurant, on the top floor, but also a bookseller and a barrister's office below. The lift was a creaky, open-sided affair badly out of date.

The restaurant had a fine reputation (10£), an excellent wine list (15£), and a fixed price list of entrees (averaging 20£) all of which, for two, set Kris back several days' wages, which he convinced himself was an investment. It was located a short walk from Smedley's apartment and only a step or two beyond Larsen's flat.

The next morning, Miss Smedley—who had become "sweet Susan" among other friendly names—called Kris' office early, only to be told that "Mr. Larsen has a meeting across town and will not likely be in before noon." Susan then called her own apartment and was greeted by a groggy Kris who said, "I thought you might try that trick. I'm in a meeting and can't talk now."

"Meeting my backside! I'm not surprised you're worn out. What do you think about me?"

"I thought I answered that question last night. I think a lot of it."

"Of what?

"Y'er backside. That's probably not what I called it. Y'know, we should be on the same committee. We could just meet here and save a lot of shoe leather."

"So, adjourn it and get your lazy arse out of the sack or I'll come over there and get it out for you."

"Good. It's only a couple of doors down the street."

Kris knew she was upset. The front door slammed, and she stormed into the bedroom, snow still on her hair and melting on her nose.

"That's cute," said Kris.

"Cute snoot," Susan said, as she dropped her coat and outer garments on the floor and crawled into bed. "Now, warm me up. If Sir David were here he'd say that's what you need to do."

"Well, I'm glad he's not here. "Now," as he stroked her back, "you say we have work to do? We'd best get about it."

Susan said, "Mmmmmm..."

CHAPTER 19

WILLY IS FOUND

AT SUSAN'S REQUEST, the personnel office had located two employees of the agency who matched the description given by Susan. One of them, it happened, was in Canberra on a short assignment and the other right here in Thames House.

Susan called Willy Westbrook's supervisor and asked that he be sent to Sir David's office to be interviewed for an assignment. When an order came directly from Sir David's office, now meant now! Westbrook appeared in five minutes looking confused and a bit apprehensive. Kris introduced himself and took Willy to an adjoining conference room. He appeared to be a pretty good match for what he thought Bransky might look like.

"How long has it been since you climbed a tree, Willy?"

Visibly taken aback, Willy replied, "Since I was a kid. Probably twenty, thirty years, sir"

"Drop that 'sir' business. You and I are going to be well acquainted, living and working together for the next few weeks. I'll explain that later. Now, I want you to go home, pack some clothes for maybe a week. I will have a car and driver waiting in the street at ten tomorrow morning. The driver will take us to the airport where we will board a Foreign Office plane, and we'll sleep at our Washington embassy tomorrow night. It will be late afternoon when we get there, but just figure that we pick up four or five hours because of the way The Almighty constructed things."

Willy's head was spinning but he replied, "Yes, sir."

While airborne, Larsen explained their mission. Protection of the former Prime Minister and President Truman was their most important objective, and its success depended in large part upon Willy being able to climb the tree in the circle drive on the Westminster campus. Larsen had asked a clerk at the embassy to go to the second-hand clothier's to buy a well-worn black suit to fit the agent known to Susan Smedley in Sir David's office. There was scarcely enough time for any necessary alterations.

Wilson met them at Washington National Airport and delivered them to the British embassy and invited them to a seafood restaurant on Maine Avenue. Rationing was still in full force in England. They agreed readily and were ready to go when Wilson picked them up at seven.

Dinner, of course, was excellent and full of talk about the job that lay ahead of them. Willy was still in a state of confusion about their assignment. He sat quietly, soaking up every word until a stomach full of lobster and a bit of jet lag put him asleep—he and Larsen had tried to cram too much into one day.

Following a restful night at the embassy, Willy and Larsen were treated to a sumptuous breakfast in their room. They met in one of the offices to learn more about their mission while waiting for the car to take them to Wilson's office at Treasury.

While Willy had had many assignments in the Isles and in Europe, he had never been to the U.S., and he was taking in all of the sights as they drove down "Embassy Row," past "Old State" and the White House. On their way to Wilson's office at Treasury the next morning, their driver took a loop around The Ellipse so that Willy could see the south facade of the White House.

Frank Wilson welcomed the visitors as they pulled into the parking area at Treasury and walked them to his office. When everyone was seated and coffee was served, Wilson opened the conversation with "Okay, gentlemen, why the great urgency that we be acquainted, and why the great secrecy about it?"

Willy was still in the dark about much of their mission, so he sat silently, listening to every word. Larsen led off with "You know, of course, that Mr. Churchill will be making a speech in Missouri in March."

"Very much so," said Wilson. "Several agencies are already working on this and will be for the next month or so. We are also aware that due to his importance internationally, your MI5 and probably the Yard as well are involved. Another visitor, we were recently informed, is one of our 'friends' from the east, one Feodor Bransky. Now, I know Bransky by reputation only, and it is not a good one. In fact, the word would be 'dangerous.' I suppose you gentlemen are posted here to keep an eye on him?"

"Exactly," Larsen responded, "but even more than that. We are here to see that he is properly prepared for his trip back to Europe. Willy here is my photographer, and he has a new long-range lens that should produce a very nice picture."

CHAPTER 20

THE PROFESSOR WANDERS (1996)

WHILE WEATHERLY STUDIED file 1612 and scanned mid-1940s news-papers
from Britain, Scotland, and the United States concerning Churchill's visit, he
kept an eye out for any reference to Sir Hugh St. John, but turned up no mention of him. Apparently, due to the nature of his continuing service to the Admiralty, news of his exoneration was kept from the press. A month after his return from Scotland, Weatherly found he had exhausted his work with the file and repeated calls to the Justice Department convinced him his request for the American version of 1612 was bottled up in the Department of Justice bureaucracy and he was stonewalled in his efforts to secure its release.

He called Clive as much for a chance to discuss his frustration as to delicately request St. John's advice and possible influence in finding a solution. Three days after Weatherly left requests on both his office and personal phone, St. John called him back.

"I'm very sorry for the delay in responding to your messages, but I had business away from the embassy for a few days and returned only late last evening. So tell me, Hamp, how goes the research project?"

"Thanks for asking, Clive; your question goes directly to the purpose of my call. I have pretty well covered all the leads in MI5's version of 1612, and I'm afraid I will not get access to the U.S. version in time to satisfy my publisher. I really don't know where else to turn. Are there any avenues you can suggest I try to reach someone in a position to move on this? I hate asking since you have done so much already in my behalf, but I don't know where else to go."

After a short pause, St. John cleared his throat and spoke with a deliberation that told Weatherly the agent, while not stalling, was choosing his words with care. "My contacts in your Justice Department are somewhat tenuous. I have worked with some in the CIA—even consider a couple of them as friends—but it would be a bit awkward to request a favor of this nature, unrelated to our agencies' official cooperative relationship."

"I fully understand your position, Clive, and I said at the outset I will not impose on your friendship in any way that could impinge on your position. It's just that I have spent more time and effort lately seeking, checking, and verifying data in newspapers, books, and other documents at the Library of Congress than most of the staff there."

"Have you enlisted the help of your friend, the Secretary of State?"

"I have called and written him, but so far he has not responded. My researches have led me to conclude that I probably should go back to Glasgow and the libraries there, both as a change of scenery and to explore some areas I overlooked on my previous trip. And by the way, have you been in touch with Mr. McTavish at all?"

"I've written him, suggesting we arrange to meet the next time I go back to Britain, but he has not responded yet."

"Well, when I go, I will as a matter of courtesy call on him, and I'll convey your greetings to him as well. And of course, while I am there, if I find anything new on your father's life and career, I will pass it on to you."

What he did not share with his friend was his intention to deepen his research into Sir Hugh's career, beginning with another interview with McTavish.

Weatherly began at once to plan his trip back to Scotland, securing his tickets for a week hence, and writing to McTavish of his arrival and asking about lodging on or near the university.

He spent the following week organizing the pages of notes he had accumulated during the months of research he had conducted since beginning the project. He had begun with a working outline of the project on his computer, which he developed and revised as he acquired data. Now that he was nearing the end of his research, he had to determine the content and shape of his book, which meant that a significant portion of all the data he had gathered would not be included. Although as strictly factual as possible, he intended it to be a story of real events involving real persons. The attempt on Churchill's life had proven a bombshell, of far greater consequence historically than he had anticipated. It was a revelation it seems no other historian had discovered and would shock historians across the globe. It was this feature that compelled the professor to finish his work, get the book written as quickly as possible. Despite the efforts of MI5, the Justice Department, Clive, and himself, once the manuscript left his hands the secret was out, and the responsibility of absolute accuracy and solid, verifiable support and evidence weighed heavily upon him. He would strive to present it as honestly as possible, providing the context of the event and a clear, honest depiction of the people, the times, and places involved.

An "old school" scholar, he was more comfortable with hard copy—typed or hand-written pages garnered from his sources. The voluminous notes he had taken (at the Library of Congress, Strathclyde and Glasgow Universities, and from books, history articles relevant to the occasion, newspapers, file 1612, and numerous interviews) he had typed up shortly after gathering them. The interviews he had taped when the subject allowed it, and he had transcribed it into type-written pages, editing out irrelevant material as he worked.

His working outline now was several pages long, and he had to shape it into the outline of his book—turn it into chapters and the chapters into a sequence that would convey what he wanted to say about his topic. Then he could review all his notes, all the information he had accumulated, and determine what would be included and where. This task was not quite completed when he flew to Scotland, brain-weary and grateful for the diversion from such a tiresome task.

McTavish had responded promptly to Weatherly's letter indicating his plans for further research in the MI5 files and other sources, both for his book and his interest in Sir Hugh St. John's career in the Admiralty. McTavish's reply was as hearty as he, almost insisting that Weatherly stay in the provost's home and make free use of the accommodations as well as the resources available to him in Glasgow.

Chapter 21
SCOTLAND REVELATIONS (1996)

WHEN WEATHERLY CLEARED customs in Glasgow, he headed to the baggage claim area and was approached by white-haired stranger, a trim looking, middle-aged man sporting a worn but well-pressed chauffeur's uniform. He doffed his cap as he approached, asking, "Excuse me, sir, are you professor Hampton Weatherly?" in a strong Scots accent.

"I am," Weatherly replied, stopping.

"My name is Clifford Compton of the Motor Services Department at Glasgow University. Our provost, Mr. McTavish, sends his greetings and is waitin' on ye' in 'is office."

"I am pleased to meet you, Mr. Compton," Weatherly replied, extending his hand. Compton grasped it, gave it two vigorous pumps, and turned to move smartly toward the baggage claim area, the professor in his wake.

When they had retrieved his luggage, Compton insisted on carrying both pieces at the same brisk pace he apparently always used. The vehicle was a large, aging, but spotless black Bentley with a capacious trunk ("boot" to Compton) where he stored the luggage, then opened the left rear door for Weatherly, shutting it firmly when his passenger was seated. He made no conversation on the trip to the university but muttered, half under his breath, a constant stream of complaint and mild invective at drivers, cyclists, pedestrians, and road conditions—in a brogue so thick Weatherly could not comprehend much of it.

At the campus, Compton brought the vehicle to a gentle stop and popped out of his seat to open the rear door before the professor could reach the handle. "Ye' know your way to th' provost's office, neh? I'll deliver yer bags t' the house." He turned, stepped to the car, then turned back to face Weatherly. "And wilcome back to Scotland, sir," he said, touching his hand to his cap before turning back to the car.

"Thank you, Mr. Compton," Weatherly managed before the man pulled his door shut.

He paused in his seat, his window open. "Yer wilcome, sir, an' if ye don't mind, you can drop the 'Mister'; just Compton will do, thank you." He closed the window and nodded, then eased the car away from the curb.

The door to the provost's outer office was open, and Weatherly stepped inside, where McTavish was standing in front of his secretary's desk, his back to the doorway. When his secretary leaned sideways to greet Weatherly, the provost turned and broke into a smile. "Hampton, so good to see you," he said effusively, rea'[ching for Weatherly's hand and gripping it firmly as they shook. "I was just telling Mrs. Edwards here that you might enjoy a cup of tea after your long flight. The stuff the airlines offer I find barely palatable myself, but how was the trip? Bearable, at least?"

"Oh, yes, much as I expected—like the tea, bearable." He turned to the secretary, a formidable looking woman—white hair, firmly coiffed and sprayed, starched lace bodice over her ample bosom, and a dark gray woolen dress tailored to her substantial frame. "It's nice to see you again, Mrs. Edwards," he greeted her, shaking hands lightly. Her smile was coolly polite. "Likewise, I'm sure," she responded as she left the room

"Come in and sit down, Hamp," McTavish urged, his hand on the professor's back. "The tea will be up shortly, and I am anxious to hear what your researches have brought you." He ushered Weatherly inside and closed the office door behind them. He motioned his guest toward an upholstered chair near the windows, facing his desk, and seated himself in the large, black leather overstuffed executive chair behind his desk and scooted it sideways to face his guest more directly. "Are you back for any specific data or new leads, or looking for verification of what you already have? Mr. Ballard has renewed your pass for the classified section and has arranged for the same access at Strathclyde University's library." He leaned back in his big chair, smiling.

Weatherly thanked him profusely, which McTavish waved away, assuring him he was very glad to help, but he beamed under Weatherly's expressions of gratitude. A light tap on the door preceded its opening to admit a slight, middle-aged man with a badly fitted brown toupee pushing a tea cart with a white cloth covering its load.

"Ah! Thank you, Albert," McTavish said heartily, then watched as the man carefully plucked the white cover off, folded it deftly, and draped it over his left arm, revealing a large silver teapot, two full-sized cups with saucers, and three silver domes topped with wooden handles. He poured a cup of steaming tea into a large china cup, which he placed on a saucer and looked up at Weatherly.

"Sugar, honey, lemon, or milk, Sir?" he asked, tipping his head slightly to the side.

"A teaspoon of honey and a bit of cream, please."

"Very good, sir." He opened a small stoneware container and spun a teaspoon of honey on it, neatly placing it in the cup. He lifted a small folding table from the side of the cart, opened it, placed the cup and saucer on it, and placed it and a small china beaker of cream and a heavy white napkin in front of Weatherly's chair. He moved the cart to McTavish's side and filled a cup, placed it on a saucer, and stepped back. "Will there be anything else, sir?"

"No, thank you very much, Albert," McTavish replied.

The man dipped his head slightly. "You're very welcome, sir," he replied, turning quickly to disappear through the door, which closed quietly behind him.

McTavish stood, rubbing his hands together and smiling as he looked over the small table, then lifted each of the domes, one by one, and exclaimed over each, "Ah! Crumpets—and they are warm—with butter and two kinds of jam! And teacakes! Ooh! Candies as well! What is your pleasure, Professor?"

"I'll start with a crumpet—just butter, please."

McTavish lifted one of the domes and with a small tongs placed a scone on a small plate with a butter knife and brought it with the butter dish to Weatherly's table, waiting as he buttered his scone, then returned to the table and settled into his chair, where he leaned forward and placed two scones, two teacakes, and the butter dish in front of him, lifted his cup in a salute and took a small sip. The professor mimicked his moves, and both men settled into their elegant repast. Before he had finished half his scone, McTavish was pressing the cakes and candies on him; he accepted one of each, repeatedly rejecting his host's urging him to take more.

At length, McTavish wiped his lips and fingers, topped off his tea mug, refolded his napkin, and leaned back in his chair. "Now then, Hamp, how is your new friend, Sir Clive? I must confess I have been remiss in not responding to his very polite and careful letter suggesting he come by to pay his respects to an old family acquaintance. I believe the last time I saw him was shortly after he joined the navy. He and his father paid me a short visit, and the next thing I heard was that his father had died and was buried at sea. I sent my condolences and got a brief note of thanks several years ago."

"Yes, he told me he had written you about a possible visit, but I don't know how often he comes back to Britain, and Scotland in particular. His mother, I understand, is in a home near Liverpool, but in an advanced state of dementia and may no longer even recognize him."

McTavish shook his head and looked down. "'Tis a sad state of affairs, and Clive has never married." He raised his head and looked out the window. "I wonder why that is. He was a fine-looking young man, and his parents to all appearances had a good marriage. Odd that he wouldn't wish to carry on the family name and title."

"Well, he says the title has little meaning for him, since there is no estate, and he's the last of the line. While I know little of his career, I believe he's had postings in several parts of the globe and he is dedicated to his service."

McTavish nodded and looked back out the window. "That's admirable, to be sure, but odd that no lass has ever taken his fancy enough to lead him to the altar."

Weatherly, slightly piqued by the provost's remarks, leaned toward him. "I haven't known him long, of course," he said, "but we have become friends—perhaps in part because I too find myself regarded as odd because I have never married, and though I have traveled extensively, I have remained in the same small town for half a century. I take it that you yourself, sir, are married."

"A widower now, for five years and more, with two fine sons and five grandchildren. I can't imagine life without them." He paused and looked intently at the professor. "Do you consider Clive St. John a close friend, Hamp?"

Weatherly paused, returning the provost's steady gaze. The question was unexpected and Weatherly wondered at McTavish's intentions in asking it. "I don't know if I would describe our friendship as close, but there are not many among my friends much closer, though in perhaps different ways. I like him and think this regard is mutual, much as our respect for one another."

McTavish looked at him speculatively, a slight smile on his lips. "And he has never mentioned me in your conversations about his father?"

"No. He suggested my looking into information about his father at your university, and perhaps at Strathclyde. My meeting you was just my good fortune, and I conveyed your knowledge and interest in his family and urged him to contact you."

"Thank you very much, Hamp," McTavish replied. "I would be most interested in talking with him after all these years."

"If I may ask, were you close friends with Sir Hugh? I know your knowledge of the family is extensive."

McTavish leaned back and again directed his gaze to the window. "No, not close, I would say. He was always polite but a bit cool. He and his wife may have had tea with us once or twice, but I doubt if he had close friends anywhere. I found him intriguing—the nature of his work in the navy, and the fact that he had a title and all that, but we seldom got beyond small talk in our conversations."

"And you had no contact with his widow or his son following the news of his death?"

"None, unfortunately. She never so much as acknowledged my note of condolence." He looked away again and was silent, his expression grave. "I always had great respect for him, but his reserve toward me was almost chilling, and he never spoke of his family except in short answers to my inquiries about them." He was silent again, then he shook his head slightly and stood.

Weatherly rose also, recognizing that his host was terminating their conversation. "Thank you so much for your hospitality; I shall impose on it as little as possible."

McTavish smiled and extended his hand. "'Tis always a fair pleasure talkin' with you, Hamp, and I look forward to a pipe and a dram with you soon and often. And you'll keep me informed of any wee nugget you turn up in your research on the St. Johns?" At Weatherly's nod, he went on, "They've become a bit of a hobby with me."

"I will, and I may take advantage of your interest in them, anything you might want to convey to Clive, or remember about his family would be welcome."

The provost nodded, a slight smile on his lips. "You remember the house I pointed out to you on your last visit?" At Weatherly's nod, he went on, "Mr. Compton's services are available to you as well; his apartment is above the garage, though he's often on campus during the day."

"Thank you very much for that offer. I prefer walking as much as the weather allows, but if I need a ride, I'll let you know." He stepped out of the office, and the door closed softly behind him.

McTavish stayed on his mind as he strode briskly down the stone sidewalk to the nearest street on his way to the provost's residence. *It almost seems McTavish has some ulterior motive in encouraging me to pursue Sir Hugh's military history. Surely he has had access to these library resources. Could it be that, like Clive, his position or his reputation might be compromised if he showed his deep interest in the St. Johns? His curiosity is odd. I will ask him about it the next time we sit down together.*

CHAPTER 22

THE CHAUFFEUR OPENS UP (1996)

HE WALKED TO THE Strathclyde University library, presented his access card and made his way to the Archive area, and spent the afternoon perusing the regional newspapers from 1941-1945 for any mention of Quayloo or Sir Hugh and the Admiralty.

Back at the provost's residence, he hesitated briefly at the door, wondering if he should ring, but Compton appeared quietly and let him in, nodding briefly. He waited as Weatherly set down his backpack and removed his jacket. Compton took it from him and picked up the backpack. "I'll acquaint ye' with the house and show ye' your room." He faced Weatherly with the jacket over his left arm, which held the backpack, and gestured. "Me rooms are over the garage just around back, and ye' ken reach me by the phone here." He pointed to a small desk with a worn but comfortable leather office chair. The phone was a dated desk model with push buttons. "Ye' just push the nine to ring me. Most of the day when I'm not drivin', I'm near the outside door where I dropped ye', and ye' have the number to reach me from the provost." He stepped around the professor and crossed the room to a set of stairs carpeted in a worn but clean maroon runner. He ascended, Weatherly following, and opened a wide, heavy door of darkly stained wood and stepped through it, holding it for his guest. Weatherly found himself in a long, wide hall dimly lit by a skylight recessed into the ceiling. A quick glance revealed a door at each end of the hall, with four other doors, not across from each other, two on each hallway. Halfway down each hall was a smaller doorway.

"Mr. McTavish's rooms are at the end of the right hallway," Compton explained. He turned and walked down the other hall. "At the end there," he went on, "is Mrs. McTavish's sitting room, which has been locked up since she died about four years ago. And this one will be yours for as long as ye' stay." He opened a door on the right and waited for Weatherly to enter. He left it open as he placed the professor's belongings on a small, varnished writing desk near the large single window across from the door. "There's extra blankets if you need 'em on the shelf in the closet." He turned and pointed to a single door close to the queen-sized bed, covered with a substantial figured spread; two large similarly covered pillows leaned against the wooden headboard. Compton waited as Weatherly took in the furnishings: a heavy looking dresser of dark wood, a wine-colored overstuffed chair with a matching footrest before it, and a set of shelves holding several hardcover books of varying sizes. Compton strode back through the main door and stopped, turning to face Weatherly. "Ye're lavvy is here across the hall on ye'r left, and as ye're the only guest, 'tis only you'll be usin' it. Ye' have any questions?"

"Only one for now, Compton. Where might I find a good meal nearby late this evening?"

A small grin touched the chauffeur's lips before he answered. "Mr. McTavish has invited you to dine with him at the Highland Hotel restaurant about seven-thirty this evening. He regrets he can't join ye' here tonight, but I'll be takin' ye' both there. It's a bit posh, but ye' don't have to dress up."

"And you'll be joining us at dinner then?"

"I'll be havin' a mug and and somethin' to eat at the bar there," Compton replied, looking him in the eye.

"Well," Weatherly replied, shaking his head. "I'd be honored to have your company too, and you've been very gracious. Perhaps at another time?"

"The honor would be mine," Compton replied, nodding, "but on me own time, say this weekend?"

Weatherly pondered for a moment, then suggested, "What about tomorrow then? It's a Saturday, and if you don't have other plans, I would like to take you to breakfast at your favorite place." He raised his hands to keep Compton from objecting. "And I insist it's my treat. I would like to learn a bit more about you—get acquainted."

Compton's brow wrinkled. "I appreciate the offer, sir, but I'd rather pay me own way or take you as my guest. I'd be more comfortable that way."

Weatherly thought a moment, then held up a finger and reached into his pocket for a coin and placed it on the small table. "How about we flip for it? If it's heads, I'll treat; tails, breakfast is on you, okay?"

A rare smile of delight lit the chauffeur's face as he nodded. "Your coin, I'll flip, if ye' don't mind then."

Weatherly smiled back and nodded. "Let's do it."

Compton picked up the coin and showed it to the professor. "Heads," he announced, then turned it over on his palm. "Tails"

Weatherly nodded and Compton flipped it neatly into the air so it landed on the tabletop between them. They both leaned over it. "Tails," they said in unison, and both laughed. "I'll meet ye' here at ha' past eight tomorrow, if that's suitable. No need to dress up, but it might be chilly enough for a jacket," Compton said. "It's a bit of a walk, but a pleasant one. I can acquaint ye' with the neighborhood a bit. We'll be leavin' in about an hour, sir," he said, turning toward the door.

"One other thing, if you don't mind, Compton," Weatherly said. "I don't fully understand the protocols here very well, but I'd prefer you address me as Hampton, or Hamp, rather than 'sir,' if you don't mind. I recognize the differences in our 'stations,' I think you call it, but like most Americans, I think, I'm a bit uncomfortable with it, coming from a working-class family myself. My father worked for a large grain company in a small town, running the elevators—the big grain storage facilities next to the railroad."

"I'll try," Compton replied, "but only in private. Mr. McTavish would not approve."

Weatherly nodded. "I understand. Thank you for making the effort. I'll be down shortly, after I store my stuff and freshen up a bit."

Compton nodded and exited, closing the door softly behind him.

On the drive to the hotel, Compton, his two passengers in the back seat, drove silently, occasionally looking into the rearview mirror. McTavish was affable, pointing out sites of interest, and commenting on aspects of life in the city

When they pulled up in front of the hotel, Weatherly and McTavish were quick to open their doors before Compton could hop out to assist them. "I'll meet you just inside then," he said, driving smoothly away as the two men headed inside. Before they were seated, the maitre d' placed their menus on the table and took their coats, bowing slightly as he left. When Weatherly opened his menu, he noticed there were no prices for the items listed. McTavish smiled as Weatherly glanced up.

"Yes," he said softly, "it's a special menu, arranged by Mrs. Edwards—and the tip's included." He leaned forward and gave Weatherly a conspiratorial wink.

Both men turned to the "Libations" section at the back of the heavy menus. Weatherly found the list of beers, ales, stouts, and other rather daunting, so he turned to his host, who had laid his menu aside. "The ale we had on my first visit was excellent, but is there another from this rather extensive list that you might recommend? With so many choices, what do the people with good taste seem to prefer among the local choices?" Weatherly inquired.

The provost leaned back in his chair and smiled. "I can say without boasting that I have tasted pretty much every beer, ale, stout, and lager in the land, so tell me what your preferences are and I can suggest something. How about something unique to this part of Scotland?"

McTavish leaned forward again. "I can't say I know you all that well, Hamp, but here's what I'll do, since you asked. We can get three samplers and go from there. I can't say I know what most people here drink, but you can try an ale, a stout, and a beer, picking from among what I like, and we can discuss what you think of them and find something that appeals to you."

"Thank you, that will be fine. Now, if I can impose on your good tastes for the rest of the meal, I'd like some advice about the entrees as well. I was considering haggis, which I have not tasted, but understand it's a signature dish here."

"Ah, you're in for a treat then. And here's Mr. Boyle to get us started."

Boyle was a slender man with dark, thinning hair combed back and oiled, and pencil mustache. He nodded at McTavish and answered in a carefully modulated tone, "It's good to see you again, Mr. McTavish, and what can I offer you to begin your meal?"

"Professor Weatherly is from the States and would like a small sample of what you consider your finest local beer, ale, and stout, and I shall begin with my usual."

"Very good, sir. And it's a pleasure to make your acquaintance, Professor Weatherly," he said, nodding slightly.

"And I am glad to meet you also, Mr. Boyle," Weatherly said, returning his nod.

McTavish turned his full attention to Weatherly, folding his hands on the table, his head slightly tilted to the side. "Tell me, Hamp, how are your researches progressing? Are you finding the material you need here, and if not, perhaps I can suggest other avenues available in Glasgow."

Weatherly paused, composing his thoughts. "The information on

Churchill's visit was interesting but scant, but I have what I consider sufficient details about the event, and I was a small part of it, during my freshman year."

"So you're nearing the end of your research on the book. Now what have you learned about the St. Johns, which is of more interest to me?" he asked eagerly.

Weatherly again paused before answering, "Well, I cannot thank you enough for getting me access to the files in both libraries. I learned quite a bit about Sir Hugh's career and his court martial and its aftermath. The staff in both institutions were most helpful. I copied my notes and those documents I was allowed and sent them to Clive. I'm looking forward to discussing all this with him when I get back."

Boyle returned, deftly balancing a tray holding the tasting glasses and a double shot of a rare scotch, and a small bowl of chipped ice with an elegant looking silver teaspoon. He plucked the two folded napkins from atop the tray and handed one to each man. Each place mat bore the name and logo of its beverage. The scotch was served in a tumbler etched with wheat grasses. In a few seconds, Boyle stepped back, placed a napkin on his arm, drew his feet together, bowed slightly, and smiled. "Daniel, will take your order and serve you. Is there anything else I can do to make your dining experience as pleasant as possible?"

"Thank you, Boyle," McTavish responded. "I know that Danny will take good care of us." Boyle nodded, turned, and marched back to his station.

Weatherly lifted the small glass of lager, sniffed it, and held it up to check its clarity and effervescence. "Here's to you, Mr. McTavish, for your hospitality and generosity. I appreciate your leaving me to do my work, and for the services of Mr. Compton. I'm looking forward to breakfast with him tomorrow at a place we can eat well and talk."

McTavish drew his brows together slightly. "Your treat?" he asked.

Weatherly put his drink down and chuckled. "Quite the contrary. He's picking up the tab." McTavish's eyebrows went up, and then he smiled. "He's a competent fellow, circumspect, neat, and very capable. I could probably name the place you will probably go to in three tries, but I am surprised that he's invited you. I'm not sure what you will find to talk about as he hasn't opened many conversations with me."

Weatherly smiled. "Actually, I invited him, aware that Saturday was his day off and he probably had other plans. He seemed a bit uncomfortable, so I asked about someplace within walking distance. We both wanted to pay, so before he could suggest separate checks, I suggested we flip a coin. He flipped, and I won, so he's paying."

McTavish shook his head and looked down. "He can afford it well enough, I should think. His wife died a few years back, and they had no children. He pays a small rent for his lodgings, and he has access to the university fleet when he chooses to travel, but insists on paying for the petrol on these infrequent trips. His salary is more than adequate for his needs, and he's a careful man, aware of his place, but he doesn't talk much about himself." He paused, looking down again, then lifted his scotch and smiled. "And here's to the success of your book, and I look forward to reading it." He passed his glass under his nose and closed his eyes for a moment before lifting the glass to his lips and smiling as he savored the drink, rolling it in his mouth before swallowing.

Weatherly took a more generous sip of the lager and let it run over his tongue as he swallowed. He nodded at his dinner companion. "I am no connoisseur, but I find this excellent." He took another deep swallow and nodded in satisfaction.

McTavish nodded, took another sip, and set his glass down. "With all this information you found, I wonder if you've formed a sense of Sir Hugh's character; what kind of a man do you think he was?"

Weatherly stalled before answering, draining the glass of lager and setting it aside. "I have the sense that he was very good at his job, his role as double agent, which took great courage. He must have had nerves of steel, knowing with any misstep in his dealings with the Germans and the Russians, he could have been killed—or worse, threatened or tortured if his cover broke. But of his assignments and exploits after the war when he was sent on secret missions in Asia and South America, and who knows where else, I found no information whatsoever, and I doubt that the Admiralty would release any such files as there might be for a long time. I plan to make a visit to the Orkneys to get a feel for the place, possibly find someone who was there at the time."

McTavish grunted and smiled. "Huh! You might find those islanders a bit close-mouthed and clannish. I visited some of the major islands a few years back and found them courteous but cool toward strangers, and it's a poor, cold, windy place." As he spoke, Weatherly finished his ale, wiped his lips. He lifted the stout to his lips, took a mouthful, and tipped his head back to roll it around over his tongue before swallowing.

"I've never tasted anything quite like that," he noted, "and I will finish the sample, but I prefer the lager, perhaps because it is familiar, and with a subtle complexity that I find delicious. I hope I can find it in the States, but I don't recall seeing it there."

McTavish nodded and smiled, then turned and waved a finger at Mr. Boyle, who was waiting near the door. He came almost immediately to the table and stopped, his heels together. "How can I help you gentlemen?" he asked in soft, deliberate tone.

McTavish responded by nodding at Weatherly and explaining, "Our American friend here was quite taken with the lager and would like a pint, please—and you might bring me another as well. And thank you."

"You are most welcome, sir; Daniel will be by shortly with your drinks." He stepped back and turned smartly to march back to his station, beckoning with his finger toward the kitchen.

"When do you plan to make the journey to the Orkneys, Hamp?" McTavish asked.

"As soon as possible, actually," the professor replied. "I assume it will take most of the day, going by train to Aberdeen, a ferry to Kirkwall, and then find my way to Quoyloo, where I hope to find lodging for two nights and then return."

McTavish nodded as Weatherly spoke. "It will be an entire day each way, but one day will very likely be sufficient to learn all you want about the place. I will have Compton make the necessary reservations for the travel, and he can take you to the train station Monday morning."

"That's very hospitable of you, but I don't wish to impose on your good will."

McTavish waved him off, insisting it would be no trouble. "Just consider it a small favor—and I shall expect a full account of your findings when you return."

Daniel, a stocky young man in a crisp white shirt and dark trousers under a starched white apron, appeared at the table, a covered tray balanced neatly in one hand at shoulder level. He swept the white linen cover from the tray as he lowered it and deftly placed the large crystal mug of beer in front of Weatherly, then the glass of whiskey before McTavish. He neatly placed the empty glasses on the tray and covered them. "Will there be anything else, gentlemen?" he asked. When McTavish shook his head, Daniel nodded and lifted the tray and stepped back. "I shall be back to take your order shortly," he promised, and strode back toward the kitchen.

The two men returned to the menus. After a few moments, McTavish folded his menu and looked across the table at Weatherly. "Still leanin' to the haggis, then?" he asked. "Or has somethin' else caught your fancy?"

Weatherly smiled. "I would be remiss if I came twice to Scotland without trying haggis. This seems a great place to find it authentic and well prepared."

McTavish nodded. "You are right on both counts—and you do know what you are getting, nae?"

"I think so, at least basically," Weatherly replied. "I know it is boiled in a sheep's stomach and contains organ meat, some small grain—oats, perhaps—maybe some vegetables and seasonings."

McTavish savored a generous sip of his drink before replying, "That's it briefly, but every cook who makes it develops his or her own recipe, and I find that here it's a savory dish. I'm not a true fan m'self, but I eat it at least once a year in January, when it is featured as a traditional feast."

Daniel returned shortly, and McTavish put in their orders, then leaned forward, saying, "Tell me a bit more about your new friend Clive St. John. What was his response when you told him you and I had met?"

Weatherly sipped his beer to gather his thoughts before replying. "He remembered you as a neighbor and an acquaintance but said you were not close. He mentioned your note of condolence at Sir Hugh's death but indicated that you had not been in touch since, so far as he recalled. He did indicate he was interested in hearing from you as a source of information about your relationship with his family."

McTavish leaned back and took another long sip of his whiskey, his look thoughtful and distant. He glanced at his guest, then away, and asked, "How did he respond when you told him of my interest in his family?"

"I don't recall any particular response. We mostly discussed what I had learned and the documents and data I had to share with him. We would both be interested in any insights you might have to share about Sir Hugh."

Sandy looked down and smiled, shaking his head. "Clive was right. Sir Hugh was not a particularly close friend, and I only knew Clive as a child. My interest in the family was piqued by his father's service with the Admiralty, and something of his heritage. Three generations of agents in the country's security services indicates they held some highly classified state secrets—and as a titled family with such a low profile that Clive has largely ignored it. Intriguing, to say the least, nae?"

Weatherly nodded and took another drink, just as Daniel showed up with what seemed a very large tray balanced on his hand. He lowered it to the edge of the table, removed the linen covering, set steaming plates in front of each man, and arranged the accoutrements, then stepped back to ask, "Will there be anything else, gentlemen?"

"Not for the moment, Daniel," McTavish responded. "Thank you."

Daniel nodded and turned away as both men reached for their napkins and arranged them on their laps, Weatherly leaning forward to sniff the steam rising from his plate. He lifted his crystal mug, still half full, in a salute. "*Bon appetite,* sir; this is a genuine gustatory adventure for me, and I am most grateful for your hospitality."

Sandy raised his cocktail and nodded. "I'll be interested in your assessment of the haggis. Don't hesitate to tell me if after you have thoroughly tasted it's not to your liking. As you saw, there are several delicious entrees, if haggis doesn't please you."

"Thank you, but there is such an array of very attractive sides I could be quite satisfied just with them." He cut into the membrane, and the hot, savory smelling contents fell onto his plate. As it cooled, he buttered a bit of the fresh bread and ate a bite.

Their conversation during the meal was light, much about the food, with Weatherly expressing gratitude for the opportunity to try the Scottish national dish, which he found palatable enough that he finished it while admitting it would likely never be a favorite.

Over snifters of high quality Scotch whiskey, Weatherly asked, "If you don't mind, tell me your impressions in retrospect of young Clive. What sort of lad was he, and when did you last see him?"

McTavish leaned back and studied Weatherly's face for a moment, then looked down into his drink before he replied. "It was shortly after he joined the navy, and it was a short conversation with all three in their garden. His father and I chatted a bit about general topics, but neither Clive nor his mother said much, except to answer questions directly put to them. Clive thanked me for my congratulations on his enlistment, but he seemed reluctant to share many details about his training. We all shook hands before parting, and we've had no real contact since, except as I've already told you." McTavish drained his drink, dried his lips on the napkin, folded it, and pushed his chair back, but did not stand. It was clear he was finished, and their conversation lagged as Weatherly finished his scotch and thanked his host. Compton, waiting near the door, left when they appeared to bring the Bentley to the curb. He opened the door for Weatherly while McTavish went round the car and seated himself. There was little conversation on the way home. Once there, McTavish told the chauffeur to make the necessary arrangements for his guest's trip to the Orkneys, accepted Weatherly's gratitude for his hospitality, and each went off to his room.

When he came down the next morning at 9:50, Compton was seated at the table, reading a newspaper, but he rose at Weatherly's arrival. He was dressed in sharply creased tan trousers, a vest, and a lined hunting jacket over a black pullover, and oiled leather, high-topped walking shoes. A narrow-brimmed plaid wool hat and a hand-carved walking stick rested on the table. He nodded briefly at Weatherly's "Good morning, Compton," and responded, "Good morning, Professor; I trust you found the accommodations suitable."

"Oh, yes, very comfortable. I was tired from the flight and retired early, and slept very well. I had tea and a couple of the scones at the kitchen table, thanks to you, I assume."

"Aye, but weekdays Mr. Pierre Lucien, the butler, will prepare your meals. He's a fair hand in the kitchen, and pleased to be of service here, though he's a bit stiff and formal in 'is manners." Compton moved toward the door, picking up his plaid tam and his stick from the table. He held the door for Weathlerly, then stepped out in a brisk march up a slight incline, the cane tapping a steady beat as they strode along. Neither spoke as they climbed, but when the street leveled out, not as breathless as Weatherly, Compton observed, "I see you also like walking. Not a lot of men younger than you can keep a quick-march at this angle." He gestured back down the street with his stick.

"Indeed," Weatherly responded. "It's the best way to acquaint oneself with a city, getting oriented to its layout, and something of the culture as well, which you can't get on a tour bus or while driving."

"I noted your hat and those handsome walking shoes as well," Compton, noted, "and your gait. Ye've a good walker's stride."

"Well, thank you, Compton," Weatherly responded, smiling at the dapper-looking chauffeur beside him. "I'm both flattered and impressed by your comment and your powers of observation."

"A grand part o' walkin' is th' observin', don't ye' agree?" He looked up and down the street they were crossing.

This is obviously a test question, Hampton thought. *We're not just trading complements here.* "For me it's the greatest part," he answered.

"I try to engage all my faculties to learn the tenor and atmosphere of places I've never been before."

Compton did not look at him for a time as they marched along, enjoying the hike, and Weatherly, anticipating what he might learn from the careful and self-aware gentleman beside him, almost missed Compton's sudden turn to the left, pulling open a large, worn wooden door with forged black, heavy looking hinges in an aged brick building. He nodded Weatherly inside—dimly lit, the air tinged with tobacco smoke. Almost simultaneously, three male voices spoke up: "Aye, it's Mr. Compton—good mornin' to ye." "Aye, Compton, come and join us. Ye're just in time to treat us to the next round." A low murmur of chuckles and "To your health, Compton," followed by the bump of mugs on the tabletop.

"Thanks mooch fer yer generosity," Compton replied—with the first tinge of irony Weatherly had heard in his voice. "This is Perfessor Hampton Weatherly from America. He's lodgin' at the house fer a time, and we're just gettin' acquainted." Five men, all of retirement age, nodded, some lifting their beer mugs in a slight salutation. One turned and offered his hand, which Compton shook briefly, nodding at the other man, who also turned to shake hands with Weatherly. "Welcome t' Glasgow, Perfesser. How long will ye' be among us, eh?"

"I leave tomorrow for the Orkneys, but I'll be back in a week or so for a couple of days."

"Well, we hope to see you again then. Take yer mackintosh—it's mostly wind and rain up there."

"Thanks for the advice," he replied, tipping his hat slightly as he followed Compton to the far corner and a small, heavy looking wooden table, with a pair of chairs of the same construction, each with a thickly padded seat.

"Let me take your coat, Professor," Compton offered. He folded it neatly and laid it across the back of an empty chair behind his own, then removed his own jacket, laying it with his hat and cane on the seat of the empty chair. He pulled a chair out, directing Weatherly to sit, then seated himself in one across the table, and pulled it closer. "If it happens that yer' allergic to tobacco smoke, we could ask for the smoke-free dinin' room. It's vented and there's a tight door, but it's plain and very private, if ye' know what I mean."

"Thank you for the offer, but I'd prefer to stay here. I like the feel of the place, and the smoke is little more than a fragrance that fits it. I'm an occasional smoker myself."

"Good. Then we're agreed on the place. One o' the folks workin' here will be by for our order, and they may offer a menu, but as you're a stranger here, let me recommend the local brew, and the 'Fish 'n Eggs' platter. It comes with whatever local vegetables are in season, scones, and tea. The server can rattle off the rest of the menu if you'd prefer somethin' else. It's all good food, but many folks come here for the platter."

"Thank you, Compton, I shall take your advice, as I'm here to learn all I can about the area—especially during the war—I'll be pickin' your brain, as we say in the States, so I'll be in your debt for your time and efforts, as well as for the breakfast."

Compton regarded him soberly for a long moment. "I'll be glad to tell what I remember, but it's been many a year and I have forgotten much, besides which, much of my service time was spent away from here, and we don't talk much of that time."

Pleased at the man's frankness, Weatherly smiled. "It's another generous and pleasant act, Compton, and as an American, I prefer my friends call me Hamp, if you please."

"But not in other company, Hamp."

A stout woman with lightly salted dark hair, wearing a full white apron, appeared at the table and greeted Compton cheerily, "It's good to see you again, Mr. Compton, and I'm pleased to make the acquaintance of yerself, Perfessor. Will you be havin' your usual, Mr. Compton?"

"Indeed, yes, Helen, two orders of your specialty, a pot of tea and two pints of the usual." When she had left, he looked at Weatherly. "Our breakfast will be awhile, but the beverages soon, so let's talk a bit. Don't be afraid to ask anything, but if ye' ask somethin' I can't answer in good conscience, I'll beg your pardon and we'll go on."

Helen appeared, bearing two mugs of a dark ale and two heavy looking teacups and a full-sized teapot under a cozy on a serving tray she held in one hand. She deftly laid out cloth napkins, the teapot on a small saucer, cream and sugar, and the ales while holding the tray. "Anything else for the moment, gentlemen?"

Both men shook their heads as Compton thanked her, and she strode back to the kitchen. Weatherly took a small notebook and pen from his inside pocket and laid them beside the ales. When he looked up, Compton raised his mug in a toast. "Your health and well-bein', Hamp," to which Weatherly responded, "And to yours, Compton. I'm pleased and honored to have made your acquaintance." He took a sip of the dark golden brew and found it slightly sweet at first, melting into a slight bitterness of the hops as he swallowed. Compton, he noticed, took a deep draught, swallowing heartily a full quarter of the mug. "Ah...the top o' the mornin—this puts a fresh bloom on th' day. Drink up, Lad—'tis not a sippin' drink, but a hearty one."

Hamp obliged, taking a deep swallow, but not nearly the quantity of the chauffeur's. Compton's smile was warm as he asked, "How does that suit your fancy, now?"

"Excellent," he responded, "pure pleasure all the way down." Taking another deep swallow, Compton looked at him across the small table, a soft smile on his lips, his posture notably relaxed.

He's fully coherent, Weatherly thought, tipping back a deep swallow of ale and nodding. "A good brew indeed," he said, smiling. "Now tell me what you can about Mr. McTavish and his obsession with the St. John's family." But the waiter arrived with two fresh mugs, followed by Helen bearing a heavy tray draped with a large, white linen coverlet, a small folding table hooked over one arm. With two quick moves, she caught the table in her hand, snapped it open, and placed it close to the two men. She whisked off the coverlet and set two large plates of the fish and eggs on the table, with a small basket of scones under a linen napkin. Salt, pepper, and a small jar of honey finished out the order, and she stepped back, her hands on her ample hips. "Will there be anything else then, gentlemen? Can I pour ye' a cuppa tea?"

"I'd appreciate a cup of tea," Weatherly interjected before Compton could dismiss her. She lifted the cozy from the pot and poured the steaming beverage into Weatherly's cup. She glanced at Compton, who was shaking his head. "None for me just yet, Helen, thank ye'. One beverage at a time for me."

"I figgered as much," she said, gathering up her linens and the table. "Enjoy your breakfast, gentlemen."

Compton tucked his napkin into the vee of his vest, picked up his ale, and took a deep draught, then sat back, a knife in one hand, fork in the other, and smiled across the table at Hampton. *"Bon appetite, mon ami,"* and dug into his meal with surprising gusto. Weatherly buttered a scone and turned his attention to the generous portion of fish and cooked peas, carrots, and small boiled potatoes. Both were silent for several minutes as Compton neatly, efficiently, and quickly dispatched a fair portion of his meal before Weatherly had taken three bites. Weatherly recognized everything he tasted, but its unique aromas and precise and simple presentation made it delightful. He paused and lifted his mug in a salute. "Well recommended. Fine dining indeed. Thank you." He drained his mug as Compton brought the level of his to half. Almost immediately another mug was set before him.

"Ye're more than welcome," the chauffeur replied, "and here's to your good taste in recognizing it." Compton returned to his meal with quick, deft moves, punctuated with hearty swallows of his ale. When he finished, he wiped his mouth and folded his napkin, lined up his silver on the plate, and sat back with a sigh of pleasure. Hamp found himself sated, despite having eaten but half his meal. He wiped his mouth, folded the napkin, pushed his chair back from the table, and drew his tea closer. "I hope we can take the remainder of my order away with us. It's another full meal for me."

'It's a complement to 'em, Hamp. Now, have ye' got any more questions for me?" He winked. "I'll order up another round, and maybe it'll loosen up me tongue—and yours when you finish your tea."

"I'll stay with the tea for the time being—and the half-mug of this fine ale. Then we'll discuss your generous offer. Now, tell me what you know or can tell about Mr. McTavish and the St. Johns." He pulled his pen and notebook closer, looking directly into Compton's somewhat reddened eyes.

Compton reached back and fumbled in the pocket of his jacket, pulling out a curve-stemmed pipe, already loaded with a dark, pleasantly scented tobacco. He produced a matchbook and carefully lit up, spreading the flame evenly over bowl. He shook out the match, licked his thumb and forefinger, and pinched out the match head; he tucked the dead match into the matchbook and returned it to his pocket. "It's me secret vice," he explained with a slightly rueful smile. "I like a couple of smokes after such a meal. You're welcome to light up if you like. They'll bring an ashtray."

Weatherly shook his head. "No thanks. I smoke only rarely, and almost never when I travel. Like you, I am a careful man about many things, including my health, but I do enjoy smoking, moderately. And your smoke has a fine aroma to it."

Compton nodded. "It's a blend a local shop carries for me." He paused, took a puff, and looked back at Weatherly. "I've given this matter considerable talk since you asked me to share what I've heard and what I think about it. I'm not sure where to begin. It's been ten years and more now I've been with the man, and his wife and sons, and he seldom talks of them since Mrs. McTavish passed away."

"Did she ever talk of them with you as you drove her around?"

"Not s'much, except to complain a bit about his obsession, which she didn't seem to understand much either."

"Okay, so tell me the first time you remember him mentioning St. John, or the first things you heard about them."

"I think that might have been on our first trip to Manchester on some university business or other. He didn't talk much when we were in city traffic, but country miles either put him to sleep or set him to talkin', and I don't think it mattered much whether I was really listenin' to him or not. He asked me if I'd heard of the St. John family, and when I said 'neh,' he went on anyway. Said they had a title and both Sir Hugh and Clive, his son, had served in the admiralty—code work in the First War, and Sir Hugh as a secret agent or a spy." Compton paused and tamped the ashes on top of the tobacco in his bowl before reigniting it.

"How did he seem to feel about them, based on what he talked about?" Weatherly asked, leaning toward his host.

"In part he was jealous of their title—and Sir Hugh's not taking it seriously enough. 'They neglected the responsibilities that go with the privilege,' he might have said. But there was a lot more to it than that. I think much as he denigrated them for not having made more of themselves—distinguished their name somehow—he seemed a little afraid of them." He paused to take another long swallow from his mug. Weatherly noticed that his brogue had become more pronounced. Having finished his tea, Weatherly pulled his half empty mug closer.

"Aye, lad, drink up now. Ye'r fallin' behind already, and I'm needin' another." He waved at Helen across the room and gestured toward his mug. She disappeared into the taproom and returned with two mugs, setting one before the professor, shaking her head slightly, but not speaking. Both thanked her as she bustled back with the empty mugs.

Weatherly waited for him to go on, and when he didn't, he asked, "And do you know what he was afraid of?"

"'Tis a difficult question," Compton replied, leaning forward over his fresh drink, gripping it tightly. "He never come out and said what it was, but over the years I pieced together enough to know it was somethin' highly personal between them that made the St. Johns cold toward him, but he never said what it was." Compton paused again, took a long drink, wiped his mouth with the back of his hand, and drew on his pipe. "Some o' the lads I drink with here, and other pubs occasionally, sharin' the local gossip and tellin' stories have hinted at some of Mr. McTavish's private affairs and interests." Compton paused, looking pensively at the wisp of smoke rising from his pipe.

Weatherly took a swallow from his mug, and Compton did the same—a moderate sip for the first time.

"And you think some of the gossip might have been legitimate, that is, based on truth?" Weatherly asked.

"I can't say I could prove it, but something came up in different places, from sources not known to each other." He paused again, stroking his chin as though in deep thought.

Weatherly waited for him to go on, then realized Compton wanted him to ask, so he did. "And what was it that 'came up' in these conversations?"

Compton laid his pipe in the ashtray and took another swallow of ale. He leaned forward and looked up and down the room to see if anyone else was listening, then turned to Weatherly. "I think it needs to be told," he said in a low voice, almost as though talking to himself, "but I'm much torn about bein' the teller." He looked away and drew a deep breath. "The word is that Mr. McTavish had a particular interest in boys and young men." Compton paused, visibly shaken at his own words, anxiously watching for Weatherly's reaction.

"And you think something might have happened between Clive and Mr. McTavish?" he asked.

Compton took another deep swallow, then shook his head. "Aye, I *think* it *might* have but I kenna be at all sure. It jibes with what I surmise of Mr. McTavish after ten years of observin' and listenin' t' the man."

"Well," Weatherly responded, "I have neither reason nor interest in impeaching the man's reputation, but I am sure your revelation is prompted by more than idle pub gossip. So I will ask what you can tell me what else there is." He emptied his mug and pushed it aside. Compton moved the full one left by Helen closer to Weatherly, who was beginning to feel the effects of his unaccustomed indulgence.

"'Tis a hard thing," Compton said, running his hand over his face and wiping it on his trousers. "Aside from his personal oddities and tastes, he's good man, respected in his position at the university. He has always treated me squarely. On one occasion, may have hinted that we might become 'more intimately acquainted,' as he put it. I ignored it, acted like I hadn't been listening or something. He never spoke that way to me again. However, young men, staff, faculty members, and students occasionally accompany us, and some I've seen coming from his room in the early mornin'. There may have been complaints, but no charges made I've heard of." He paused, now sweating, not meeting Weatherly's carefully neutral gaze.

Uncomfortably aware of Compton's agitation, he pushed his chair back and stood. "Please excuse me for a moment, and tell me where the loo is."

Still shaken, Compton half-rose from his chair, and gestured to the far corner of the room. "Just around there, by the taproom." Weatherly thanked him and turned away as Compton slumped back down in his chair.

When he returned, Compton's elbows were on the table, his hands wrapped around his empty mug, into which he seemed to be staring. When Weatherly approached, he raised his head, and with some effort, focused his bloodshot gaze on the professor. "Ye' ready for another round then, my friend Hamp?"

"Thank you for the offer, but I've had all can handle for now. I could do with a bit of fresh air, however. If you're up for it, I'd enjoy a little walk with you. Seems a fine day for it."

"Ye' don't have any more questions for me then?"

"I have quite a few of them, but what you've shared with me gives me an unexpected perspective, and I need to think on this, but I very much hope we might do this again when I return from the Orkneys."

Compton stared at him for a moment, his face slack. "Sure you won't stay for another round, then?"

"Not today, Compton. I sincerely appreciate your hospitality and conversation, but I've sat so long I need to move around a bit. I think I'd like to head back to the house and finish up my packing as I would like a morning train to Aberdeen, and you have my tickets reserved, right?"

"Aye," Compton responded quickly. "They're awaitin' ye' at the station, fer th' 8:45 departure. We should leave around eight." He sat up in his chair and brushed the front of his vest and lap. Weatherly reached for his jacket as Compton struggled to his feet, leaning heavily on the table.

"I'll see to the tip then," Weatherly said, pausing a moment, ready to help Compton into his jacket, but the man waved him off. Compton settled the breakfast bill with Helen, complimenting her on the quality of the meal and her service. Compton was weaving slightly on his feet as he returned, his hat and cane in hand. Weatherly donned his jacket and his cap, following the careful steps of his new friend to the door.

As they stepped out on the sidewalk, a gust of wind tugged at them, and Compton leaned on his cane to keep his balance, then began marching up the sidewalk, his cadence much slower than their earlier walk. Weatherly stayed close to the older man in case he wobbled or tripped, but except for an occasional drift from side to side, Compton marched steadily on, but there was little conversation on the hike back to the Provost's residence.

Once inside, Compton resumed his careful bearing, shaking Weatherly's hand as he thanked him for his good company. "There's a meal in the kitchen should be hungry later and breakfast when ye'r up for it. I'll be in me quarters should you need anything—or I'll see you in the marnin." He nodded, then turned to the door, his back straight, his steps steady.

THE ORKNEYS BY LAND AND SEA (1996)

WHEN WEATHERLY CAME DOWN on his way to the kitchen at 7 a.m., he found Compton, back in uniform, drinking tea at his small table near the telephone and reading the *Times*. He half-rose from his chair as Weatherly raised his palms and shook his head. "Please don't stand, Compton," he said. "I'm just going to breakfast. Have you eaten yet?"

"Aye, and yours is in the icebox, courtesy of Masseur Lucien."

"*Tres bien,*" Weatherly replied, smiling. He received a nod and polite smile in response, but Compton's gaze was reserved.

He found his breakfast on a large plate of two sausage patties, fried potatoes with diced red peppers, and scrambled eggs, with bits of onion, chives, pepper, and, he found later, a distinct portion of curry. A saucer held a sliced tomato. Weatherly put the plate in the microwave, poured his tea, and carried it to the counter, where he found his silver, a linen napkin, and a small empty drinking glass. He carried that to the refrigerator and poured orange juice into it. Within fifteen minutes he was putting his dishes in the sink and pouring a second cup of tea, which he carried with him back up to his room. Twenty minutes later, he carried his small suitcase and a leather backpack holding his notes and notebook, pens, pencils, and other supplies into the reception area. Compton rose and retrieved the suitcase and offered to take the backpack, but Weatherly waved him off, smiling as he thanked him.

As the bag was stowed in the "boot," as Compton called it, Weatherly stepped to the left side of the Bentley and opened the forward door. "If you don't mind, Compton, I'd prefer to ride in the front seat so we can chat more easily, and I will see more of Glasgow here. That is, unless it would distract you."

"Nae, sit where ye' like; you won't distract me from me drivin.'"

The heavy doors closed with a muffled thud, and the Bentley purred to life. When they pulled into the street, Weatherly turned to Compton to ask, "Would you mind answering a few more questions about McTavish and the St. Johns?"

"I'll do me best, though my memory isn't as good as it once was, ye' understand."

"I understand that very well, having a similar weakness, and I'll keep it in mind. I'd like you to tell me what you know of the St. John family, based, of course, mostly on whatever Mr. McTavish talked about."

Compton was silent for a few moments, in heavy traffic. "I know Sir Clive was in town and they chatted when I was first employed here, but I never met him meself. If Mr. McTavish talked about that visit with me I don't recall it. But his name came up often when McTavish was talkin' about Sir Hugh and what he knew of him."

"Can you recall any specifics of what he said?" Weatherly asked. Keeping his gaze on the traffic, a brief smile flickered across his lips. "I recall a couple of trips when Mr. McTavish was frustrated about the university's strict interpretation of 'secret' in reference to 'Secret Files.' He took offense when they denied him access to some of the files on the St. Johns, father and son."

"How long ago was that?"

"Oh, it might have been fifteen years or so. He was more jealous of his position then. More than once when I picked him up from the library, he was as angry as I've ever seen him. 'I'm the university provost, for God's sake, and this is the university's library! They've allowed me access to more critical files than these, and they blame the Admiralty for denying me access? They trust the university with this data but not the university's provost?' He contacted the Admiralty and MI5, and it took a long time for them to reply, despite his several calls to them. I don't recall that he ever said exactly what he was lookin' for, and I never heard if he got it."

"That explains his interest in my research, though Mr. McTavish is never mentioned in the material I've examined, which I'm sure is not all there is in those files. Clive, you know, was turned down on the 'need to know' restrictions, and he was delighted to get my notes and recollections of the Sir Hugh data that was denied to him. I'm sure he and perhaps Mr. McTavish have higher clearances than me, but I was cleared and they were not. And because this involves two government bureaucracies, it might take years to find out why."

Compton nodded as Weatherly spoke, then glanced at him with a rare full smile. "He seemed much more interested in the St. Johns at that time than he's shown of late, but he's obviously not lost all interest in them. I'm sure there're folks who knew both families, and I wonder if Mr. McTavish would introduce you to 'em if you asked."

"It's in my notes to ask that very question," Weatherly answered, "the very next time we meet. But what do you recall McTavish saying about them or about their chilly relationship?"

"Well, I know he relished the news of Sir Hugh's conviction by the Admiralty court, and I twice drove him up to Orkneys where he treated some o' the locals to drinks and quizzed them about Sir Hugh and his son. He handed out his card and invited them to call him, but they obviously didn't tell him all he wanted to know. We Scots by nature are wary of strangers an' their questions, and those in the remote villages even more so. From what I overheard when they asked why he wanted to know, he passed it off to curiosity about his old acquaintances—his closest neighbor. His manner and tendency to talk too much pu|t them off, though they treated him with courtesy, and thanked him for the beer. He complained about their coolness toward him on the way home. Said it was as if they were protectin' the St. Johns; 'close-mouthed as Hugh himself' was his way of puttin' it."

As they neared the station, traffic increased, and Compton moved smoothly into the left lane, turning into a line of slow-moving vehicles entering the departure area, maneuvering the Bentley neatly into an open space next to the curb. Both stepped out of the car and moved to the rear. Compton retrieved Weatherly's bags and set them on the sidewalk. "The ticket counter is well-marked, with signs to guide ye' to it. When ye' come back, call me at this top number." He handed over a small card with the phone number in clearly printed handwriting. "Or ye' can call Mr. McTavish's number, the second one there. Either will tell you when to expect me. Be modest in yer tippin, if ye' do it at all. Ye'll lose respect as an American if they think you rich and uncouth."

Weatherly smiled and shook his hand, thanking him for his time and his kindness. "It's been a pleasure, Hamp, and I look forward to your return." He tipped his cap as he slid into the Bentley and glided back into the street.

Weatherly shrugged into his backpack his tickets, passport, wallet, and a small tablet and paper inside a zippered compartment on the side of his bag. He strode as briskly as the crowds allowed to platform B, stopping at a kiosk for an *Aberdeen Journal* to read on the two or three-hour trip to his departure city. He hoped to take in the scenery from a forward-facing window seat. He arrived fifteen minutes before the scheduled departure, but this being Sunday, the crowds were much smaller than on weekdays. He found an empty bench in the waiting area, sat down, and took out his camera and the tablet to make notes of his observations on the ride, using a kind of shorthand of single, abbreviated words: "smell of pipe smoke, red tam, car cold." He called them "trigger words" to evoke other senses. When he heard the 8:45 train coming, he stood, put his tablet and pencil in a jacket pocket, and moved toward the rear of the line-up where he could walk on to a car only half-full of passengers. He had a choice of for-ward-facing window seats and chose the one facing the baggage racks at the front of the car where he stowed his small suitcase. He pulled off his backpack and removed his camera and notebook and set the pack on the floor between his feet. He pulled the newspaper from his pocket and began to read, glancing up to nod at the passengers passing in the aisle. Many were traveling alone, like he was, but there were couples of all ages and a few with children. Most were well dressed, but a few were laborers in their work clothes, with a few long-haired teenagers in flamboyant retro garb. As the crowd thinned out, he noted that there were empty seats behind him, and no one was standing or looking for a seat.

The whistle blew, the doors closed, and the train started with a slight jolt. Weatherly folded his paper and set it on the seat beside him and laid the backpack atop it. The scenery outside his window was dreary, the sky dark and a heavy fog-like mist hung in the air. Away from the station, they entered an industrial section of the city: warehouses, business buildings, industrial plants, dark and block-like in the mist. Shortly they were sliding through tenements—aging concrete and block buildings, depressingly similar, reeking of poverty. These gave way to blocks of modest suburban homes, duplexes, and shopping centers. Weatherly reflected that what he'd seen of Glasgow and its environs from the train looked like much of the western hemisphere—with many of the same logos, advertising signs, and products he might have seen in Chicago, Memphis, or Melbourne, Australia. As they approached the countryside, the winds increased, and the fog turned to raindrops. Through the precipitation and brief breaks in the blowing winds, he noted the train was slowing as it crawled up a steep hillside, passing cliffs, and great, dark boulders, some nearly covered with lichens and mosses. The car rocked as they rounded a sharp curve, and he could see a deep chasm dropping steeply off to the left of the tracks. The train accelerated down to a small valley, then slowed as it started climbing again. Small towns and villages slipped by, almost indistinguishable in the rain. Weatherly sighed and retrieved his newspaper. When he finished it, he dug out a novel he had started reading on the flight to Glasgow, finally looking up when they slowed to enter Aberdeen.

When the train came to a stop at the terminal, Weatherly waited in his seat until the aisle was clear, then donned his backpack, picked up his suitcase, and went searching for an information desk where he got walking directions from his stop to the ferry terminal and its ticket office. There Weatherly donned his jacket, stowed his tickets in one if its pockets, put on his hat, stepped from the train, checked the time, and opened his umbrella. Recalling the directions to the ferry terminal, he set out on the half-mile trek, grateful for the chance to loosen up after sitting for most of the day. The rain persisted, though not so heavily as it had been, and the wind came in short gusts from at least three directions. At the terminal, a bored looking agent examined his ticket and rather brusquely directed him to the proper dock, where he sat on a cold, hard bench in a protected waiting area. The ferry backed in twenty-two minutes behind schedule, and a handful of passengers disembarked before the trucks and cars got under way. Weatherly waited until the boarding passengers headed to the gangway and found himself at the end of the line, waiting for the boarding agent to tear the stub from his ticket and usher him to the stairway that took him two levels up to the glass-enclosed lounge. There he found a small forward-facing table with two padded chairs. He removed his hat, backpack, and jacket and placed them on one chair, sat down in the other, and pulled out his notebook and camera, and looked around the almost empty room for one of the wait staff to appear. None did for some time, as those who had driven aboard trickled in, damp and red-faced from the wind and rain that swept across the moored vessel, even though it was protected on three sides by solid-looking port structures. The small barroom quickly filled, and when the crowd was seated, one of the bartenders emerged with his notepad and began taking orders from tables of patrons like Weatherly not yet served. Before he reached Weatherly, he returned to the bar and posted his orders, chatted with the other staff members, then ambled back to ask, "And wot's ye're pleasure t'day, Sare?"

"A double shot of the best of the Orkneys, please."

"That'd be the Highland Park Reserve, then. Have you tried it befare?"

Weatherly shook his head. "Not that I recall, but it's what you'd recommend, then?"

"'Tis the best of the islands, and ye're in for somethin' special, like no other whiskey around. Part of it's the hard spring water, and some is due to the particular peat bogs we use. But it's a bit steep: ten pounds fer a shot, fifteen fer a double "

Weatherly leaned back to look into the man's face. "Thank you for the warning, but I'll go for the double and trust I'll find it a bargain, right?"

The man smiled. "For a Scot, ten-pound a shot whiskey hardly seems a bargain, but it's somethin' ye' should try if you've the means fer it."

"Bring it on, then, please," Weatherly replied. "I trust it will help counter the chill even here in the lounge."

"Practically guaranteed, sare, but you'll want to savor it. Anything else then? Maybe glass of water and a bite to eat?"

"What goes well with Highland Park Reserve?" Weatherly responded.

"Maybe some crackers and a bit o' a local cheese, eh?"

"I'll take your word for it," Weatherly replied, nodding, "and that glass of water as well."

"I'll be bringin' it soon as it's up, and thank ye'." He nodded before turning back toward the bar, passing the other patrons without looking at them.

There was a slight murmur in the room as the ferry began backing away from the pier. Once clear of the docking area, the ferry shuddered as it shifted forward, making a long, slow 180 degree turn toward the open sea and gradually picked up speed. The sky was dark, and rain pelted the windows so that Weatherly could not see the prow of the vessel, and he turned his attention to his fellow passengers, most of whom seemed to be working adults, ranging from teenagers to those in or near retirement. From their clothes, he deduced most were laborers, some with waterproof clothing which suggested fishermen or crewmen on working ships or offshore oil rigs. Some of them, men and women, were carrying shopping bags, and small groups in easy conversation indicated they were well acquainted. Some carried briefcases, which they opened on their tables and extracted work papers and began reading and making notations. A few pulled out newspapers, and others settled into books.

The ferry rocked and swayed in the winds and heavy seas, but his fellow passengers seemed to ignore the motion except for holding their drinks and snacks to keep them from sliding off the tabletops. The waiter took a few remaining orders, moving across the shifting floor with the easy balance of a seasoned sailor, then began serving, balancing a tray bearing drinks and paper containers of snacks and light lunches—sandwiches, fish and chips, sausages, salads, and dessert sweets. When he reached Weatherly, he set the heavy glass of scotch down, followed by a small bottle of water, and the cheese and crackers sealed in cellophane along with a packet containing a plastic knife, fork, spoon and a large, heavy paper napkin.

"Ye'll want to keep a grip on the scotch and an eye on the rest or ye'll be pickin' em off the floor," he warned. "I'll be checkin' t'see if if ye' find the scotch t' your likin', or if there's anything else I can do for ye." Weatherly thanked him and watched as he moved across the room, rocking slowly from side to side as the ferry rolled in the churning sea.

He opened the cheese and popped a small square into his mouth, savoring its smooth, creamy texture and the slight sharpness released when he chewed. He followed that with a bite of cracker, then took a swallow of water, and lifted the clear, caramel colored whiskey to his lips, noting a faint smell of peat. He sipped and let the drink slide across his tongue—at first cool, then gently lighting up the back of his tongue and pleasantly warm in his throat. A second, more substantive sip yielded more complex flavors: a hint of mineral—probably in the spring water that had flowed over the ancient rock—and a stronger sense of the peat from that region. The warmth was stronger on his throat, and it seemed to grow in his stomach. He leaned back in his chair to seek a clear description of his first experience with the Orkney Scotch whiskey. He had sampled—and enjoyed—other Scotch whiskeys but hardly considered himself a connoisseur enough to make comparisons. *I don't precisely recall their tastes, but I know this one is unique in my experience. Some others tasted strong, others seemed milder, but this is a distinctive taste, with, I think, more mineral-like, maybe more "natural," but clean, maybe medicinal, but pleasant and interesting. I shall ask McTavish's opinion on it. I'm sure he's familiar with it. It will be a delectable companion on this trip.*

Full darkness came slowly, and the seas calmed slightly as Weatherly slowly downed the tumbler as he reviewed his notes on Sir Hugh's secret assignments, from various sources besides the journal: Compton, McTavish, and Clive. His expectations were low, given the nature of the topic, and the decades that had passed since he served up there. Of course, he hoped for some lucky connection that might reveal a heretofore hidden aspect of the man or details of his work.

He finished his scotch and, later, a pot of tea and an order of fish and chips half an hour before they docked in Kirkhill. The waiter appeared with his bill, and Weatherly added a modest tip as he handed over his credit card. When the waiter returned, he nodded slightly and thanked Weatherly pleasantly and wished him well on his visit to the Orkneys. It was fully dark when he left the ferry, grateful to escape the rolling motion characteristic of sailing those occasionally treacherous waters. He asked for recommendations and directions to comfortable lodgings in Kirkhill that were fairly close, as the rain abated to a heavy mist, and the wind softened. His room featured a double bed, clock radio, a telephone and private bath with thick, soft towels, and a desk large enough for him to spread out his notebook. The desk clerk directed him to a modest restaurant and recommended the fish and chips for a light meal, and promised a modest dinner menu and well-prepared fare. He was not disappointed and returned to his room after arranging for the bus trip to Quoyloo the next morning. Pleasantly weary from his long day of travel, he turned off his bedside lamp at ten-thirty p.m.

EXPLORING QUOYLOO (1996)

FOLLOWING A HEARTY BREAKFAST at the same restaurant the next morning, Weatherly pulled a heavy wool turtleneck sweater over a thick flannel shirt, put on his vest and his lined jacket, checked his backpack, which was fully stuffed, and shrugged into it. He donned a woolen cap, picked up his walking stick and his suitcase, looked around the room, and locked the door. He dropped the suitcase off in the lobby, confirming he'd be back two days hence, and set out at a brisk pace for the travel center where he booked a coach ride to Quoyloo, a small farming community about half an hour away. He took an empty double seat, but at the first stop, several people boarded, and a man of ruddy complexion, probably in his fifties, carrying a rather worn briefcase settled in across from him. He placed his briefcase on the floor behind his knees, turned to Weatherly, and stuck out his hand. "The name's Sandy," he announced, grasping Weatherly's hand and shaking it vigorously. "I'm from Kirkwall by way of Aberdeen, and I take it ye're from the United States." His eyes were a pale blue, with deep laugh lines, and his smile was bright, revealing what was obviously a full set of dentures.

Taken by the man's natural good nature, Weatherly smiled back at him. "My origins are that obvious then? My name is Hampton Weatherly, and I am recently from Washington D.C.—by way of Iowa, my home state."

"Well," Sandy replied, looking away and stroking his chin, "me U.S. geography's not what it might be, but I'm guessin' from your accent it's somewhere in what they call the Midwest, right?"

"Indeed," Weatherly replied. "Just north of the middle of the country."

"And ye're not just tourin' the Orkneys, so what brings you clear out here, Hampton?"

Weatherly took a moment to gather his thoughts before replying, "I confess that sightseeing in part brings me here, but I intend to do a little research on behalf of a friend—from Scotland too, by the way—whose father served in the Admiralty in the last world war, part of the time in the Orkneys, including Quoyloo. I hope to get a feel for the place, see if there's any reference to him in the public records. With luck, I might turn up a friendly resident who remembers him from nearly fifty years back."

Sandy gazed at him intently, his eyes still merry, smiling. "So you're writin' a book then?"

Weatherly leaned back on the bench and folded his arms. "I am writing a book and will shortly return home to finish it, but my book has little to do with my interest in Quoyloo. I am coming as a tourist, and doing a favor for a friend by looking into historical data regarding his father."

Sandy turned in his seat, crossing his legs in the aisle, and Weatherly firmed himself against the urge to distance himself further. Sandy put an elbow on his knee, resting his chin as he smiled and returned Wetherly's cool, focused attention. "Do you know anyone living there?" He cocked his head slightly.

Weatherly shook his head and uncrossed his arms. "No one. I will walk about, take some pictures and notes, then try to get in touch with the local authorities and maybe the churches about accessing their records. Should I get the opportunity, I'll ask if there's anyone living nearby who might remember rumors about a British military spy there during the war. I am sure there were more than one."

"I lived in the area for some thirty year and more, includin' the war years—which were excitin' times for a lad with all the strangers and local folk frettin' about so many strange outsiders among us, some of 'em maybe spies and such like, but it brought some prosperity t' the village too.

"It was and is a wee town, and very few remain who were there during the war. Most of the strangers in town were military, one way or another, there for short stints. Others showed up for a day or two, and some of 'em came back periodically for just a day or so, and few long enough to become familiar, but I might not recognize any of 'em if they showed up today, fifty years older."

"Thank you very much, Sandy, for sharing your insights, but I must ask, just on the off-chance you might have heard something about a Scotsman named Sir Hugh St. John who served here in the latter years of the war."

Sandy looked at him for a moment, then shrugged and mumbled, "Ye'r wilcom, and I wish ye' well, but I can't recall anyone of that name. It's not to say I never met him, but it's probably unlikely." He glanced out the window at the bleak uneven landscape, the sky almost the color of the giant gray rocks jutting from the ground. Then he turned again and faced Weatherly across the aisle. "What d' ye know of the Orkney population?"

Somewhat taken aback at the question, Weatherly paused before responding, "Very little, actually. It's my first trip here, and I haven't been here twenty-four hours yet, so I haven't met many. You're the first I've had a conversation with, other than the waiter on the ferry, who introduced me to Highland Reserve as the best drink in the Orkneys."

Sandy's smile broadened as he sat up and asked, "Did ye' find it to your likin' then?"

"I thought it fine, unlike any other scotch I've tasted, which are not all that many, so I'm no expert."

Sandy nodded again. "'Tis a fine drink, to be sure, though not to everyone's liking, and it's dear, and most won't spend that much on their booze. I know because I have been travelin' all over Scotland, Ireland, and Britain's many islands for over twenty years, supplyin' mostly scotch, but other whiskeys, wine, and even American bourbons to pubs and stores all over the land."

Weatherly smiled and nodded. "You, I guess you are a traveling salesman, then, or a liquor agent perhaps."

"Aye, part now of a vanishin' breed, replaced by the telephone and the internet, so I'll be takin' my retirement soon, grateful the company's kept me on this long. But I'll miss the travelin' and the folks I've gotten to know and understand."

"Unlike you," Weatherly responded, "I have done more traveling since I retired than I did during my teaching career. I love going to new places and taking in the atmosphere, getting a sense of the local culture and how the landscape and history has shaped it."

"We've got only a short time, but I could give you a head start, if you're interested," Sandy said. "We're both students of human nature, you might say, and it might help you a bit with your quest here if you knew little more about the folk and their ways in these islands."

"I can't tell you how grateful I would be for your insights, and if you don't mind, I'd like to take notes and ask questions. And also, I'd like to know your full name."

Sandy reached into an inside pocket and withdrew a card, which identified him as "Calum Ballard, Purveyor of Fine Spirits, of Kirkhill, Scotland," with a phone number and a small logo of a whiskey bottle tilted over a glass. They exchanged cards, nodding seriously as they faced one another in the window seats.

"We north Islanders are clannish by breedin' and nature, and while we trust each other by necessity and common sense, we're curious and much aware of our neighbors near and far, and of strangers." Sandy's manner was intense, his eyes bright, but no closer to Weatherly than halfway across the aisle. "You'll find us guarded, a trifle suspicious, but coolly polite, with a high tolerance for individuality. Meet us eye to eye and we'll help you all we can, but with a strong sensitivity to slight or arrogance. The weather and the climate are hard, and we can be too—in the best and worst of ways." He sat up and looked at the strangely beautiful landscape of thin topsoil and rocky outcroppings, the narrow, paved two-lane highway snaking in and out of view before and behind them. He turned back to face Hampton again, smiling. "Jis' be yourself and don't try to impress us."

Returning Sandy's smile, he shook his head. "That's quite a sketch you've given me, and I am grateful for it. I take it I should tip modestly, if it is proper to do so." He looked expectantly at his new acquaintance.

Sandy reached up and rubbed his temples, his eyes closed. "It's a matter of respect, of course, on both parts: your gratitude for our service, and ours for your acknowledgment of it. There are few people of wealth livin' here, and it's unlikely you'll deal with them; we're careful with our resources and understand you may be too."

The bus came to a stop at a roadside pub, where a few cars and trucks were parked nearby.

"This is your stop, Hamp. The folks inside can guide you to some lodgings. And good luck to ye' in your wanderins and yer research."

Weatherly shrugged into his vest and coat, retrieved his stick and his backpack, and shook hands with his new acquaintance. "I am in your debt, sir, for sharing your insights and advice. I would welcome the chance of seeing you again before I return to the States."

"T'would be a privilege and an honor, Perfesser, and best of luck on both your pursuits here." He nodded several times, then resumed his seat to fix his stare at the scant activity in front of the pub.

Quoyloo consisted of a several sturdy-looking family homes, many built since the war, he noted as he strode up the main street of the village, nodding politely to the few residents he met, delighted to find the Boots and Spurs pub was still there, under an old-fashioned but brightly painted sign featuring a brightly attired rider on white horse extended in full gallop. Inside, he explained to the barman ("Ben," according to stitching on his apron) that he was an American college professor doing a bit of research on the area and was favored with a pint "on the house." After thanking the man, he took a seat on a stool at the bar and glanced around at the five other patrons—a middle-aged man in heavy denim work clothes, a mug of beer between his scarred and calloused hands, and four older men at a small table playing cards around a half-filled pitcher of beer. Turning back to his host, he said, "One Sandy McCallum, whom I met on the bus, suggested I might find someone in Quoyloo who remembers the war years here."

Ben's smile widened. "So you met Sandy McCallum, then. He's an interesting fellow, well-known around here," he replied, his gaze steady, a slight smile on his lips.

"Yes," Weatherly replied. "He said there might be a chance someone might recall the war years here, and that part of local history interests me. He also shared some of his insights into the local culture."

"Well," the barkeep responded, leaning across the bar, "Sandy grew up here, related to people all over the islands, has traveled abroad a fair bit, and loves to talk. One of the best salesmen I ever met. What did he tell you about us?"

"Not much. He suggested native Orkandians were shaped by the landscape, which I think I understand a bit. It is really quite beautiful, but not an easy place to live."

Ben nodded. "'Tis not a thrivin' community. We have a couple of schools, but most of the graduates leave to make their fortunes elsewhere. There's as many sheep as citizens, but few large farms. There's work in the brewery not far away and few other small businesses like the pub here, but many of the residents are older folk, and a fair number of them have to move away when they can't abide the weather—especially the long, dark winters. That would include most of 'em who were bairns here durin' the war."

Weatherly downed his ale and thanked Ben for the sketch of Quoyloo and inquired if the Boots and Spurs still offered lodging, as it had during the war.

"Aye," Ben replied. "We've a few rooms upstairs, a couple of 'em all made up, and they're available.

"I learned that Sir Hugh stayed here—or a place of the same name—during the last days of the war. Would you mind if I took a look at one of available rooms?"

"Ye're more than welcome," he replied, crossing over to open a drawer beneath the brew taps. He handed Weatherly an old-fashioned skeleton key attached by a ring to a heavy carved wooden stick about three inches long, rubbed smooth by thousands of hand over the years, the initials "B & S" over a large neatly carved into it. Ben gestured to a single door at the back of the room, and Weatherly left through it, finding himself in a kind of alley. To his left was a set of weathered wooden steps leading to a full balcony. He mounted them and looked at the tin numerals on each door, finding "2" just to his left. His key opened the door with a loud click and he stepped inside.

The room looked unchanged from when Sir Hugh had stayed there. It featured a full-sized bed with a wrought-iron frame, neatly made up with a worn patchwork quilt and two standard sized pillows, a small writing table with a straight-backed wooden chair. There was no closet, but six pegs set into the wall for hanging garments, and a three-drawer cabinet nest to the bed. A narrow door with hook-and-eye fasteners on both sides opened into a closet containing a narrow metal shower stall with a plastic curtain, a stool with an elevated tank operated by a pull-chain, and a small sink with a used bar of soap. Weatherly pushed the single tap to the left, but no heated water issued; pushing it to the right yielded warm water after about three minutes. A single door on the opposite side with a hook-and-eye lock indicated the bath was shared.

Considering the quarters adequate for his needs, he returned to the bar and paid with cash what he felt was cheap.

CHAPTER 25

EXPLORING QUOYLOO (1996)

WHEN THE SUN ROSE the next morning, Weatherly was washed, his backpack loaded with his camera, walking stick, rain shroud, a woolen knit cap, his notebook, and small items that stayed with his pack. He locked his room and descended the stairs.

After a hearty Scottish breakfast featuring two meats, eggs, toast, beans, and black pudding the next morning, he stepped out under a lowering gray sky and chill, damp breezes. The ground fog was light, broken up by the winds as he set off toward the shoreline, comfortable in his woolen cap and layers of clothing. A short distance away, he turned and surveyed the little town of scattered modest dwellings with small service businesses interspersed among them. Ascending a small hill, he looked back over broad green fields and meadows, mostly treeless, with little movement or signs of life in the region. He tried imagining it in wartime, more crowded, bustling, but the buildings now were modern and the layout undoubtedly altered. He continued toward the sea as the grasslands gave way to a challenging rocky shoreline, which he skirted, pausing to look through his binoculars for signs of gun emplacements or monuments, but he found nothing to draw him closer to the formidable wet, sharp rocks pounded by the surf. He paused to snap a few photos of the view, both seaward and toward the town.

He continued along the seashore, then turned toward the town to enter from the side opposite his departure. At the first street he entered, he slowed and began walking to the end, then turning onto another street, following it with the intention of traversing every public thoroughfare in Quoyloo. As he walked, he met few pedestrians, each of whom nodded politely as they passed, but closer to the few small businesses, he seemed to draw more attention. When he paused outside a small pub, a middle-aged man dressed in in work clothes stopped and looked at him, smiling. "I ken ye're a stranger here; can I help you find anything?" in a clipped and almost musical local accent.

"Actually, I am looking for someone—anyone who might tell me a bit about local history, particularly about Quoyloo during the war. And by the way, my name is Hampton Weatherly, from the United States." He offered his hand, which the man shook warmly.

"Ai'm pleased t' maet ye," he responded. "Ai'm Robert McGrath, late of Aberdeen. Been here goin' on fifteen year, and like most, I know about everyone in town—includin' their bairns, dogs, and in-laws." He paused, smiling, and looking at Weatherly expectantly.

Hampton smiled back. "If it's not too early, Mr. McGrath, I'd like to ask you a few questions over a pint—or a pot of tea, if you've got the time."

"Aye," McGrath replied heartily, "'tis a good day t' stay inside where 'tis warm and there's peanuts with the beer." He held the door open and followed Weatherly inside.

The single room was small, and smelled of smoke and stale beer. Two patrons sitting at the bar greeted Robert by name and raised their mugs in a casual salute as Robert led the way to a small table farther back. Weatherly shrugged out of his jacket and hung it on the back of his chair, laying his backpack and stick on the floor near his feet.

"Your usual then, Robert?" the bartender asked.

"Aye, and the same for me generous new mucker, Hampton, from the States."

"Wilcome t' Quoyloo, Hampton," one of the men replied. "What brings you here so far from home?"

Hampton smiled as he sat down. "It was recommended by a friend whose father served in the navy here during the war."

"What was his name?" the man asked.

"Hugh St. John, but he wasn't from these parts, just assigned here in the latter days of the war and for a time afterward."

"Sorry, I never heard of 'im," the man responded, "an' I was a bairn in Edinburgh at the time."

The barkeep, in a soiled white apron over his evident paunch, arrived with two glass mugs holding a dark amber brew, which he set before them, wiping his hands on the apron as he stepped back. "Will there be anything else, then?" he asked.

Robert glanced over at Weatherly, who shook his head. "We'll start with the peanuts fer now, Ian," Robert responded. Ian nodded and headed back to his station behind the bar, where he scooped up a bowlful of unshelled peanuts and a couple of brown paper napkins and brought them to the table. Weatherly folded his hands and leaned a bit forward. "My friend's father, Sir Hugh St. John, was sent by the navy to keep track of foreign shipping patterns—and, when possible, to gain the confidence of the captains and crews without revealing his real purpose and station. He was later brought up on charges of spying for the enemy and was ordered back to Quoyloo while his case was settled. I want to hear anything you can remember about the Orkneys during wartime—anything at all." He paused as Ian delivered their beers. Looking at Robert, he smiled. "It's just a subject of discussion, and it might give me some insight into the character of these residents, some of whom are direct descendants of people who were closely aware of the presence of agents and spies among them."

Robert was holding his beer with both hands, staring down at it, his face serious. When Weatherly stopped speaking, Robert raised his head, shook it slightly, and looked across the table. "As long as you don't expect much information and the beer holds out, we can talk about anything you want." He smiled as Weatherly nodded.

"Let's start by your memories of the war," Weatherly began. "As a child, what do you remember about the war? How did it affect you and your family?"

"Well," Robert responded after a large swallow of his beer, "I was just a bairn livin' on the outskirts of Aberdeen, but I remember the rationing and some pretty scant meals, and we heard lots of news of the war from the radio, and the bombings, of course. A lot of bombers flying overhead and we were hustled to the basement or a refuge, if we were in school. Some of 'em got pretty close, makin' the house shake. And the screamin' of damaged planes as they fell out of the sky was awful. Our house was damaged while I was in school, and some men came by and helped patch it up enough t' keep the weather out. I was too young t' follow the news, and couldn't 've found the Orkneys on a map." He paused to take a deep draught of his beer, looking at Weatherly over the rim of his mug.

"You must have heard a few things from the locals once you settled here," Weatherly ventured. "It was a boom time; there was building and housing, the Churchill's barriers were constructed, German subs lurking near and military forces moving in and many more moving through; they must have talked about it—probably still do. I don't have the time to stay here and get their stories, and I wouldn't know quite where to start. You must have made friends here, found some interesting drinking buddies from that time who either grew up here or maybe came as part of Quoyloo's war effort. I'm just looking for some tidbits, trying to get a feeling for the place."

Weatherly paused and took a good swallow of his drink while Robert drained his pint, and Weatherly signaled Ian for another. Robert tipped his head back and briefly closed his eyes as he pondered his response.

"The truth is, Hamp, while I know some muckers who were here then, but I can't recall the details of their tales. What I do recall is a bit mixed up with me own mimries o' that time. An' much of it is jist pub talk. I kin tell ye' with so many lads here there was much competition for the lasses— if you ken what I mean." He grinned as he lifted his drink for a large swallow and winked at Weatherly over the foamy rim. "It was said the lasses were mostly no great beauties, but cold toward t'ward these lonesome lads. An' drinkin' often led to fightin' o'coorse.

"'Twas hard times too, with the rationin' and hunger. I heard there was a pretty busy black market workin' then; a fair amount of military food rations kept some from starvin', but not many talk about that o'coorse."

Weatherly nodded at these revelations, then asked, "Did you ever hear anything about spying by various countries and agencies then?"

Again Robert closed his eyes and leaned back in his chair, then sat up and looked intently at the professor. "Years ago now, not many after I arrived here, I was sittin' with some o' my new mukkers, and few aulder gents. I kinnot recall their names, if I ever knew them, but they was half blootert, havin' been there awhile, talkin' aboot the war and such, and a man they called 'Hugh,' who they remembered from the war and afterward. Seems he appeared and disappeared, sometimes for months, sometimes for days, and was likely a spy of some sort, but polite and generous. They could never pin him down as to his business there, nor quite where he was from. He was full of interestin' tales, an' a good listener. Pleasant company, but just a bit odd." Robert frowned, as if in deep thought, then shook his head and smiled at Weatherly, who was listening intently. Robert shrugged and drained his pint and set it down.

Weatherly signaled Ian for a refill, then leaned back took a generous sip of his beer. "Is there any chance you might remember anyone else who might have been there at the time?

Robert shook his head, looking a bit sheepish as he replied, "'Twas a long time ago, and I might have been a bit sozzled at the time. It's a bit of a miracle I remember that much. Wish I could be of more help."

"Well," Weatherly replied, "it confirms what I knew, and I have enjoyed your company and your insights on the people of Quoyloo and its history." He paused as Ian delivered another pint and stood up when the barman left. "It has been a pleasure meeting you, Robert, and I appreciate your good taste in beers." He shrugged into his coat, and the Scotsman stood up with him.

"Glad to have made ye'r acquaintance, Perfessor, and thank ye' v'ry much fer yer time and generosity."

They shook hands and Weatherly paid Ian the tab, leaving generous tip. "It's for you, Ian," he said, "unless you want to treat my new friend. I take it you know what's in his best interests. And a good day to you as well." He shook the man's hand, went out, and resumed his stroll, making his way eventually back to his room, where he shed his damp jacket and cap, removed his boots, and laid out his notes and worked, arranging his impressions and thoughts and writing them carefully in his notebook.

He dined that evening in the pub downstairs and learned there was a bus back to the ferry in the morning.

Retracing his way back to Glasgow seemed shorter than his trip in, but it was early evening when he phoned Compton to pick him up.

CHAPTER 26

CASE SETTLED (1945)

THE ADMIRALTY COURT was in a difficult situation, having found Sir Hugh guilty of espionage but knowing, albeit off the record, that Sir Hugh's activities were ordered by the Admiralty and, as an officer of the Royal Navy, he had obeyed. The court apparently reached a compromise with itself when, according to public record, it was ordered that Sir Hugh be sentenced to a residential detention at an unnamed location. This was fortunate indeed for Sir Hugh in that had the court's found him guilty of a treasonous crime of espionage, he would be subject to execution. The court apparently reached a compromise with itself when it sentenced Sir Hugh to detention—in Quoyloo in the Orkney Islands—which was where he had spent some of his clandestine assignment—which had led to his being charged with treason. The document in a sealed envelope sent by courier from the First Sea Lord informed him of the court's decision. A small sealed envelope among its pages contained a hand-written note.

Hugh, this was the best I could wrangle from the judges on the court, given that the charges were somehow leaked to the press. I am both very proud of your service and I shall continue to do all I can to stay informed of your situation and do my best to protect you. I'm sure you understand why you must destroy this missive at once. Johnny

Each of the four parties to this unfolding drama—Sir Hugh, German naval command, the Russian navy officers in Leningrad, and the Admiralty—tried to determine what the others' reactions might be, and each developed and revised their plans accordingly. The Germans terminated Sir Hugh's contact frequencies immediately, fearing that he would "go public." Similar Russian fears caused their termination as well.

Sir David Petrie called an urgent meeting after he had met with Ivan Maisky, the Soviet ambassador to the Court of St. James. He asked his secretary to reach Churchill. Five minutes later, she opened the door. "I beg your pardon, Sir David, Mr. Churchill is at Chequers and a Mr. Christopher is visiting for the weekend. Should I let him know that you are insisting on his presence?"

"By all means and tell him to bring Mr. Christopher. We need him as well."

When these participants were seated in an irregular circle, facing each other, Maisky was the first to speak: "My colleagues, this is a most important and at the same time the most embarrassing announcement I have ever made, but I will not mince words. The Soviet Union is bankrupt...'broke,' I believe is the word. It is not that we cannot meet our obligations—we can and we will. We are technologically bankrupt. The leader of our Tekburo passed away yesterday afternoon, and aside from him, no one in his office had the slightest idea how our system works."

"I can vouch for what he said," Petrie volunteered. "But I need to be clear about just what the problem is. Let me lay out what I have heard. There are two leaked versions. One is that the equipment is modern, state of the art equipment and you do not have the technical training to operate it. The other holds that the equipment is of moderate age but in need of maintenance and repairs."

"A bit of both," said Maisky. The system was acquired about six years back, so while it is not the most modern system, I am told it still has a lot of service life. Therefore, we must determine if it is of operational efficiency, but we will need operations assistance."

"Then," Petrie stated, "we must send a team to make a technical assessment and whatever repairs we can."

It would take weeks, maybe months to assemble a proper team, get the authorizations, train and deploy them, all in secrecy, so Petrie suggested that one Sir Hugh St. John be sent ahead in order to lay the groundwork on the ground in preparation for the larger team. Delivery and equipment would come through the British Izmir base.

"Just a moment," Churchill interjected. "Isn't this the chap who was recently charged with treason for collusion with the enemy?"

Sir Petrie sighed, removed his glasses, and massaged his temples with his other hand. "Yes sir, but the Admiralty Court dropped the charges and sent him back up into the Orkneys on temporary detention until the matter cools down. Far from being a traitor, he was actually on a secret and very dangerous mission to dupe the Germans." Petrie paused briefly to decide not to mention Sir Hugh's arrangement with the Russians, then went on, "He fed them some false rumors and plans from the Admiralty, along with just enough truth to bolster their belief that he was a turncoat. He turned over very useful data for us to capture and destroy a lot of supplies and even a few u-boats. In the closing days of the war, he was kidnapped by the Germans and traded back to the navy in exchange for some valuable German prisoners we'd acquired—some as a result of his activities. When they get around to it, he'll be due some of the Admiralty's highest medals and honors. He's absolutely brilliant at coding, and one of the few experts knowledgeable in electronic transmissions."

Churchill removed the dead cigar he'd been chewing on and leaned toward Petrie. "You know him personally, then?"

Petrie shook his head. "I've never met him, but I do know he's highly regarded in the top echelons of the Admiralty."

Churchill studied Petrie for a few moments, then sat back and turned to Maisky. "What do you think, Mr. Ambassador? I will make some calls to some of my old cronies I know up there, but he sounds like the man for the job."

CHAPTER 27

A BRIEF ASSIGNMENT (1944)

THE LOCALS IN QUOYLOO were aware of Hugh's presence. It was a small town after all, and his duty—ostensibly to track sea traffic in the North Sea—meant he was frequently in town—along with many other sailors, men and women civilians, all strangers who appeared and left in considerable numbers every day. Considering that he appeared intermittently, he was known only to a few naval personnel and by sight to a few shopkeepers and bartenders who did not ask his name. The one exception was the owner of the Boots and Spurs pub where he lodged in an upstairs room, along with other occasional guests.

When he walked through the front door of the Boots and Spurs, the clerk greeted him, "Good afternoon, Mr. St John. We thought you might have deserted us. Will you be staying with us? We have a room ready."

"Thank you," he replied. "I am not sure how long I will be here, but please see if I have mail."

As he headed to his room, he thumbed through a small stack of mail handed to him. His attention turned to one with a return address "Admiralty; Glasgow" and a notation of "Confidential."

"When will those blokes at Admiralty ever learn not to call attention to themselves?" he muttered as he sat down in the lobby to scan the letter. In part it read:

"You are ordered to report to Royal Navy Lt. Commander Newsom on Wednesday next (28ᵗʰ) at the office and guest quarters of the Duncansby Head Lighthouse east of John o' Groats, at two p.m. This is a secure facility of HM Royal Navy. Lt. Commander Newsom will offer identification. Newsom will be accompanied by a person to whom you will be introduced and who will hand you your orders."

He glanced at the calendar on the wall behind the clerk's desk. *Hmmm. That's tomorrow.*

At two o'clock sharp, Hugh's taxi pulled into the Duncansby Head Lighthouse parking lot, and he was approached on the tarmac by a man in a civilian suit. "Sir Hugh, Lieutenant Commander Newsom here. Nice spot here, wot?" He handed Hugh his identification card.

"Spot on for view but not my choice this time of year."

As they entered the lobby, Hugh noted a man seated with his back to the door reading a newspaper. He rose to meet them, and Newsom introduced him as Kiril Demetrevich. Demetrevich extended his hand, smiled, and said, "You may address me as 'Kiril."

"Mr. Demetrevich represents the naval forces of the USSR," Newsom said. "You two need to talk. The dining room will serve luncheon until four." Newsom nodded at each, then left abruptly.

When Sir Hugh and Demetrevich were seated, Demetrevich took some papers from his pocket and handed them to Sir Hugh.

Strange indeed for an officer in the Royal Navy to receive orders at the hand of an officer in Stalin's navy, he thought.

"Effective immediately, you will place yourself under the command of Commander Demetrevich on temporary duty and subject to the following:

A. Recall at any time by HM Navy
B. Duty is for the purpose of developing improved radio-telegraphy service with the navy of the USSR and none other.
C. Your personal effects will be collected for you from the inn at Dounby.
By order of Adm. John Cunningham, First Sea Lord."

Sir Hugh nodded toward Demetrevich and gave a short salute. Demetrevich smiled, and they filled out the menu selection form on the table.

Hugh opened the conversation: "I notice, Kiril, if I may, that your very good English has a slight Oxford accent. Did you, perhaps, study there?"

"Yes, I did. I have never been able to disguise it. It was a great experience. We have nothing like it in the Soviet Union."

"Now, tell me," Hugh said firmly, looking Demetrevich in the eye, "where are we going and when?"

Demetrevich, not meeting Hugh's look, replied, "You will learn that tomorrow."

"I am sure that your people are aware that I speak no Russian."

"I will be your interpreter for at least two weeks." He went on, "We understand from Admiral Cunningham that you were not too happy with this cold and nasty weather."

It was evident to Sir Hugh he would get no further information from his Russian interpreter. Even his attempts at small talk about Demetrevich's experiences at Oxford elicited little more than short answers. After the meal, they shook hands, and Sir Hugh was driven back to his room in Quoyloo.

His orders and their immediacy made Sir Hugh curious. He pulled a little souvenir booklet from his pocket and began making notes, not starting a diary, but notes of the day's happenings and what little he had learned. This was on the small cabinet next to his bed the next morning when a knock came at the door.

It was Commander Demetrevich accompanied by one of the pub's waiters pushing a cart.

"Good morning, Sir Hugh. I assume that you could use a little breakfast."

"You assume correctly." The waiter made two trips up the wooden stairs and laid the table in seconds and disappeared.

"Tell me, Kiril," ventured Hugh when they were seated, "what is the news from Stalingrad this morning?"

Demetrevich's face froze. "That cannot be discussed."

"Very well," Sir Hugh responded. "When we get to this mysterious station, I can get the news there while we get to work setting updating your electronic communication systems."

"To receive any outside news in that manner is not permitted."

Hugh leaned slightly forward and held Demetrevich's eye until the Russian looked away.

They finished their breakfast in silence until Demetrevich said that they must leave at once for a flight to Crimea. "It will be cold in the mountains. Get a jacket." As Hugh went into the bedroom for his jacket and luggage, Demetrevich spotted the notepad on the table where Hugh had left it. When Hugh returned, Demetrevich said, pointing to the pad, "This sort of thing is not permitted. You should know that. This is a top-secret mission, and time is of the essence. We are not to be bothered with news of the war. Do you understand?"

"I suppose so. Are there a lot of places like that in the area?"

"Not enough. But there will be when this war is over. Stalin will see to that. We will not discuss this further."

"Well just what the hell can we talk about? We are allies. Surely we can have friendly conversations as colleagues working on an important project, no?"

Instead of answering, Kiril put his finger to his lips to silence Hugh; he reached down beneath the table and pulled a small black electronic device up and showed it. Hugh recognized it as a transmitter, and his eyebrows went up. He shrugged and nodded to the Russian, who replaced the device and stood up.

"I see you are packed up and ready to go then," he said. "I will give you a hand with your luggage." He went to the door and spoke to the waiter, who was leaning against the rental van. They quickly loaded up, and Demetrevich followed Hugh to the front desk where he paid his tab, offering the clerk a tip, which he insistently refused. They drove without speaking to the naval station, where they stopped about twenty yards from a large single-engine plane with two rows of five seats. Hugh noted the two trucks idling, one on each side of the aircraft, their beds covered with canvas. The van stopped when two armed guards waved and escorted them to the plane. The trucks carried more guardsmen in full battle gear, seated with their rifles on two benches in each vehicle. Their escorts stopped and saluted Hugh and Demetrevich, offering to stow Hugh's luggage as they approached the stairs that were folded down from the doorway into the plane. One of the guards took Hugh's luggage up into the plane; Kiril nodded to Hugh, indicating he was to board. Hugh selected the second seat behind the co-pilot. Demetrevich spoke briefly to the two-man crew, then took a seat one row back from Hugh's on the other side of the plane. The pilot ground on the starter until the engine started, sputtering and emitting dark smoke before settling into a brief roar that was quickly idled down. Two RAF fighters blew past them and climbed into the air.

A signalman guided the aircraft to the runway, holding two flags crossed over his head as the pilot tested his gear, checked his instruments, and pushed the throttle to a higher roar. The signalman dropped his flags to a horizontal posture and trotted out of sight as they trundled down the runway, picking up speed until they lifted heavily into the air.

Twice during their flight, Sir Hugh broached the subject of how he might approach his work once he had access to the equipment, but he drew few responses from the taciturn Russian.

Demetrevich maintained his stone face throughout the flight to Sevestapol except when he snored louder than the engines just outside his window and drooled as his head bobbed on the bumpy flight. On the ride to the military post in a battered and smoky truck pock-marked with bullet holes, Hugh was relegated to a rear seat while Demetrevich bounced around in the front seat, occasionally shouting at the driver for speeding over the pot-holed surface. At the naval station, they were waved through the armed gate and were driven to a low, gray building with twelve doors, each with a small, crude patio. They stopped in front of the third door, and Demetrevich dismounted and walked up to the door, pulled an old-fashioned skeleton key attached to a thin wooden plate the size of a playing card with Cryllic letters on it. The driver got out and picked up High's bags and carried them to the room. Sir Hugh stepped inside and noted that with three in the room it was crowded. To his left was a wooden frame attached to the wall—a single bed with a thin mattress, holding a thin, stained pillow, a couple of folded woolen blankets and a set of grayish sheets. A rusty clothes rack with eight wire hangers, two fatigue uniforms and one stiff-looking dress uniform, and two towels stood next to a battered wooden desk with three drawers on each side of the kneehole.

"This is the junior officers' quarters," Kiril explained. "The fully furnished bathroom is the third door down." He turned and stepped through the door, followed by the driver, and they made their way to the bathroom where they washed up. They drove to the officers' mess hall, now nearly empty, where they were served generous portions of warm cabbage soup, black bread with sliced salami, and slices of a heavy tan colored cake without icing, and mugs of strong black coffee. Their conversation was slow and intermittent, dealing mostly with remarks about the meal and the weather.

On their way back to their quarters, Demetrevich explained they would hear the bugle at five a.m. and he would meet St. John at the mess hall an hour later.

On his first morning in Sevastopol, Hugh showered and shaved with three younger officers, who ignored him as they chatted among themselves. Back in his room, he allowed himself a few minutes with his pipe. He pulled out the little booklet where he had made some hurried notes. He read through them and jotted down some of his impressions of his experiences so far. When he finished, someone knocked at the door, and he opened it to admit Demetrevich.

"Good morning, Sir Hugh," he said with a forced brightness. "I trust you slept well after our long day."

"Well enough, thank you. With a little tea and a bit of breakfast, I should be ready to begin our duties here."

"Good," the Russian said, then he looked down at the small notebook Hugh had been writing in. "This is not permitted," he said without looking at Hugh. "If I see it again, I shall be forced to confiscate it." He turned and stepped outside as Hugh buttoned the booklet into the voluminous side pocket of his fatigue pants. He took his jacket and stepped out, turning to lock the door and pocket the key. The two men marched to the mess hall without speaking.

Over breakfast among other officers, Kiril's manner softened, and he seemed genuinely interested in what Hugh told him about himself as Kiril revealed that he was married and had two children in Moscow. He seemed eager to share information about his family life.

The atmosphere was cordial until Hugh asked about news from Stalingrad. "It is not permitted to pay attention to such news from the outside. Facilities here are for our troops to enjoy rest and relaxation and not to concern themselves with other matters."

"Okay. Never mind. When we get to the station I can pick up all the news."

"As I told you in Quayloo, it is not permitted to receive news in such a manner. It will be cool on the mountain. Please bring a jacket."

Demetrevich was silent and expressionless on the bumpy drive to the transmitter station. They were waved through the guard gate and delivered to the front door of a building set apart from and above the rest of the base. It was about twenty feet square with a flat roof and one door conspicuous for it its heavy steel construction. The siding showed signs of wear not unusual for such remote military stations throughout the world. "Now, Kiril, where is my office?" Hugh asked as he toted his gear from the van. A younger enlisted man carried Demetrevich's large leather briefcase. "I assume you will arrange for me to be delivered here each day until I get a handle on our problems here."

"No. I will see that you are delivered here, but I am not permitted to leave you here alone. Safety, you know."

"Safety? How can I be safer than here on this mountain top?"

Kiril ignored the question, and his expression was stony as he escorted Hugh into the small, bleak building with one window and jammed with radio equipment of indeterminable vintage among the working radio-telegraphy equipment, small colored lights blinking on the monitors. He hung his jacket over the back of the worn office chair at the console table. "Please close the door when you leave"... and he belatedly added, "...Kiril," in an insincere attempt to be cordial.

"It is not permitted," Kiril responded as he sat in the office chair.

"What do you mean 'it's not permitted?' You brought me here to help your navy update its electronic communication equipment. Now you have to get out of my way and let me do my job."

"It is not permitted," Kiril repeated, stone-faced.

Hugh sighed and turned his back to survey the equipment. The clerk manning the station stood by, looking nervous. "I don't see your manuals, except for these in Cyrillic," Hugh said. "Where are your English manuals? At least some of this equipment I recognize, though much of it is pretty outdated."

The clerk shrugged, embarrassed. "No English," he mumbled in a thick accent.

Sir Hugh turned back to Demetrevich, paused, and rubbed his face as he gathered his thoughts. "Surely, Kiril, you understand it is almost impossible for me to do anything by way of improving operations here without manuals I can understand. This station has been cobbled together with parts from all over the world and perhaps some of the orders and manuals are not even available in English. However, the British Admiralty has access to nearly everything in the field of electronic communications. If I send them descriptions and model numbers, they can get them to me within a few days."

"It is not permitted. You may communicate with England only through official channels and after approval by the authorities."

"You, my friend Kiril, are full of feathers. I must communicate with the Admiralty for the help and support I need to complete our mission here."

Kiril stood and faced him and took a deep breath. "Sir Hugh, this will make it very difficult for me to do my job. I cannot perform my assigned duties if you will not cooperate. Together we can get the job done. But you must cooperate—"

Hugh interrupted Kiril, "Meaning to do what you say?"

"Yes. I am ordered to help you fix our communication system and to see that you do not violate any regulations." Kiril reached into his pocket and handed Hugh several printed pages. "Should you need to communicate with England you must fill out these forms for approval. Return them to me and I will see that they are properly filled out."

Without responding, Hugh held out his hand for the forms and saw that they were printed in Cyrillic. He looked up, but Demetrevich would not meet his gaze. Instead, he looked down, but did not take the papers from Sir Hugh's hand. Looking very uncomfortable, he asked, "Do you understand what you are to do with these papers?"

"I cannot read Cyrillic, but I know what you can do with them. You would be very uncomfortable sitting in your chair, and it won't solve the problem."

Now sweating, Demetrevich took the papers and, still not meeting Hugh's gaze, he said, "I must report this to my superior."

"Please do. And explain the situation to him. It is not complicated. In the meantime I will make an inventory of the equipment here and what we will need to accomplish this mission; I will fix what I can to keep it operational. I will prepare a detailed report for you. I will also let you stand by when I send it to England, to assure you I am not feeding them top-secret data."

Kiril was shaking his head. "It is not possible. My orders are clear: no direct communications with foreign powers."

Sir Hugh's response was steely. He leaned forward, his face inches from Demetrevich's. "Then we must cancel this operation. Report that to your superiors and tell them to inform the admiralty I am prevented from performing my duties here and requesting extraction ASAP—which means 'As Soon As Possible.'"

Demetrevich blanched, and he took another step back, shaking his head. "It is not possible. This will take a little time. I will try to explain this conundrum to them, but the orders are from Moscow, and it will take a few days to get their response. Please do not try to contact England. Your transmissions may be monitored, intercepted, do you understand? That could mean being cut off. Please let me explain to them that you cannot perform this mission, which they requested, under these restrictions. They do not want it aborted, I am very sure of that. Just proceed with your work and your report, and I will tell them this is of the highest priority; they should respond in a few days."

Sir Hugh took a deep breath. "Very well, I will do as you suggest—for a few days. I will keep sorting and patching this tangle of wires and junk, and I will concentrate on preparing the report detailing our needs to bring this station up to speed, but when I have finished—in no more than two weeks—I will transmit it to England, detailing what we need to accomplish this mission in the written report. Agreed?"

Without responding, the Russian turned away and left the building.

While he worked through the equipment, Sir Hugh kept his conversations with Demetrevich to a minimum, only asking him to translate his questions to the young aide who spent most of his time outside the facility, talking with other personnel and smoking. It was evident he knew only slightly more than Demetrevich about the operation there, but was able to provide some information about what had gone on there in the last few months. It was impossible for Hugh to determine how much was reliable, but clearly it had been a slipshod, complex organization run by people poorly trained and supported in their assignment, which was to keep the station operating, despite breakdowns, delays, and confusion and dissension among the staff.

Meanwhile Demetrevich's disposition deteriorated. When Hugh asked him about the progress of relations with Moscow and his request for permission to directly contact the Admiralty, Demetrevich invariably looked down and shook his head. "The request has been sent to Supreme Headquarters in Moscow, but we haven't received their response yet."

As Sir Hugh's deadline drew nearer, he asked Demetrevich if he had any contacts in the naval bureaucracy who might have heard something of the request or its status. Kiril shrugged, then turned as though he was looking out for eavesdroppers. "There is much competition and mistrust, much that is held to be top secret in this echelon. No one openly trusts anyone, so every secret is seen as a tool in the competition for influence. Just my asking would bring suspicion upon me. So, I try very hard to carry out my orders. My rank and position are due to my value as an interpreter and my experience abroad in England. My service in the navy is my life, and I do love my country."

Sir Hugh studied Kiril for a few seconds. Then he smiled and said, "You have my sympathies and respect for your rectitude, Kiril, and I wish you well in your career, but I will resign from this operation and request extraction from here in a few days if I cannot directly contact my superiors and experts in my country."

Demetrevich looked at Sir Hugh sadly, and his shoulders sagged. He looked tired and worried, and the stone face did not appear. Then he stood up and straightened his shoulders, and he looked up and again spoke to a spot just above Hugh's head, "Both Russia and I are grateful for what you are trying to do here, and I hope you will be able to stay and accomplish your mission." He turned and stepped out of the control room and resumed his place in his chair, looking out the window. In the ensuing days, he spoke only when called upon to translate requests he could not personally fill to other personnel, such as tools, batteries, and parts. Such requests seemed to be answered quite promptly, and the men delivering them treated him with obvious respect.

Sir Hugh in the meantime continued his inspection and inventory, detailing in his notes specific instances, along with suggestions for necessary upgrades and what was needed for each step. Back in his quarters in the evening, he typed his reports, based on these notes, and submitted copies of them to Demetrevich every morning, keeping his own drafts hidden in a paper box secreted among the mess of useless parts that cluttered the work area.

The situation deteriorated for a week past the deadline. Demetrevich grew more haggard every day. He lost weight and often fell asleep in his chair, mumbling in his sleep and waking suddenly wide-eyed and pale. Hugh kept silent, but when he had completed his inspection and submitted his report, he contacted the Admiralty:

30 April 44. Hugh St. John to Adm. Cunningham. My work here is not progressing due to obstructionism by one Cdr. Demetrevich, who serves as my interpreter but who functions as my shadow. He hovers over me at all hours, interfering with my work. The equipment here is beyond repair – antiquated and poorly maintained, if indeed maintained at all. There are no manuals in English, and I am forbidden to contact you except by written forms, in Cryllic, which are submitted to Moscow. Since I have not had any response to these missives, I assume they have not been forwarded. In light of these facts, I see my presence here as futile, and it puts me and Commander Demetrevich at risk. I therefore request that you withdraw me from my present location..."

The door crashed open and Demetrevich all but fell into the small room. "It is not permitted! You are corresponding with England. It is not permitted; do you not understand? It is not permitted! I must contact my superiors at once!"

Hugh replied coolly, "I hope you will do so and please send a copy of your report to Admiral Cunningham. They need to know that your naval bureaucrats have not permitted me to get my work done. That's why I have requested withdrawal. I care not a farthing if your incompetent, rinky-dink navy rots away and sinks to the bottom of the Black Sea."

"This is not permitted! Not permitted! Do you not understand?"

"Yes, and the cable has gone. Gone. Do you not understand?" Hugh's accent reverted to his native Scots. "But I do not understand how a bloke of your intelligence can believe what ye're mouthin'. We are allies, for God's sake. Allies! Friends! All I am trying to do is the job I was assigned. It is your navy and your state bureaucracies that have made this impossible."

The situation deteriorated for two more days, as did Demetrevich, who developed a persistent twitch in one corner of his mouth and the stumbling gait of an old man.

Hugh again transmitted to Admiralty: *"Get me out of here ASAP. Their equipment can't be fixed without the required manuals and parts. They will not let me explore what they need; I am about to damage relations with our ally."*

Demetrevich heard the unmistakable sounds of Hugh's transmission and opened the door, holding it for support and trembling as he spoke. "This is not permitted; I must contact my superiors at once."

Hugh looked at him, sighed, and said, "Kiril, sit down. I want to tell you something and you must listen."

Surprised by this command, Kiril wobbled back to his chair and sat.

Sir Hugh's voice was steady and firm. "I am leaving. Do you understand that? Leaving!"

Demetrevich seemed to sink into his chair as he said, "I must report immediately or I will be charged. I will be shot or exiled to Siberia. I don't deserve that."

Hugh took pity on him and waved him to the chair in front of the console. As Demetrevich began his slow and deliberate typing, Hugh closed the door and sat in Demetrevich's chair.

CHAPTER 28

THE ADMIRALTY TAKES ACTION (1945)

PETRIE USUALLY VISITED the Glasgow office of MI5 at least monthly. As usual on these occasions he had lunch with his affable friend Admiral John Cunningham.

"Johnny," Petrie began, "I have heard nothing for some time about your loaning Hugh St. John to the Soviet Navy. I must say that it was a generous move on your part to engineer that whole operation. How is it going?"

Though he did not say so, Petrie had serious reservations about sending Sir Hugh to the Crimea. He was more deeply concerned about the entire operation of Cunningham's Glasgow division of the Admiralty. He had discussed his concerns with Admiralty officials in London, most of whom shared his concerns about Cunningham. London officials had called him "a peacetime admiral" who could play golf and drink whiskey with visiting officials, but his military assignment—getting vital paperwork through the chain of command—was critically inefficient, unreliable, and poorly led by the second son of a royally connected family.

"Oh," Cunningham replied, "I was about to prepare a report to you. Sir Hugh is in Sevastopol, and his work there is going according to plan according to Soviet navy headquarters. He reports that their equipment is aged and should be replaced soon. We expect regular reports from him."

This response was unrealistic at best and, worse, a dishonest, uninformed report when Petrie was entitled to facts. As he was about to change the subject, a yeoman knocked and came into the office and saluted. "I beg your pardon, sir. This cable just in and it looks as though it may be important." He handed the cable to Cunningham and left.

Cunningham read to himself: *Hugh St. John to Admiral Cunningham: re: TDY with Soviets. Operation here a disaster. Equipment is aged and beyond repair; must be replaced if operation is to continue. Soviet official assigned to me does his best, but the bureaucracy is uncooperative to the extent that I cannot get my work done as I am forbidden even to make these communications. Because of these conflicts, I feel at risk and urgently request my immediate extraction. In fact, he is most likely monitoring this cable. My presence here...*"

Cunningham handed the cable to Petrie who read it and said, "Are you going to withdraw him?"

"Oh, yes. Most certainly. Plans to withdraw him should be ready in a week or so."

With that Petrie rose from his chair to his full six feet two inches height. "A week or so? A week or so!" he shouted almost in Cunningham's face. "Johnny, we have been friends for a long, long time, but his sort of thing cannot be written off to friendship. Blimey, Johnny," resorting to a little of his old navy salt, "You've got one of your most valuable men in immediate peril, and you want a week or so to rescue him? You have the resources. Use 'em. Rescue your man, dammit, Johnny; get St. John out of there now!"

As Petrie spoke, Cunningham sank lower and lower in his chair. Petrie towered over him and continued, "If you need someone to take the rap for this inexcusable delay, I'll take it. Now, get your arse up out of that chair and rescue your man!"

"David, you've never talked to me like that..."

"We'll discuss that later. Now, GO...GET...YOUR...MAN!"

Cunningham reached for the phone and called his executive aide. "I say, Tommy, I need you here. No, not in twenty minutes. Now!"

Tommy, a young ensign, appeared, breathless, as Cunningham hung up the phone, casually returning the junior officer's crisp salute.

"Damn the salutes and all, Tommy. Sir Hugh is in some kind of trouble, and we have to extract him. Contact the Coastal Forces station at Peterhead and tell them to stand by with passenger aircraft for a top-secret long-range mission. Now!" Tommy snapped a quick salute, about-faced and sped off. With unaccustomed alacrity, Cunningham prepared an urgent encrypted message to the Admiralty detailing the situation.

1630 hrs, GMT, London.
"Cunningham to Petrie, London: Admiralty urgently needs
Commando Unit E6 for rescue mission from Sevastapol. Further
details to follow. Also cable Soviet Naval Headquarters, Sevastopol:

*Our order placing St, John on TDY with Lt. Cdr. Demetrevich is re-
voked effective immediately. Cunningham."*

*RNHQCFP: URGENT! Under a white flag of truce, extract Com.
Hugh, St. John, by first available aircraft from Sevastopol Russian
naval station ASAP. Please confirm. Notify HQ USSR NavCom
Sevastopol when in range. Refuel with maximum efficiency tomorrow
a.m. under mutual treaty obligations."*

All arrangements were promptly confirmed. Cunningham ordered a
coded message to the Russian operations officer in charge of Sevastapol's
fueling facilities allowing fueling of British military aircraft flying white
flag carrying high-level passengers. At five a.m. Coastal Forces HQ wired,
"Refuel request denied." Cunningham took the reins and fired off a cable
to USSR HQ Sevastopol:

*"Your treaty obligations require your cooperation. Contact Moscow
immediately and confirm you will assist. This is an emergency of extreme
urgency. British aircraft entering your airspace within 24 hours.*

Eventually, a message crackled through Hugh's antiquated equipment:
"We're enroute. ETA 1630 GMT."

Meanwhile, Demetrevich, who had been sleeping restlessly in his chair
when Hugh began his communication, suddenly burst through the door,
his eyes wide and red, his hands shaking. "I tell you this is not permitted!
Not permitted! You must stop all transmissions immediately. I will report
this to my superiors." Demetrevich left the small equipment room, slam-
ming the door behind him.

Momentarily he returned. "I need that equipment to report this to my
superiors."

"Sorry," Sir Hugh replied. "I am working with it now. That's my assignment. I can let you have it in a couple of hours"

"A couple of hours! I cannot wait that long to inform my superiors.
They will have my head. This delay is not permitted."

"Sorry, I have work to do—"

Kiril's tone softened. "Please, Sir Hugh. If I do not report as required,
they must either have me shot or reassign me to Siberia. I don't deserve
this."

Hugh looked at him, but Demetrivich would not meet his gaze. After a
moment, he handed the mic to Kiril, who was sweating and deeply

disturbed. Still not looking up at Hugh, he said, "And you have not heard that our valiant army has killed a million Germans. What few are left are in full retreat."

His work there finished, Hugh gathered up his meager baggage and copies of his reports and waited until Demetrivich turned from the controls, and sighed deeply. "Kiril," he said in an urgent tone, "what did you learn in your communication?" Demetrivich shook his head, not meeting Sir Hugh's penetrating look. "Listen to me, man," Hugh ordered, putting his hand on the Russian's shoulder. "You have to understand that a British aircraft is on its way here even as we speak. The Admiralty has ordered my extraction from this impossible situation, and I am leaving." He put both hands on the Russian's shoulder and gave him a sharp shake. "Do you have any idea what will happen to you in the fallout of this event? Have you any means of defense for the abortion of this ill-conceived operation?"

Demetrivich looked up, his features slack, his eyes reddened, deeply troubled. "I am ordered to accompany you with an armed escort to the fueling station to facilitate your departure, making certain you are not carrying contraband or secret files. I am then to stand by for further orders. I fear the worst—taking the blame for the failure of the operation. I could be imprisoned, exiled to Siberia, or executed, which I might prefer."

Hugh had never seen a man thoroughly crushed. He released his grip and patted Kiril's shoulders, shaking his head. He took a step back. After a long pause, he spoke with an insistence that made the Russian sit up in his chair. "I have a plan, but it will require a very high degree of courage on your part. Now listen!

"Go back to your quarters, shower and shave, and put on your dress uniform, including all your ribbons and stars. Pack your biggest briefcase with your essentials and any documents that might be useful to you abroad. Put on your strongest military face and bearing. Walk upright and fast, like a confident and important man on a serious mission—and stay close to me. Can you do that? And do you want to leave Mother Russia, perhaps for the rest of your life?" Sir Hugh's own confident, commanding manner mirrored what he had advised the terrified Russian.

Kiril looked back at Hugh for a few moments and then dropped his gaze, slumped and hapless. "What will become of me abroad? I have no connections outside of a few KGB and other security agents who will always be on the alert to send me back to Russia to be hanged or abolished to a Siberian work camp where I will shortly die." He sighed deeply. "If I stay, I may be able to convince my superiors this disaster was not entirely my fault. However, I know I will make a convenient scapegoat for those in the bureaucracy far removed from here who are already scrambling to distance themselves from this operation. My life will be hell if I can avoid detention, which would probably be another kind of hell." He looked up, sad and dejected.

Sir Hugh sighed and managed what he hoped was a small, encouraging smile. "If we can get you aboard that plane and back to Britain, I will do what I can to secure your safety, but you would have to give up everything you know about your navy, your security apparatus, and anything else useful to British security, both military and civilian. You will be closely guarded, and any outside communications will be monitored. Eventually, you may be allowed to emigrate under a new identity; I would advise you to leave Britain. And I would advise you to decide soon; the plane is in the air, and you have only hours to decide if you want to be on it."

Demetrivich rose shakily to his feet and looked Hugh in the eye, though his voice was husky and he was close to tears. "This is all too much, and I cannot make such a grave decision at the moment. I will return to my quarters and dress as you have suggested and try to come to a decision before we leave. Thank you very much for your offers of help. I can't tell you how much it means to me that you are willing to take such risks for my welfare." He hesitated a moment, then stepped forward and embraced Sir Hugh, hugging him hard, kissing him on each cheek. He stepped away and left the building without looking back.

Sir Hugh gathered his jacket, gloves and cap, along with the box of his reports and documents in his sea bag, stepped out of the shack and walked over to Demetrivich's jeep. His aide drove to Hugh's quarters, and Hugh dismissed the driver. Inside, he showered and donned the clothes he had worn on his arrival and hung the garments he'd been issued back on the rack. Everything else he packed into his sea bag. He stripped the bedding from his cot and folded it neatly, spread the worn and scratchy blankets on the mattress, and laid down to wait for Demetrivich's arrival. He slept for an hour, then got up, stretched, used the head, combed his hair, and sat down in the only chair, facing the door to wait.

An hour later, the aide returned with the jeep and indicated it was time for chow. He was silent during the drive to the Officers' Mess and sat with friends while Hugh sat alone at one of the tables to eat. He bussed his dishes to the large table outside the kitchen and returned to his seat. In a few minutes, the aide returned him to his quarters

The next morning, Demetrivich showed up replete with ribbons, pins, and other marks of distinction, and with his driver. He met Sir Hugh in his quarters. He looked nervously around the small room and asked, "Do you have everything you brought with you and nothing else?"

Recognizing Kiril's stiff formality as a cue, he replied, "Yes, Commodore," in a formal manner. Demetrivich climbed awkwardly into the rear seat and gestured Hugh into the front. They were silent on the way to the officer's club, the Russian carrying Hugh's sea bag and valise. Inside, Kiril led Sir Hugh to a small table with two chairs near the noisy kitchen and bar area. He gave an orderly instructions concerning their breakfast and leaned across the table to speak softly to his companion. "This place is rife with hidden microphones and cameras, but with the noise from the kitchen, I think we can speak safely." Sir Hugh nodded, expressionless. "I was interrogated at length last night by a couple of my superior officers and three men in civilian clothes about our relationship. I assured them that I was present when all your forbidden transmissions were made, despite my orders, to the Admiralty, and that you had not been left unsupervised in the station. I cooperated fully and was informed that an armed escort will accompany us to the plane." He sat back and smiled broadly at Sir Hugh, who grinned back at him, nodding.

They continued their charade of light conversation as Demetrivich explained matters to Sir Hugh in hushed tones, broken up by pauses, during which Sir Hugh cheerfully responded, occasionally laughing, though his words and questions were deadly serious. Demetrivich described the layout of the fueling station and the officers they were likely to encounter. "The station is heavily fortified and guarded; there will be manned machine guns and other weapons trained on the aircraft from the moment it appears until it is out of sight, and we will be watched by armed guards, both visible and hidden."

"Will I be frisked and my bag dumped and examined?" Hugh asked, his tone light.

"Possibly, but I will carry the bag, and I trust nothing of interest is in your valise," delivered with a hearty chuckle.

Their meal was delivered, including a cut-glass bottle of vodka and two glasses. Demetrivich thanked the orderly dismissively and poured a double shot of the vodka into each of the glasses and raised his in a toast to Sir

Hugh. "Here's to a safe trip, and my regret at the failure of the mission. We both gave it our best shot." He drained his glass in one large swallow while Sir Hugh took a modest sip from his. They unfolded their napkins and lifted the metal domes from their large plates, releasing a small cloud steam.

Hugh lifted his glass. "And here's to you, Commander, and to your success in your next assignment." Demetrivich lifted his empty glass in response, a sardonic expression on his face. They finished their meal in relative silence; their table was cleared, leaving an urn of coffee, two cups, the vodka, and the glasses on the table. Demetrivich topped off Hugh's half empty glass, filled his own, and poured two cups coffee.

Sir Hugh chuckled and leaned across the small table and asked softly, "And will you be accompanying me on the flight?"

Demetrivich's smile was strained as he shook his head, then downed a generous portion of the vodka, sighed, and said, "My orders are to stand by here until I am contacted and given my next assignment." His gaze was steady but grave. Then he shrugged. With a strained smile, he leaned toward Sir Hugh, and his look became serious. "Despite the failure of this assignment, I still love my country and hope to be of service to her in some capacity. I think my fluency in English, French, and German will keep me from exile, and I will be under watch for many years, and it is unlikely I will ever leave Russia again, which is painful to me." He sat back and gave Hugh a grim, almost defiant look, but his eyes were misty with barely contained tears.

Sir Hugh held his coffee cup with both hands in front of his mouth and leaned forward, his elbows on the table, speaking softly. "I wish you every success and peace in your life and career, Kiril. I am glad we met, despite the frustration for both of us that our assignment was doomed from the outset."

Demetrivich pushed back his chair and stood up. "Your plane is expected shortly, perhaps within the hour. We will wait in the senior officers' lounge and drive to the refueling station when we get word your plane is on the ground." He fairly marched from the room, his posture erect, his bearing confident, Sir Hugh following in step. They retrieved Hugh's baggage and stepped into a long, unadorned hall. After passing two unmarked doorways, they stopped in front of one with a small sign fastened to it, the words in Russian, a keypad on the wall beside it. Demetrivich punched in a series of numbers (which Hugh memorized out of habit) and pushed the door open. At the far end, a single soldier in fatigues manned a snack bar offering coffee, tea, beer, and vodka along with sandwiches and other light fare. Kiril turned toward it and stopped at the nearest booth to deposit the luggage and gestured Hugh to the bench facing the snack bar as he sat facing toward the door. "I regret that we have no reading material in English and little left to talk about, but we will not be here long. The head is to the left of the snack bar, and I will accompany you should it be necessary." His look, aimed directly at Sir Hugh, was grave, with a hint of warning. Hugh nodded and sat back in his seat. Demetrivich pulled a Russian newspaper from his briefcase and opened it. He glanced up in surprise when Hugh pulled out his small pocketbook pad and began writing in it. "You know," he said softly, "that will be confiscated before you board the plane."

"It's a note to the KGB," Hugh replied. "I'll hand it to you when we leave." Kiril shook his head and returned to his paper.

Dear Comrades and fellow spies, he wrote. I wish to thank you for your hospitality and support during my brief time of service here. This is a beautiful spot of land, despite the rather trashy appearance of your temporary presence here. Because I am unfortunately ignorant of your language and have been constrained to a very small part of your establishment, I was unable to explore the lovely surroundings of the facility, nor to become at all acquainted with the local residents. I have been treated with respect by everyone I have encountered, and especially Commander Demetrivich, whose leadership and professional endeavors have been noteworthy, and deeply appreciated.
It will not surprise you to learn that I found the bureaucratic structure of your government inefficient, complex, and dense, seriously impinging on our efforts to complete the assignment. You have my sympathies in carrying out your responsibilities under such a frustrating environment. All large governments seem to devolve into such a state, as I have learned in my career in the royal navy. I wish you well in your endeavors for so long as we are allies, and we should all be proud of our success in destroying the scourge of the Nazi regime. May peace prevail in our efforts to respect one another as we rebuild what the war has grievously inflicted on countries across the globe. Peace be with you.
Hugh St. John, Lt. Commander, His Majesty's Royal Navy

The door opened suddenly, and a small crowd of men uniformed in battle dress, most bearing small arms—pistols, rifles fixed with bayonets, and other weaponry entered the lounge as Demetrivich and Sir Hugh stood, and Kiril came to attention as a trim, graying officer whose rank Hugh could not determine stepped forward and acknowledged his crisp salute. The officer drew a folded sheet of paper from his pocket and read it aloud. Demetrivich responded "Da!" followed by a string of Russian words as crisply spoken as the other officer's reading. Demetrivich picked up the sea bag and handed Hugh his valise as they filed out in the middle of the heavily armed escort. The commander assigned a junior officer armed with a heavy pistol to Demetrivich's jeep, placing him in the rear seat next to Hugh while he took the other front seat. They left in a small parade of vehicles surrounding Sir Hugh's and drove about a mile on dirt road to the airstrip. They stopped outside the perimeter of the twin-engine RAF cargo plane, whose engines were running, and the officer dismounted, nodding to Hugh and Kiril to follow him. Kiril, carrying the sea, bag spoke briefly to the officer and set Hugh's sea bag on the ground. There was a brief exchange between them, then Demetrivich opened the bag. The officer glanced inside, moved a few around, then stepped back, and Demetrivich saluted him with a few words and turned to Sir Hugh. "Good bye, Hugh," he said, rather stiffly. Hugh nodded and said, "Good bye, Kiril." Hugh reached into his pocket and handed the small notebook to him, and Sir Hugh extended his hand for a brief, firm handshake, picked up the sea bag, and marched to the waiting plane and mounted the steps into the cockpit, which closed behind him. He was directed to a seat behind the pilot, stowed his bag and buckled in, and glanced out the small window next to his seat. As the pilot revved the engines, the co-pilot turned to Hugh and said, "Welcome aboard, sir. If you need anything, let us know." Hugh gave him a thumbs-up and turned see the rest of the crew: flight engineer and navigator seated in the three seats behind him. At the end of the runway, two fighter planes took off over them as they taxied into the after-blast, turned, revved the engines, and slowly picked up ground speed and lumbered into the air, turned left at low altitude, and rose, thundering, into the cloudless sky. Sir Hugh never heard anything of Demetrivich again.

CHAPTER 29

A SCOTTISH FAREWELL (1997)

WITH HIS LUGGAGE STOWED in the boot of the Bentley, Weatherly seated himself in the left front seat with a tired sigh. Compton glanced over at him. "A long day, nae, Hamp?" he said, a trace of a smile on his lips.

"Indeed. It was an interesting excursion, but I am quite ready to get back home. I trust you are well, and Mr. McTavish also."

"Aye, we're back into our usual routine, but he's been less talkative of late; I think something's on his mind, but I've no idea what; probably something to do with his work."

Weatherly told Compton of his visit to the Orkneys and the people he'd met there, and the chauffeur nodded, not taking his eyes off the traffic, occasionally responding with brief observations on the place. As they unloaded the luggage at McTavish's home, the provost welcomed Weatherly, detaining him in the parlor as Compton carried his bags up to the guest room. "I trust your trip was interesting, and did you find the Orkadians hospitable?" he asked grinning.

"I didn't become acquainted with but a couple of them, but found those dealing with the public to be courteous and helpful. It's a bleak environment, requiring tough, hardy people used to looking out for themselves, and I can't say I learned much about the object of my excursion, Sir Hugh St. John, but enough by hearsay to verify that he was indeed there during the war."

Compton came down the stairs and into the room, nodding briefly at both men as he passed through.

McTavish stood, and Weatherly also, recognizing that the provost was ending their brief conversation. "How long will you be with us now, Professor? You're welcome to stay as long as you like, and there's much of Scotland you've not seen yet."

"I can't tell how much I appreciate your hospitality," Hampton replied. "But I'm sure you understand that I have much work to do with all the data I have acquired with the excellent resources you've made available to me. I will stay another day to pack up and rest for the tedious trip back to Missouri, but I am hoping to catch a flight the next day."

"I'll have Mrs. Edwards arrange your trip tomorrow, and Compton will see you through the airport. There's a good chance your flight could be early in the morning so you will want to retire early tonight. However, I would like to invite you to lunch tomorrow at the university, if you haven't other plans. I want to hear more about your discoveries about the St. Johns, if you don't mind."

"It would be a pleasure, but I am much in your debt for your generosity as my host. Perhaps I could invite you as my guest, though it is a scant token of gratitude for your hospitality."

Sandy shook his head, smiling. "Nae, the pleasure is mine. I've taken the liberty of reserving a private room for our last conversation—one of the perks of my position. Shall we say, one o'clock? Compton will pick you up around 12:45."

"That would be fine," Weatherly responded, "but if you don't mind, I would prefer to walk from here. I've done little but sit all day long, and it will be more of the same getting home."

The provost nodded. "Of course, I understand, and the walk will whet your appetite." He shook Weatherly's hand and walked toward the stairs, where he stopped and turned. "Good night, then, and sleep well."

Weatherly waited until he had ascended the stairs, then went quietly up to his room.

Weatherly slept well but woke when he heard McTavish leave his room. He remained in his bed, anticipating their upcoming conversation and what he would have to report to Clive when he returned to Washington, where he would spend at least a day packing up his car and closing out his apartment and other affairs. He was now anxious to get home and down to the final steps of writing the rough draft of his book, some details of which he would surely discover he needed. But he first had to arrange his notes and papers on Sir Hugh, most of which he'd already forwarded to Clive. The provost's relationship with Clive was a delicate matter. How much could he trust Compton's revelations about McTavish? What did Clive remember about him? He could hardly press McTavish about the matter, but he might be able to delicately ask him about their relationship or what he recalled about Clive as a boy and a young man. He had grown to like and respect Clive, hoped they could stay in touch. They had not covered all the details of file 1612. But first he must prepare for the conversation with McTavish.

When he heard Compton and McTavish leave, he rose from his bed, showered and dressed, then sat down with a notepad and began listing in a kind of shorthand just what he wanted to learn from the provost and how he might direct the conversation to those aims. He went back to his typed notes and reviewed their previous conversations, and what Compton had revealed. He wrote a list of questions in his pocket notebook he could refer to at lunch and afterward. At 10:30 he donned his jacket and set out to explore what he could of Glasgow, which was cloudy and cool but dry. He arrived at McTavish's office at 12:42.

Mrs. Edwards invited him in, explaining that the provost was out of the office for the moment. He sat down across from her desk, and she picked up a plastic folder and handed it to him. "These are the best arrangements I could secure on short notice, but you have a reservation, and with your passport you should have no trouble getting aboard. You are booked on British Airways, and there is a stop of about two hours at Heathrow. "

Weatherly accepted the folder and thanked her for her efforts in his behalf, rising to shake her hand across the desk.

"We are pleased to be of service, and I hope you have enjoyed your time in Scotland."

"Oh yes, very much," he assured her, "and I hope someday to return for a more leisurely visit."

"You will be welcome, I assure you, Professor," she said primly and glanced down at the surface of her desk.

Weatherly sat down in his chair and waited, his cap in his lap, until McTavish bustled in. Wetherly rose and shook his hand, and McTavish spoke briefly to Mrs. Edward, explaining he would be back later in the afternoon.

The university's faculty club was a well-lit facility on the top story of the main administrative building, with windows on all four sides. The main room featured a full bar and restaurant and several small tables and three larger ones that could be combined to hold nearly the entire faculty. The furniture was heavy, with overstuffed chairs and sofas. Several tables were occupied by small groups, and a few patrons sat alone at or near the bar. Off the main room were several smaller facilities for small groups. McTavish led him to one of these with a small table and two padded, straight-backed chairs facing each other. As they sat, a waiter appeared with water and menus, greeted them, and left, closing the door behind him. McTavish glanced through his and set it aside. "The food is fair, though not outstanding," he announced. "We have a trained chef and a small staff of cooks, and the service is excellent. I think I will start with two fingers of scotch."

Weatherly had been looking over the menu and made his selections. "It's a bit early in the day for me to drink, and I think I'll try today's feature of coq au vin, with water and tea at the end." He folded his menu, and the waiter appeared almost instantly with two tall glasses of ice water.

McTavish looked up at him. "Professor Weatherly has chosen the coq au vin, and I will begin with a shot of my usual, and the stew." The waiter nodded, picked up the menus, and left, closing the door quietly. McTavish sat back in his chair and smiled at his guest. "Well, Hamp, I can't wait to hear what you have learned of the rather elusive St. Johns, starting with Sir Hugh."

"Well, Sandy," he replied, "my best source was a rather brief journal that he began following his court martial and continuing through his assignment in Sevestapol at the end of the war. It seems he was picked up in the Orkneys and sent to Sevestapol to help organize their one of their communication stations and improve its operation. The Kremlin naval intelligence bureaucracy managed to scuttle that operation in a matter of weeks, and he was extracted and returned to Scotland. In the war he was, as you suspected, spying on both German and Russian shipping and was recruited by both as a mole, and ordered by the Admiralty to serve as a double agent. It must have been a very delicate dance for him to avoid detection at least until the war was effectively over. Churchill himself was in on his assignment in Crimea. After his return and the settlement of his court martial, he was sent on other missions in several places around the world. The last was apparently to Afghanistan. He sickened, died, and was buried at sea on the way back to Britain. I was unable to get any further information about it, and neither could Clive. He earned several distinguished commendations, but the details of those exploits were not available."

During Wetherly's report, the provost listened intently, and when Weatherly stopped, he shook his head and looked down at the table. "So,

I guess he was indeed a hero. His exploits would make quite a tale. Are you considering writing about it?"

Weatherly shook his head. "Not presently. I will turn everything I have on him over to Clive and let him decide if wants to do anything of that sort. I have all I can handle with the book that started all this."

"I must ask you, Hamp, if there was any reference to me or my family in that diary?"

Weatherly glanced up from his meal, smiled, and shook his head. "I'm afraid not. There was no mention of his wife or Clive either, and little about his duties. It seemed to be something he wrote when he had time on his hands, and he never mentioned where he was or even what he was doing. I find it remarkable it wasn't confiscated when he was captured, but it was among other classified documents, and I was not allowed to copy and print it, but I copied it by hand and typed it up to send to Clive."

Their waiter appeared at that moment and laid out their meal with a quiet efficiency, asking, "Will there be anything else then, gentlemen?" before he left. Weatherly spread his napkin in his lap as McTavish savored his drink, swirling it slowly before taking a generous sip and sighing softly in satisfaction before addressing his meal.

They unfolded their heavy linen napkins, and McTavish raised his drink. "Well, here's to your efforts and to the success of your book, Hamp. I hope that we might stay in touch, and I'd love to have a copy."

"Thank you, Sandy," Hampton replied. "It will be awhile before there will be any copies, but I promise that you will get one of the first."

They dined in silence for a few minutes, then Weatherly looked up briefly at his companion, and still holding his fork, he asked casually, "What can you tell me about Clive as a boy growing up almost next door?" Weatherly returned to his meal, looking down as he cut a piece of the chicken on his plate.

McTavish paused in his eating, looking across the table. "As I've mentioned, I didn't see much of him, actually. You know he was sent away during the war, and when he was schooled he enrolled in a tech school, so our paths never crossed that often. My recollections of him then seemed he was a good-looking lad, grew taller than his parents, and was...how should I put this... he was carefully polite, always a bit deferential, rather studied in his manners."

Weatherly nodded, and then asked, "Was he friends with your children?"

"Not really," Sandy replied. "He was a bit older than them, though he did give some of his toys to my older son, including a rather crude radio he had constructed in his youth. He connected a battery to it and showed Robbie how it worked, but they were never close."

"I guess you didn't get to know him very well then, as he was apparently only home for short periods of time."

"Aye, that's the short of it. I invited him over for chats now and then, at his home and mine, but he seldom responded. Like his father, I guess, whom I never really got to know either. They would come and go without so much as letting me know they were there. A strange lot; kept their own close counsel, and there was nothing neighborly about them. I guess that's why I became so interested in them." McTavish swallowed the remaining scotch, returned to his stew, and they finished their meal in relative silence.

When the waiter reappeared to clear the table, McTavish ordered a glass of Benedictine, urging Weatherly to sample it or something else to "settle your meal," as his host put it, but Weatherly demurred, explaining that he planned an hour or so of shopping and needed time to finish his packing.

"Well, then, can you spare the time to walk back to the office with me?" the provost asked, a bit sharply. "It may be we'll never meet again in person, and I'd appreciate your sharing your sentiments regarding Scotland and Glasgow, and maybe some bits about the St. Johns you've overlooked."

"It would be a pleasure," Weatherly responded, looking the Scotsman in the eye. "And who knows, I have enjoyed getting acquainted with your country, and I could happen to return, as I have found it a hospitable place, thanks to your kindness toward me, and your great help in getting me access to your libraries and other sources. I am in your debt." The waiter returned with McTavish's *aperitif*, and he swirled it under his nose before taking a sip, closing his eyes as he savored it in his mouth.

"Is there anything you'd like me to convey to Clive on your behalf then, Sandy? He'll pick me up from the airport, and I hope we'll have time for some conversation while I am vacating the apartment and closing up my affairs in Washington."

"Ye'v taken quite a liken to him then, I take it," McTavish replied. "Close friends then?"

"I like him very much," Weatherly replied, "but we're not what I'd call close friends. We've not spent much time together, and I know almost nothing of his personal history or his private life. He's done me some great favors in my research, and I feel in his debt. And I have found his father's story fascinating also, and look forward to talking with him about it."

McTavish tossed back the dregs of his drink and stood up, as did Weatherly. "And ye've told me all you learned about the family then?" he asked as they walked toward the exit.

"I think so," Weatherly replied.

During the short walk from the Faculty Club, McTavish was strangely silent; he walked with his head down, as though contemplating something serious. As they approached his office, he stopped just outside the entrance and turned to Weatherly and offered his hand. He shook it warmly, putting his other hand on the professor's shoulder. "It's been a pleasure meeting you, Hamp," he said, looking deeply into Weatherly's eyes. "I am truly grateful for your sharing the product of your researches into the St. Johns; though I know you might have learned things you haven't shared, I understand your position." He dropped the professor's hand and placed both of his on Weatherly's shoulders, looking down at him with a troubled smile. "Give him my highest regards, and tell him I deeply regret any misunderstandings between us." He gave Weatherly's shoulders a firm squeeze, then dropped his hands to his side and turned away. His voice dropped almost to a whisper as he grasped the door handle. "I wish you well, Hamp, in your life and with the book. I look forward to seeing it." He wiped his eyes as he pulled open the door and stepped inside, letting it close softly behind him.

CHAPTER 30

THE MAIN EVENT (1946)

THE FIFTH OF MARCH, 1946 broke clear and comfortably cool. Hampton Weatherly, a freshman at Westminster, was a good student who had settled comfortably into the Westminster environment. The faculty, having noticed his excellent work and study habits, regarded him as an "up and comer." After a week of cursory investigation into his background and character, he won the honor of retrieving and handing press passes to the authorized reporters and news teams. A tall, taciturn man in his forties introduced as "Mr. Thornton," who wore a gray suit, the jacket buttoned to keep his pistol and shoulder holster from view, took the identification document, usually a passport, and clearly pronounced the last name, spelled it, and the given name on the document. The passes were in a set of four expandable brown paper files, arranged in alphabetical order by last name. Hamp, as he was known on campus, deftly flipped through the files, retrieved the pass and a paper form, which he presented to the reporter for signature; at a nod from Mr. Thornton, he handed the press pass over.

One early arrival identified himself as Julian Sampson, Eastern European Editor for the Glasgow *Eastern Star*. He was not in the file. Mr. Thornton took a folded document out of his inner jacket pocket and handed Sampson a blank pass to fill out. He stepped aside, and using his briefcase as a lap desk, he filled out the form and walked to the front of the line. Thornton glanced briefly at the form, reached into another inside pocket, and handed Sampson a pass.

When Sampson headed up the walk, Thornton left the gate and found Larsen. They chatted briefly, and Thornton returned to the gate. About one hour and a dozen or so reporters later, a journalist presented a Russian passport and press card identifying him as Boris Kirlov, a "photo-journalist" for the Tiflis, Georgia, *Globe*. He looked enough like Sampson to be his twin, except that his suit was of a cheaper cut and fit him poorly. Weatherly was surprised when Thornton read out and spelled Kirlov's name, and Weatherly handed the form to Thornton, who glanced at it and the passport, and nodded to Weatherly to give Kirlov his pass.

When he disappeared up the walk, Hampton asked Thornton, "How often do you see that, Mr. Thornton? Two people in a group of about 100 from all over the world that look so much alike."

"I guess that just proves the old adage that somewhere in the world everyone has a twin," Thornton replied.

Shortly thereafter, Thornton met Frank Wilson, the director of the Secret Service and in overall charge of the day's security. "How's it going, Frank?"

"Pretty quiet so far," Wilson replied. The two men sat down on a bench, watching the growing crowd.

"That Weatherly kid is pretty sharp," Thornton said. "He spotted both Bransky and Willy."

Wilson said that he had just reported to Truman Ingle that all security plans were in place and operating. "And you know, John, I am even more comfortable since the task forces were equipped with this 'walkie-talkie' equipment. It keeps me in constant touch with all of the forces. I feel good about the security system we have developed for this event." A light from Task Force #4 signaled a message.

"What the hell's going on, Frank? Some idiot has issued a press pass to a Russkie, and he is authorized to park his camera in that tree right in front of the gym."

"It's okay. I authorized it. I'll explain later; no time now."

The rumble of sixty Harleys warming up became a full-throated roar. "Here we go, men. Zero slips, remember. We've got this baby under control."

The Harley sounds slowed, then stopped. "Winnie's lighting his cigar," Wilson announced to his team. "Ten-thirty sharp," he continued, "and the arrival of the principals is imminent. That safety patrol makes a great impression with those slick blue uniforms and white Harleys. I assume everyone knows his assignment and is fully prepared and in place. Answer 'Roger' if you are and keep me informed." All four teams complied.

At precisely 1:55, the stocky photographer clamored awkwardly up the tree to the spot he had picked out earlier. It doesn't take a very large bag to hold a small weapon, so his camera case had been stuffed with a professional camera including the various lenses and a plentiful supply of film. Just to make sure, the side of the bag was inscribed "Kodak" in letters large enough so they could be read easily from the ground.

"Great crowd downtown; some saying twenty-five thousand," the local reporter for NBC announced. "I don't think near that. Winnie and Harry are seated up on the backs of the back seat of their limousines so the crowd can see them better. Harry is waving his hat, and Winnie is waving his cigar. Crowd loves it! Moving into Fifth St. Crowd cheering; Winnie and Harry waving and smiling. They are right in front of me now at Fifth and Market. The Fulton High School band is just getting ready to fire up a Sousa march right by the celebrities' limousine. Wait a minute... Something is not right. The band has started the fanfare for "The Star and Stripes Forever," and now the band is marching two by two right across in front of the limousine playing that march, everyone's favorite. Mr. Hagan is waving his baton with a big grin on his face. Now they are circling the limousine and back into the formation where they're supposed to be. No harm done, I suppose, but it sure got my attention. I wonder if the Missouri Military Academy band has anything planned. Hope not. A whole pack of Highway Patrol Harleys is at Fifth and Court. The next band is at Sixth—I think that is MMA, and the Kemper band would be where Seventh Street hits Westminster Avenue. Good show. The MMA band is tuning up another Sousa piece—don't know which one."

Wilson, on the ground, moved through the crowd to a narrow alley.

Frank Wilson ordered, "Task Force leaders check in."

Five "all clear" responses followed; #4 leader added, "But I'm still nervous."

"Run through reports again. Start, Force One."

"The limousine and its escorts are progressing west on Seventh St., approaching Westminster Avenue. All clear."

Four more "all clear" reports followed; Force Four added, "Still nervous."

Minutes passed. Four again: "Four here. That Russian photographer just settled in that tree. Everyone in the field should keep a close eye on him."

Crowds along their route were variously described in newspaper reports as "excited," "huge," "disappointingly small," "even larger than expected," "unruly," "polite." Spectators had arrived on campus early in the morning. Troopers of the Highway Patrol were assigned to keep the circular drive on the campus clear should access for emergency vehicles be necessary. Despite a few minor arguments, the driveway was kept open.

As the caravan started up the circular drive towards Washington West House and the gym, Force Four signaled a call and reported, "I am more nervous and don't know why. Please cancel everything. *It just doesn't smell right.*"

Wilson's response was firm. "Four, three forces have cleared ahead of you. And I'm not going to cancel anything based on your smell! Things are under control. Just keep your eyes open and let me know specifically of anything unusual.

"They are starting to unload the dignitaries. All units, run your reports once more, starting Force #1."

All clear reports came back promptly from forces one through three. Force Four filed a reluctant "all clear," adding "*I am still nervous but suppose it's too late to cancel.*"

"Right! But keep your eyes open and call in anything suspicious."

As the limousines started to unload the guests, the crowd pressed closer and closer to the sidewalk for a better view. This affected at least one person who collapsed, apparently from heat or crowd pressure. He was promptly taken to the first aid station that had been established in the nearby chapel.

A Secret Service agent pushed through the crowd to reach Wilson.

"The victim is KGB. The invisible tattoo under the right ear lobe is clear under u/v. He was armed. Pretty convincing evidence that he wanted to kill Churchill or Truman or... or both."

"Thanks. That's probably Bransky. Armed, you said?"

"As expected."

"Forces: Make an immediate full survey of all sites under your sector and report ASAP."

Reports began to arrive: "Force One all clear." "Force Two all clear." "Force Four, I feel better. Looks good." No immediate response from Task Force Three was a red flag for Wilson. He ordered a circumferential survey of the gym and followed quickly behind them. Two fully armed agents found a man seated on the ground behind the gym, smoking his pipe, and carefully cleaning his Smith & Wesson .22 revolver: Kris Larsen, master marksman of MI5.

"Thanks for finding me, boys."

Wilson caught up with them just as his walkie-talkie signaled a message from the medical team.

"Chief, the dead guy has a press pass in his pocket. Issued to John Gerard. Is that strange?"

"Not very. I'll tell you later. He's just as dead either way, but thanks for the word." He hit the off button and headed behind the gym.

"I've got to know, Frank," said Larsen. "Was it the fellow we've been chasing for twenty years or so, or some spectator catching a glimpse of the dignitaries?"

"Your guy, to be sure. Even to the invisible tattoo they all wear. Bransky was given the pass issued to John Gerard. He did question the name on his pass and was told 'security, you know.' He never knew about the tree situation. He wanted to be a lot closer to the sidewalk when the platform party walked by."

One member of Task Force Three had a puzzled look on his face. "Excuse me, sir, but just who the hell was in that tree?"

"Oh, that was Willy, my spotter. He has a long-range lens on his camera, and he found Bransky for me. He told me that tree perch was bloody uncomfortable. Which of you brought my lunch?" Hearing no answer, Larsen said "Gross incompetence! Ten thousand leftover box lunches and the combined forces of the FBI and the CIA can't find one for me!"

Wilson's call light flashed, and Wilson stepped away to answer. He was back in less than five minutes.

"That was Barnes. Seems that when the short inbound parade was forming up this morning at the Sinclair station, Barnes stepped around to the men's room...I can hardly breathe... and... get this...he's still there and wants me to send a car for him!" Wilson nearly collapsed to the ground laughing, and he accepted a sip of nourishment offered by Chief Bledsoe. Wilson and Larsen motioned Bledsoe aside from the others.

"Chief," Wilson began, "I will need your help. It seems that someone in the outside crowd has died. Excitement, I suppose. The body is in the hands of the medical team in the chapel. They are waiting for instructions but the body carries no ID. We need to dispose of it one way or another. What is your procedure in this kind of situation?" Chief Bledsoe caught the real question and replied, "You fellows have enough on your hands. Let me handle this one. Can I call my office on your walkie-talkie?"

"Dunno. Never tried," said Wilson.

Bledsoe took the phone and then, "Hello, that you Sally?" Pause, then, "Please put me through to my office, number 6 and thanks." Pause. "Hello,

Charlie. Please send a couple of men in an ambulance to Westminster Avenue in front of the Beta house and meet me there *now!* Right away! But no lights or sirens."

Chief Bledsoe asked Wilson to have a couple of men posted at the basement level of the chapel, the downhill side, to wait for Bledsoe's men, who came along in a very few minutes and with a gurney made their way up the hill to pick up the body.

Bledsoe found Wilson. "Please clue me in on this caper! If anyone outside the five or six of us knows about this, I'll have to file a report."

"Sure, Chief. The man without ID was a Russian secret agent we've been looking for about ten years. His name is 'Unidentified,' okay?"

"With all of your planning and security, just how in hell did he get in and how did he get up into that tree without a pass?"

"He was never in the tree. That was one of the agents from British security. We knew Branksy was coming and suspected that he planned to assassinate Churchill and possibly Truman as well. We think the Kremlin ordered this caper."

"But how in hell," Chief Bledsoe insisted, "did you guys know this man was—"

Wilson interrupted, "Chief, we really appreciate your help in this delicate matter, and now we've got to see that all of those important people get back to where they came from."

Wilson picked up his walkie-talkie and called his colleague, FBI agent Warren Harriman who headed Task Force #4, inside the gym. "How much time until the party's over, Warren?"

"No way to tell, Frank. There are always ad libs and unforeseen little glitches. I'll guess forty-five minutes until Churchill is done and then probably another twenty, thirty to get the platform party organized and on their way to different destinations."

"Thanks, Warren." Wilson then headed back across the campus to meet Charlie with the ambulance.

"Where to, Chief?" asked Charlie.

"FBI headquarters in St. Louis. Quick. I'll call you with the address as soon as I know it." Bledsoe and Larsen were tagging along behind Wilson in their own golf cart. Wilson said to Larsen, "They're on their way to St. Louis. I'm going to call our HQ there for instructions. We can't keep this quiet for long."

Wilson called and asked instructions of his deputy. "Sam, I have a delivery to make. Please give me a delivery point. Two squad cars and a larger vehicle."

"Right, Frank. I will have a car waiting at Skinker and Clayton in forty-five minutes. By the way, Frank, Director Hoover is on the line and he wants to know—"

"No time now, Sam. Tell him 'more later.'"

"He says 'now,' Frank."

"Thanks for your help, Sam. More later...maybe."

Wilson told Larsen and Bledsoe, "About twenty minutes, boys. Time for a smoke."

The three of them parked at the back, downhill door to the chapel, just vacated by the ambulance with its cargo. The smoke relaxed all three, but their job was far from done.

Wilson's walkie-talkie signaled a call. He punched the "receive" button and said, "It's for you, Chief," handing the rig to Bledsoe, now an experienced hand, who said, "Sally. Thank God you're working. What's up?"

"It's the Highway Patrol Superintendent Waggoner. Wants to know what's with the ambulance on Westminster Avenue and do you need any help?"

"Tell him 'Thanks.' Just some guy who fainted and they're taking him to a hospital to check him out. Everything's okay. And ask him to stop by my office next time he's this way after the dust settles, and tell him that in addition to a back-up safety net, his Safety Squadron put on a good show. The crowd was enthusiastic with applause wherever they passed."

"He also said President McClure is demanding an immediate briefing by the leaders and coordinators of security and he wants you to round them up ASAP."

After a few minutes, the applause died down, and the band struck up "America" followed by "God Save the King," which was followed by the National Anthem. When the applause faded, the audience was permitted to leave the building.

It was a great show as the anthems ended and the platform party assembled at the gym doors, the academic regalia and flags presented a photo op for two or three minutes. Churchill flashed his "V" sign, and they descended the gym steps to the walkway to Washington West House.

There the party enjoyed a brief rest stop and light refreshments before exiting by a back door to the limousines parked in the driveway.

The Highway Patrol Safety Squadron fired up their escorting Harleys and started slowly down toward Westminster Avenue. Closed limousines carried Churchill, President Truman, Governor Donnelly, President McCluer, Superintendent Ingle, and a half-dozen Secret Service agents.

At Wilson's suggestion, "Poodle" Breid, the highway patrol trooper leading the exiting procession, slowed at the Sinclair station just south of town where they had stopped that morning for Churchill to light his cigar. Clark Barnes was watching with the proprietor, Brown Hamilton. Breid offered to relinquish his role leading the pack to Jefferson City and give that honor to Barnes. Barnes declined, and the several autos roared off to the waiting presidential train and an opportunity for some genuine relaxation, a late supper, and perhaps another hand or two of poker.

CHAPTER 31

BACK HOME (1997)

A TRAVEL WEARY WEATHERLY with a well-stuffed carry-on bag, his jacket draped over it, dismounted at Dulles International Airport and made his way to the baggage claim area to be greeted by a smiling Clive St. John, who shook his hand and welcomed him back to D.C. On their way to Weatherly's apartment, they chatted about recent events and some of Hampton's adventures in northern Scotland. At the apartment, Clive jumped from his seat and helped Weatherly with his luggage and preceded him to the door.

Upon entering he found several people. Some of them strangers, and all of whom were smiling at his discomfiture. Clive stepped forward to shake Weatherly's hand, gripping Hamp's shoulder with his left hand. "Of course you will recognize some of these people, but there are some you know about but have never met." He gestured at the attractive, slender woman with graying hair, who stepped forward and shook Weatherly's hand as Clive went on. "This is the former Miss Smedley of MI5, now Mrs. Frank Larsen." He pointed to a tall lean, white-haired man who nodded, smiling, and offered a small, informal salute. "Next to him is Frank Wilson, recently retired from the Secret Service." He was slightly older than the other strangers, balding, with a small paunch, but his eyes were bright, almost piercing, and he moved with confidence to come up and shake Weatherly's hand with a firm grip.

Weatherly smiled up at him. "I understand that you know a bit more about me than I do of you, and I am pleased to make your acquaintance. And I think I remember you among all the security people there." He stepped back and raised his voice slightly. "Have I been involved in something of my making? If so, I have no idea what it is. Before I ask for a briefing, I note that this is a rather unusual gathering in my kitchen.

Mr. Wilson, please rescue the bourbon bottle and some glasses from the cabinet there, and Clive, if you would find the ice. And your preference, Miss Smedley?"

"It's Susan, please, and I have learned to like bourbon and ginger." She stole a quick glance at Larsen.

When glasses were filled, Weatherly said, "All right, gentlemen and Susan, am I now involved in some massive drug smuggling or money laundering operation or is someone finally going to tell me what's going on here?"

Frank Wilson raised his hand. "Maybe I should do this." He turned to face Weatherly. "You probably heard that someone in the crowd passed out and was taken away in an ambulance."

Weatherly raised his hand, stopping Wilson's monologue. "I know a great deal more than that now. Through the good offices of Officer Clive St. John, I was able to obtain much of the British portion of file 1612, the official MI5 report on that operation. It was heavily redacted, but complete enough for me to piece together how Bransky was taken out before almost anyone knew he was there. That's going to make my revelations a bit of a bombshell, I hope. Despite repeated requests, I still haven't obtained anything of the American portion of the file."

Wilson shook his head, smiling. "I've heard about your insistence, and I have been able to read most of that file. For whatever reason, the State Department still officially opposes its release. However, I would be willing to sit down and have a conversation with you about it at your convenience."

Everyone watching grinned at the way Weatherly's face lit up at Wilson's offer. "Would you happen to be available tomorrow? I can postpone the few plans I have—mostly some housekeeping and a little shopping. We could meet for breakfast, or lunch any time, unless you are leaving tonight or early tomorrow."

Everyone present was amused at Weatherly's eager response to Wilson's invitation and Wilson shook his head, smiling. "We're all here at the invitation of Clive St. John, a very persuasive man who claims he owes you a debt of gratitude for some research you undertook for him in Scotland. He went to great lengths to arrange this 'Reunion of the Principals,' as he calls it, fifty-one years after the event. Our plans for tomorrow include brunch at The Lame Duck and a leisurely tour of the city. We'd like you to join us; there will be plenty of time for conversations. We Brits fly out of Washington on the red-eye around seven p.m."

Almost giddy with these invitations, Weatherly lifted his drink in a salutary toast. "Here's to one of the best days of my life, and my deepest gratitude for your presence."

"Here! Here!" cried St. John, echoed by several "Cheers!" by the others.

Weatherly made his way to the kitchen and was disappointed that that only a finger of the bourbon remained in the bottle. "May I invite you all to dinner in an hour? You choose the place and I will call for reservations and pick up the tab. All right?"

There was growing rumble of "No, no, it's our treat," and "We'll go Dutch." Wilson stood up, calling, "Wait! Wait! I've got it. Let's each pay for our own meal and drinks, and chip in enough for Professor Weatherly." Several nods and murmurs of approval settled the issue and there was a general movement toward the door when Clive spoke up. "I'll pick our friend up at say, seven o'clock? He may be in no condition to drive if we do it right, and I will make the sacrifice of limiting myself to no more than two." He lingered as the rest of the company left.

"I just wanted to stay long enough to thank you more than I can express for all your efforts on my behalf. I shall always be in your debt." He clasped both his hands around Weatherly's right, pumping and patting it warmly.

"I quite enjoyed it, frankly, and I was quite taken with Scotland," Weatherly responded. "I hope I can go back and see more of it, and maybe tackle the Admiralty to see if I can learn more of your father's career. I've come to admire him and have daydreamed a bit that we might collaborate on his biography when I finally get this book written."

St. John shrugged into his jacket and turned toward the door. "I think I would enjoy that very much, and I expect I will still be in Washington then. We'll talk it over tomorrow—and McTavish too. I want to tell you something about him."

Weatherly paused, rubbing his face, then looked up at St. John who had his hand on the door knob. "If you have a few minutes, I'd like to discuss it now, as I have some delicate questions about him for you too."

St. John's look was serious as he paused for a time, then removed his coat and sat down on a chair nearby. Weatherly pulled another chair around to face him and sat, trying to arrange his thoughts. "Mr. Compton has been McTavish's chauffeur for several years. He's the ultimate professional, with a large appetite for ale. He took me to breakfast at his favorite pub, and after what seemed to me several pints, his tongue loosened up, and he revealed some things about his boss he probably regretted the next day when he sobered up." Weatherly paused, looking directly at Clive, who was nodding grimly.

"And what was this dark revelation?" he asked.

Weatherly took a deep breath. "He indicated that the Provost was inordinately fond of certain young men, at least in his early years at the university. Telling me this made Compton very uncomfortable, even as deep as he was in cups. As I said, he takes great pride in his job and is the soul of discretion, so he almost surely never mentioned this to anyone before. I promised him I would be as discreet as he." Weatherly paused and gave Clive an almost impish grin and said, "But even he told at least one other person, depending on my discretion as I do yours."

Clive was silent as he digested Weatherly's words. Then he looked up and nodded. "I believe you told me some time ago, after your first encounter with him, that he expressed an interest in contacting me, right?" Weatherly nodded. "And this time, did he bring it up again?"

"Not directly, but he took me to dinner just a few days ago, and invited me back to his office to continue our chat. He loves to talk, as I may have mentioned, but he was strangely silent on the short walk back to his building. At the door, he shook my hand quite warmly, wished me well in my work, and said, 'When you see Clive St. John, give him my regards and tell him I deeply regret any misunderstanding between us.' Then he turned away and went inside. He seemed quite moved; I saw him wipe his eyes as he went through the door."

St. John sat back in his chair, his lips pursed. Then he straightened up, and his demeanor changed, his look hardened. When he spoke, his words were crisp and precise, his voice controlled and neutral: he was in his professional mode. "I know what you are thinking, and I know you would never directly ask, but you trusted me in sharing Mr. Compton's revelations, and I believe I can trust you the same way."

Weatherly sensed that his friend had gone into his professional "report mode," and he listened without moving as St. John delivered it calmly and without emotion, his gaze cool and focused on Weatherly.

"When I was about fifteen years old, I was on school break in Glasgow with my mother, and Father was away on duty. She went into town on some errand, and I was alone in the house. I went outside seeking some diversion, and Mr. McTavish, as I knew him, came over and began talking with me. He invited me into his house to show me some swords and uniforms he said he'd inherited from his grandfather. He handed me the kilt and asked if I would like to try it on. I said no, but he was quite insistent—said he'd like a picture of me in it. So I started to wrap it around me, and he stopped me, grabbed me by the arm. 'No, no,' he insisted. 'You must remove your trousers. Let me help you.' He reached down and unbuckled my belt and pulled down my trousers before I could move, but I held the kilt between us as he lifted my feet and removed my pants. I quickly wound the kilt about me, but I didn't know how to secure it, nor if I had it on backward. He knelt down in front of me, pushed my hands away, and started adjusting it. He reached under it, I thought to align it or something, but he instead pulled down my underwear, explaining that kilts were properly worn without undies. I remember that his face was red, and he licked his lips. My undies were still around my ankles as I jumped back in surprise and tripped over them and fell sidewise. I was trying to pull them up when he stood and lifted me to a standing position. I shrugged him off and pulled up my drawers, stepping away from him. I kicked the kilt away. He picked up my trousers and held them until I said, 'I'd like my trousers, please.'

"I was frightened enough that I was prepared to run from the house, but when I turned, he stepped in front of me and handed the trousers over. He offered to help me into them, but I was insistent. I grabbed them and started toward the door when he cried out, 'No! Please! Don't go out like that. Put your trousers on. I won't detain you.' As quickly as I could, I pulled up my trousers as he watched me closely. I was almost breathless with fear and confusion when I started toward the door. He grasped me by the shoulder, and I froze, though I was shaking. 'Clive,' he said, 'I'm very sorry. I didn't mean to frighten you. It was just an accidental touch, and I apologize for my clumsiness. I assure you it won't happen again, and I'd rather we just kept this between us. There's no reason to mention it again—to anyone, aye?' I was still shaking, and I just nodded and pulled away, desperate to put distance between us.

"I didn't tell my mother what had happened, but my father the next time he was home asked me casually what I thought of Mr. McTavish, and I responded that I didn't know him that well, but I didn't quite trust him. He was very calm and gentle, but he knew a thing or two about interrogation, and he got enough details out of me to know what had happened. He told me stay away from the man, and that he would have a conversation with Mr. McTavish, and we never spoke of it again."

Both men were silent for several moments as Weatherly considered his response to these revelations, but it was St. John who broke the silence. "At that age, my adolescent hormones were asserting themselves, and my interest in girls and women was spiking, and I pretty much put the incident behind me. Of course, I have thought from time to time what I might say to him if we ever met, but I have no particular interest in pursuing that."

"Thankfully," Weatherly replied, shaking his head, "I've not been traumatized like that, though I have been approached by men with such proclivity. When I was younger, I sowed some wild oats, as we put it here, and came close to the altar more than once—had some serious heart-aches—but I've pretty much recovered. I do enjoy the company of women, some of whom are quite dear to me, but I've heard myself described as a confirmed bachelor, and I guess I am, and quite content as such."

St. John nodded and stood up. "Our personal histories are quite similar, my friend, though I owe my bachelorhood to a particular incident. I was deeply in love, and my fiance died quite suddenly of a brain hemor-rhage just weeks before our wedding date. It took some time before I started dating again, and no one ever came close to what we felt for each other." He smiled, his hand on the doorknob, and said, "But maybe there is hope for both of us yet." He ran his hand through his graying hair. "There may be snow on the roof, but there's still fire in the furnace, nae? I will see you at seven, Hamp."

CODA (1997)

So, what have I learned from my research? I know that I was present at Churchill's in 1946 as a special "early entrance" freshman student at age 16. I was very honored that they gave me a small job far outside the inner circle of planning and execution. The event occurred over fifty years ago, and the memories of those involved have faded, as have mine. The rest of the security planning and execution was far outside my ability to access at the time, so it has all come from my research since. Many, perhaps most, of the principals featured in the book are now deceased, and while I did my best to contact everyone involved in the event, there may be others with memories better than the sources I was able to access.

Far too many others to enumerate have made significant contributions to this effort; I have a great debt of gratitude for their input in many ways, and meeting and dealing with them has been one of the great pleasures of this endeavor. You have all enriched my life, and I thank you most sincerely. H.D.W.